HUNT

RUSSELL TURNBULL

RUSSELL TURNBULL STUDIOS

Russell Turnbull Studios
Carlisle, Pennsylvania

First Edition
Trade Paperback ISBN: 979-8989088546

Cover designed by Miblart.

THE SCORPION CHRONICLES

Hollow: Book One
Dark: Book Two
Vast: Book Three
Cove: Book Four
Hunt: Book Five

I would like to thank and/or mention the following:

My wife, Tania

Keri-Rae Barnum, New Shelves Books

Ginger Sorensen, The Essential Website

Miblart, Ukraine

CONTENTS

AUTHOR'S NOTE

Welcome back to the Realm of Beornan Heafod in this, the fifth installment to The Scorpion Chronicles Saga.

As with the preceding installments, you will undoubtedly find foreign words that you cannot translate easily.

They are either archaic words not used in today's languages, or (most likely) Olde French.

I have also mixed a bit of Irish, Gaelic and Latin (among other) words and terms within, because they fit their given situations and explain things a bit better than common English words and terms could.

If you find this confusing, I apologize in advance.

(You can use Google Translate to decipher almost everything within this saga.)

I hope you enjoy this installment of The Scorpion Chronicles!
Russell Turnbull

PROLOGUE

I quickly followed my companions into the dungeon and saw Lemac sword fighting with two royal guards.

Two other guards lay dead on the floor, along with Amaliya still in her cell; smoke was emanating from her corpse, yet she didn't look like she had been burned.

Lemac, fighting two well trained royal guards, was holding his own quite nicely as he was using both fallen guards' swords at the same time.

The guards were trying their best but seemed to continue to come up short.

Lemac suddenly screamed out a wild cry as he dropped the sword from his right hand and swiftly grabbed the guard on his left's shoulder.

The guard began to scream and twitch violently, dropping his weapon and then falling to the ground in a smoking, silent heap.

Shaken and confused, the guard to Lemac's right was easily neutralized as Lemac ran his sword through the guard's neck and pushed hard, partially decapitating him.

As the headless guard fell to the floor, blood spilled out of the gaping wound and covered the wall and the floor.

Then, with a puff of black smoke, Lemac suddenly disappeared.

We were stunned at what we had just witnessed; confused and in shock and awe.

"Dammit!" Balt growled and stomped his foot on the floor, breaking the silence.

Commander Ashpin ran to the closest window and looked out, "Well," she said as we all joined her by the window, "The Exland Mountain mystery has just been solved," she pointed out the window.

We looked and observed a cloud of black smoke disappearing just behind another green dragon, soaring around the castle.

Ficolus and Lemac were on its back, flying away.

We watched as they disappeared over the horizon in the direction of The Haze.

I turned to look at Captain Magnus and found him sitting crossed legged on the floor, cradling the head of his deceased mother in his lap, crying.

"Leave him be," Loher whispered.

Commander Ashpin and I nodded and I gazed out of the window, wondering what our next move was going to be.

Now that the Grand Ascendancy was under Lemac's control, they seemed like an even *larger* threat than it did when Amaliya was involved.

Her limited protection over Captain Kuchoff Magnus was gone and he was no longer safe.

We had to be ready.

CHAPTER ONE

STRENGTH IN NUMBERS

My attention was drawn back to the window in a futile attempt to see if the green dragon carrying Ficolus and Lemac away might still be seen, but alas, no.

I turned my attention back to the Captain as two more Royal Guards quickly stumbled noisily into the dungeon.

"The prisoner has escaped," the King sighed as they looked around the room.

"I recognize her," one of the guards announced, pointing at the corpse of Amaliya, "It's been over twenty years since I last saw her, but that's her alright."

"Who is she to you?" Kuchoff asked, a bit more defensively than he intended.

"The assassin what killed the last King, she is," the guard sputtered.

"*She* killed him?" Kuchoff and the King asked with wide eyes.

"She did, Your Majesty," the guard frowned.

"Well," the King half smiled, "Justice apparently wins once again." He sympathetically looked at Captain Magnus, cradling his mother's corpse and then to the other bodies lying on the blood stained dungeon floor.

The captain gradually got to his feet, produced a sharp knife from his pack and severed the right hand from his mother's corpse, placing it, along with the knife, back into his pack.

"What are you going to do with that?" Meeka asked as the captain walked blindly past her on his way to the door.

Her question went unanswered.

"Her personal effects are being held in a room downstairs and shall be released to you," a guard told the captain, "what would you like done with..." he asked, motioning to his mother's corpse.

"Burn it." Captain Magnus coldly whispered and quickly turned toward the stairs.

"Very well," the King stated sourly, stood there for a moment looking around at the horrors before him, and then cleared his throat, "now if you will follow me..."

The King strode out of the dungeon and quickly descended the stairs back to the throne room.

He sat down on his throne, feeling a bit ill, with a thoughtful look on his face.

A guard entered the room and handed Captain Magnus a small pack of his mother's effects.

The captain thanked him with a silent nod as the guard turned and left the room.

Several moments later, the King looked at the captain with a slight grin, stood up and sent a messenger for his guards and knights.

"If you will just bear with me for a few moments..." the King crooned and began to sit back down on his throne.

"Of course, Your Majesty," we agreed.

Before he could properly rest both of his cheeks on his throne, two massive groups of armor-clad men marched into the room.

The King smiled, rising from his throne, his voice resonating through the great hall...

"My loyal knights and trusted guards, hear me well.

A grave threat stalks our kingdom—a murderer whose very presence taints our realm.

This sorcerer, marked by his missing left ear and clad in purple robes, has spilled innocent blood upon our soil.

His fingers weave death, and his remaining ear drips with silver trinkets that pulse with dark magic.

I command you: Hunt him down.

But hear me well—this is no common criminal.

His powers are great, and I would not lose a single one of you to his foul sorcery.

Move in groups, never alone. Strike swiftly when you find him, give him no chance to weave his spells.

Those who bring him to justice will be richly rewarded.

Let it be known throughout every village, every town, every corner of our realm—this murderer's days of freedom are numbered.

Go forth with my authority, and let justice be done.

And remember—I want him alive if possible.

Such crimes demand a public accounting before the crown."

The King turned and looked to the captain of the guard,

"Captain, deploy your forces. Let no ship sail from our ports, no caravan pass our borders without inspection.

He must not escape."

The captain of the guard stomped her foot and grunted in obedience, faced her men and barked, "Fall out!"

The guards swiftly exited the great hall in an orderly fashion and disappeared as quickly as they arrived.

The King turned his attention to the knights and then to us, "I'm going to loan you a couple of my knights to aid you in your task."

"With all due respect, Your Majesty," Loher began, "are you forgetting what happened to the last knight you sent with us?"

"Sir Quinn? No," he admitted, "he was young and inexperienced, these will be experienced combat veterans."

"Okay," I agreed, "under one condition...We pick them."

"You may choose two of my knights." The King agreed

"Your timing is impeccable." Lemac chortled as he found himself safely behind Ficolus, straddling the back of a young green dragon.

The young dragon suddenly dipped lower due to the sudden extra weight of the newcomer.

Ficolus regained control of the beast and then turned to look back at his pupil, "I saw what you did in there." he growled at the younger man.

"Pray tell what you mean." Lemac urged, feigning innocence.

"Amaliya is dead..."

"Killed by her son." Lemac spat, cutting him off.

"I saw you electrocute Amaliya while she was still in her cell." Ficolus argued forcefully, "Explain yourself."

The young green dragon swooped lower as they reached the Ferrum Mons.

Gliding just over the tallest peak, they circled to the south and straight for Exland Mountain.

"She was about to turn on us, Master." Lemac lied. "Her powers were enhanced by a locket she had hidden in her robes.Once that was taken from her, she became weak and powerless."

"So, you took advantage of her temporary weakness and executed her." Ficolus accused.

"They were *false powers* and she was about to *betray* us, Master," Lemac argued, "besides, we already have what we needed from her anyway. She has outlasted her usefulness."

The dragon skimmed the water, its belly just breaking the surface, sending a spray of seawater trailing off behind them.

Exland Mountain was just a few kilometers to the north, so the dragon began to ascend once again, leveling with the camouflaged door in the mountainside.

The dragon lightly perched on the rocky cliff that was adjacent to the door.

Ficolus slid down from the dragon's back, "Without Amaliya," Ficolus snapped, waving his finger in Lemac's general direction, "controlling Kuchoff is going to be even more difficult."

"Why do we even need him?" Lemac spat as he positioned his flying mount on the edge of the cliff, "Capturing him was Amaliya's idea."

"He's more powerful than Amaliya ever was," Ficolus explained, still fuming angry, "even with that locket. More powerful than even you or myself."

Lemac coaxed the dragon over the cliff and immediately took flight, "We'll see about that!" Lemac laughed, "She's gone and I'm in charge now, Old Man." He called as he dove down below the cliff.

In the expansive great hall, morning light filtering through towering stained glass, Captain Magnus and Commander Meeka Ashpin stood before the assembled Royal Knights.

Twenty-six warriors in gleaming armor, their weapons well-maintained and their faces bearing the marks of seasoned veterans.

"Those with experience at sea, step forward," Captain Magnus called, his voice echoing off ancient stone walls.

Ten knights moved forward, their armor catching the colored light from the windows.

The young King waved a bejeweled hand. "The rest of you are dismissed."

The remaining sixteen knights bowed and exited the hall.

"Step forward if you are unwilling to follow my orders as captain," Magnus challenged.

None moved, drawing a satisfied smile from the King.

Lieutenant-Commander Roash stepped forward, her Eline heritage clear in her feline grace and elven features. Black fur gleamed as she flexed her claws. "You're dismissed if you have any fear of my kind. Even the slightest hesitation."

Six knights quickly departed, leaving four.

The King's smile faded as he watched them go, disappointment clear in his young features.

"Those skilled with a bow, step forward," Lieutenant-Commander Loher McLaaud called.

Three knights stepped forward while one remained in place.

"Dammit," Balt grumbled, his dwarven accent thick, "I had guid feelin's about tat one."

Commander Ashpin laughed softly, "Sorry Balt, but it's your turn to test them."

"Right then," the dwarf grinned broadly, "Step farward if'n ye kin unnerstand me, proper like."

Sir O'cha laughed and stepped forward while his companions exchanged bewildered glances.

"Stay put, Knights," the King chuckled, "they still need one more of you."

"Can either of you use any magic?" Commander Ashpin inquired.

Both knights shook their heads.

A frown crossed Meeka's face.

"You're not being entirely truthful, Sir Gregg," came a familiar voice.

Brother Fost, the halfling priest, entered the hall. "I taught you healing myself."

"Are you here to rejoin us?" Meeka asked hopefully.

"We both are," came the crackling voice of Avilyn, the elderly elven Royal Wizard, as he too entered.

"I thought you had a non-interference agreement with Ficolus," Captain Magnus noted with a knowing smile.

"I do," Avilyn replied, "but I have no such arrangement with that coward, Lemac."

"So, it falls to us to handle Ficolus when the time comes," Brother Fost added solemnly.

"What about the dragons?" Rion asked, his lion-like features of his Eline heritage alert with interest.

Sir Gregg suddenly stepped forward, excitement clear in his voice, "If there's a chance to kill a dragon, I'm in!"

"You are dismissed, Sir Radcu," the King said, waving the remaining knight away.

Turning to the assembled crew, he added, "You have your team."

"You're not going to dissuade me from going, My Liege?" Avilyn asked in surprise.

"A mission like this needs all the help it can get," the King commented with a smile, "Sir Gregg, Sir O'cha, you are now a part of The Scorpion crew."

The two knights bowed low to their king and then took their places within the ranks.

In his private sanctuary, Ficolus materialized from a swirling cloud of grey smoke, appearing before the crackling hearth of his study.

The magical transit concluded with barely a whisper against the stone floors.

"Welcome home, Master." A plump woman in matching purple robes spoke softly, her eyes never leaving the ancient tome spread before her.

Ficolus sank into his well-worn chair, his weathered hands drawing forth a pipe from the folds of his robes. "I bear troubling news, Daph," he said heavily.

His words drew her full attention from the text. "Master?"

Drawing an ember from the fireplace with practiced ease, he lit his pipe and drew several contemplative puffs before speaking. "Master Amaliya has been murdered," he stated plainly, the words hanging heavy in the warm air.

Horror bloomed across Daph's round features, her eyes welling with tears.

"What? Who would... Why?" The words tumbled out between sharp breaths.

"According to Lemac, it was her son Kuchoff, acting in revenge."

Ficolus' voice carried a sharp edge. "But my own eyes saw Lemac himself commit the deed, not Kuchoff."

Daph sat frozen, tears streaming silently down her cheeks.

A dark chuckle escaped Ficolus' lips. "He believes himself to be in charge now."

"That's absurd," Daph managed a watery giggle, trying to compose herself.

"You're in charge, Master." She dabbed at her tears with her sleeve.

Ficolus sat in thoughtful silence, smoke curling around him like ethereal serpents.

Suddenly, his eyes sparked with inspiration.

"Daph, my dear, I require a favor that will turn the tides."

"Tide turning, Master?"

"I need you to locate a vessel called The Scorpion, captained by none other than Kuchoff Magnus."

Recognition flashed across Daph's tear-stained face at the mention of the infamous ship and her captain.

"Then – and this is crucial, so listen carefully – you must find an ancient elven wizard named Avilyn. You'll know him by his distinctive appearance; half his face appears melted and scarred."

"Melted?" she echoed, horror creeping into her voice.

"Find him and deliver these exact words: 'You were right all along and I concede.' Nothing more. He'll understand the meaning."

<hr>

Within the grand corridors leading from the throne room, our group moved as one, though I deliberately slowed my pace to let our newest recruits catch up.

Roash's predatory smile had sparked an idea too delicious to ignore.

I positioned myself between Sir O'cha and Sir Gregg with casual precision.

"One final question for you lads."

"Sir?" They responded in perfect synchronization.

"You've shown admirable comfort with our eline crew members," I mused, smoothly pivoting to walk backwards, facing them.

Then, with practiced timing, I allowed my fangs to extend as I smiled. "But tell me, how do you feel about vampires?"

The effect was instantaneous.

Their faces drained of color, eyes widening to saucers as they jerked to a halt.

Poor Balt nearly collided with them, muttering dwarven curses under his breath.

"Thunor!" My wife Loher's voice cut through the moment like a well-aimed arrow.

I turned to her with exaggerated innocence, fangs still prominently displayed.

"What?"

Despite her attempt at sternness, Loher's smile betrayed her amusement.

Behind us, Balt's deep laughter echoed off the stone walls, clearly relieved he wasn't the target of the scolding this time.

"Awe, go on wit ta pair o' ya," Balt chortled, giving our stunned knights a friendly push forward. "'E's 'armless... if 'e likes ya."

I turned back to them, retracting my fangs as I explained that I was only partially vampiric and would never harm a crew member.

To their credit—and my pleasant surprise—both knights took the revelation remarkably well.

By the time our boots hit the wooden planks of the port, they were already joining in with sea shanties and trading stories as if they'd been part of the crew for years.

⸻ ❖ ⸻

Through the misty morning air, Lemac guided his mount with practiced precision, keeping low over the waves to avoid detection.

The young dragon's scales nearly touched the water's surface as they glided silently past the shores of Dewarg. The southern face of Haze Mountain loomed before them; its peak shrouded in perpetual mist that gave the landmark its name.

"The Scorpion will be making her way downriver soon," he muttered to himself, banking the dragon in a wide arc toward their destination.

Ahead, ancient portal stones rose from the waterline like the fingers of some long-buried giant, their weathered surfaces etched with symbols of power that had endured countless seasons.

Lemac emptied his mind of all thought – a crucial technique when traveling through these portals.

The dragon's powerful wings carried them between the half-submerged stones, and in a flash of brilliant light that momentarily pierced the morning haze, both rider and beast vanished from this realm.

⸻ ❖ ⸻

The bustling atmosphere of South Port Royale thrummed with an energy born of both fear and hope. Dragons had been sighted across the realm, and with those sightings came whispered tales of The Scorpion's previous heroics.

The legendary vessel stood proudly at her mooring, her weathered hull telling tales of countless adventures.

Along the dock, a diverse crowd of hopeful recruits had formed a winding line.

Their varied appearances painted a picture of the realm's fighting forces—Dragon Hunters in their distinctive leather and scaled armor, warriors bearing weapons of every description, and magic users whose robes rippled with barely contained power.

Sir O'cha, still new to The Scorpion's reputation, turned to me with curiosity in his eyes. "What do you think they want?"

He gestured toward the assembled crowd, his Royal Knight's armor gleaming in stark contrast to the weathered gear of the Dragon Hunters.

"My guess is," I explained, watching as another group of hopefuls joined the queue, "they want to join the crew."

The growing line spoke to The Scorpion's reputation—both for taking on dangerous missions and for succeeding against impossible odds.

Ahead of us, Captain Magnus' voice carried across the dock as he addressed his tactical officer. "Hey Roash, pick out a few good ones. You know what we need."

"Aye, Captain."

The eline officer's response was accompanied by a predatory smile that made several recruits shift nervously.

She turned gracefully, her feline nature evident in every movement, and beckoned to our dwarven warrior. "Come on, Balt," she called with a playful hiss. "Captain wants us to pick out some ground team members."

In a concealed cove within Exland Mountain, where ancient stone met restless sea, a small ship lay in waiting. Though modest in size, her armaments spoke of deadly purpose.

Upon her deck, an unlikely crew of humans, orcs, and hobgoblins moved with practiced efficiency, their disparate natures united under a common cause.

"Permission to come aboard, Captain?" Daph called, her purple robes marking her as one of Ficolus' chosen.

"Granted," Captain Brooks smiled, extending a weathered hand.

As they walked toward the bridge, the pungent scent of unwashed warriors assailed her senses. "To what do we owe the honor?"

"Master Ficolus told me to find The Scorpion and talk to her captain."

"The Scorpion?" Brooks's voice carried clear reluctance. "Are you insane?"

"We're not going to attack it," she giggled, "we're going to talk to her captain."

"You're daft, Daph," Brooks groaned, "but if the master commands it…"

As monsoon clouds gathered above South Port Royale, The Scorpion herself prepared for departure.

Brother Fost approached the captain with purpose in his step, "Request permission to pit-stop in Hydan Seir for extra healing supplies, Captain?"

"Remind me when we get close," Kuchoff agreed, his thoughts clearly elsewhere.

"Aye, Captain," Brother Fost replied with his characteristic giggle.

"Actually," Captain Magnus amended, "go tell the helmsman to slow to a stop when we arrive."

The journey to the hidden shire proved as treacherous as legend suggested.

As we traversed the hidden path, Brother Fost called back, "Keep up, McLaaud. You don't want to get lost in *these* woods."

"What's wrong with these woods?" I asked, freeing my boots from clinging vines.

"Xobish."

"I thought they were extinct," I breathed.

After an hour's trek, Brother Fost produced a handful of seeds and berries. "Here, eat these. They will counteract the effects of the flowers ahead."

Meanwhile, in a distant realm, Lemac and his dragon emerged from a shimmering portal into night's embrace.

"There it is," he sighed with relief as a castle that looked as if it had somehow been twisted...like a damp rag that has been wrung out, appeared in the distance.

The structure defied conventional architecture, its towers spiraling at impossible angles and corridors bending back upon themselves.

What had once been a proud fortress of linear stone and rigid geometry now existed in multiple temporal states simultaneously.

This realm existed in several timelines at once, portions of it aging centuries in moments while others reversed their decay.

Windows looked out upon different eras depending on which side you viewed them from.

Staircases led both up and down simultaneously, their steps phasing between past and future states with each footfall.

Near the eastern tower, a particularly violent temporal eddy had caused the stone to flow like liquid, freezing mid-ripple when the initial wave passed.

The battlements twisted into Möbius configurations where sentries could patrol endlessly without ever changing direction.

In the central keep, time moved so erratically that rainfall from a storm three centuries ago still hung suspended in the great hall, droplets caught between moments.

Physical laws became suggestions rather than rules within the castle's influence.

Gravity shifted with the temporal currents, causing furniture to cling to walls or float gently near ceilings in rooms where time had thinned to near transparency.

"We must tread carefully," Lemac cautioned, watching as his own shadow fell slightly out of sync with his movements. "One misstep and we could be separated by decades rather than mere feet."

***

Back in Hydan Seir, within The Shoe tavern, Brother Fost and I shared a moment of respite once he had returned from gathering his supplies.

"I had the strangest encounter while you were gone," I mentioned over honey mead, "a red-haired woman watching me from afar."

"That would be Twig," he explained, "she's what we call a willing outcast."

"What do you mean?" I asked.

"One day," Fost began, "shortly after her birth, her family just up and left with no word of where or why."

He took a long pull from his drink.

"Several years later, she just showed up alone, but she never stays long enough for anyone to get to know her. We've invited her to remain, but she refuses to stay flat-out.

As if summoned by our conversation, a determined voice called out as we prepared to leave.

"You're from The Scorpion, right?"

The flame-haired halfling stood before us, no longer hiding. "I want to join."

"What skills do you possess..." I began, but Brother Fost interrupted.

"I'll take full responsibility for her. Come, my child, you are welcome."

Twig's frown carried years of independence. "I'm not a charity case, Priest."

She shuffled from one foot to the other, "I possess a skill set unique to my race. I am unknown to your enemy and can find useful resources that most people commonly overlook."

"I should inform you that going after dragons is basically a suicide mission." I warned.

"Your point being?" Her matter-of-fact response drew admiration.

"You're not afraid?" Brother Fost inquired.

"Yeah, but they're dragons!" she exclaimed, as if that explained everything.

"I like you, Twig," I decided.

"Good luck with that," she laughed, gathering her curious arsenal of sharpened twig-darts concealed within her wild red hair.

—◆—

As twilight painted the peaks of Ferrum Mons in hues of gold and purple, The Scorpion resumed her journey, her crew now complete.

Somewhere ahead, beyond the horizon where sea met sky, Lemac and his dragons waited and destiny beckoned.

Chapter Two

A Hint or a Trap?

Veering left upon exiting the mouth of the river into the Strait of Avilyn, we ventured close to the island's southern shoreline near Guadium.

We were hoping to get lucky and catch a glimpse of another ship or a dragon before the sun had completely set, but the sea and sky showed nothing, so we continued to sail past Avilyn Harbor.

The Dragonfly was the only ship moored at the harbor docks and the sky was clear, so we decided to circle around Haze Mountain and the portal stones.

The sun had finally set and the lanterns were lit.

The captain decided to slow The Scorpion down a bit so we would arrive at just the right time.

———— ◆ ————

"I suggest we depart at first light," Captain Brooks stated and pointed at the setting sun, "we're not going to be able to see much tonight."

"Agreed," Daph smiled, "I could use a good night's rest, considering I was unaware of this mission until about an hour ago."

"About this mission," the captain began to ask, "what can you tell me about it?"

"Master Ficolus wants me to deliver a message to an old elven wizard, and Captain Magnus knows where the wizard is. That's all." She answered.

The sun was just coming up as we made our final approach to Haze Mountain, making visibility within the already naturally hazy waters a bit better.

"Keep your eyes open." Captain Magnus announced to the crew as the haze began to surround us.

Roash decided the harpoon was the best place to be, so she positioned herself at the controls and kept watch.

Our resident errfords assumed their places on the rails, ready to shield as two dozen archers strategically posted themselves around the ship.

"Stay far enough away from those portal stones, Helm," Captain Magnus directed.

"Aye." Helm complied.

Haze Mountain grew larger the closer we got to it.

The psi creature Amaliya had left as a deterrent was already weak and fading away as we sailed right through it.

Most of our newer crew members were caught without warning and it made for quite an entertaining show.

I say 'most of' our newer members because our newest magic user, Jacen Feldspar, detected it moments before it appeared.

He tried to warn everyone, but Avilyn stopped him so we could enjoy the show.

After a quick moment of playful laughter at our new crew members' expense, our attention was returned to the Haze.

Lemac gently let the large stone door close quietly behind him, then he turned and began to swiftly move down a long hallway.

The interior walls of the castle were carved out in such a way that it looked as though they were made of huge blocks of green and cream limestone, flickering in the soft glow of candlelight.

Cobwebs hung thickly from virtually anything they could hang from, and the air was dank and heavy.

The further he walked, the more potent the smells of fecal matter and death became.

Along with the echoing of his footsteps, Lemac could begin to hear the faint sounds of activity in a room just ahead.

He slowed his pace and approached the doorway to the occupied room; the door was open.

Peering into the room, the first thing Lemac noticed was that the floor was missing.

It looked as though it had been burned away and crumbled to the floor of the room below.

He looked down to the floor below and saw, mixed within the rubble, a few dozen trolls tending to hundreds of dragon eggs.

"Hello, my beauties." Lemac smiled.

The colossal bulk of Haze Mountain loomed ahead of us, its barren stone rising into the clouds like a titan's spear.

No life clung to its otherworldly surface—no grass, no birds, not even lichen dared make a home on its cursed slopes.

The very rock seemed to mock nature itself, as if placed here by beings whose power had long since passed into legend.

Our path took us carefully around its base, every eye scanning the shadows until we were satisfied nothing lurked in its crevices.

Only then did we turn our bow south toward Exland Mountain.

The mists that gave the peak its name began to thin, and the rough waters gradually calmed beneath our keel.

"Captain," Navari broke the silence. "May I ask you something?"

Kuchoff grinned. "Of course."

"The hand... your mother's hand. Why keep it?"

His smile vanished. "Honestly? Pure instinct. I didn't even realize I'd taken it until I found myself putting it in my pack. Just felt... important somehow."

"Ye could always feed it tae Rion," Balt suggested with a shrug.

Kuchoff stared at him for a moment before bursting into laughter.

Balt joined in, his deep dwarven belly laugh echoing across the deck.

"I fail to see the humor in this situation, Captain." Navari said stiffly.

That only made them laugh harder.

I watched from my position near the rail, remembering similar moments of levity in darker times.

"Sorry," Kuchoff managed between chuckles. "It's just... Balt and I have been through so much together. Twenty years now."

"Has it been t'at long?" Balt scratched his beard. "Ye were just a wee lad when we started."

"Look at me now—taller than you!"

"As if ye'd let anyone forget it," Balt snorted.

"Meeka and I practically raised him," he added proudly.

"Turned him intae a proper warrior."

"The whole crew raised me," Kuchoff corrected.

"Though some aren't here to see what I've become."

I stepped onto the bridge. "We've lost good people."

"The knight Loher mentioned?" Navari asked.

"Sir Quinn," I nodded.

"And Byron." Kuchoff added, unconsciously fingering the hilt of his katana.

"Did you kill Byron?" she asked Kuchoff, eyeing the allegedly enchanted weapon.

"No. He left me this blade before he died."

"T'was Meeka what sent Sir Quinn tae his rest," Balt said. "Well, her and t'at spider."

Navari's serpentine hair writhed in surprise.

"Not exactly," I corrected, the old memories still sharp as broken glass. "The spider killed Quinn. Meeka killed the spider with a spell so powerful it took them both out."

"A memory that haunts me still," Meeka said, appearing beside us.

Something in her voice made me look twice, but her face revealed nothing. "Exland Mountain approaches. Navari, to the crow's nest. Use that special sight you have."

Navari moved with her usual fluid grace but paused at the threshold. "Commander? I would have killed that spider too."

As Navari climbed to her post, I caught Meeka studying Kuchoff's profile, her expression unreadable in the strange light.

Now that I think back on it, perhaps I should have paid more attention to that look.

"I thought you said we would be leaving at first light!" Daph screamed at the still sleeping captain.

Captain Brooks sat bolt upright, "Huh?" he groggily asked, still half asleep.

"Do *you* call this 'first light', Captain?" Daph continued screaming into his ear and pointing at the sun.

Now wide awake with ears ringing, the captain pulled on his boots and ran for the hold.

"Where are you going?!" Daph screamed after him, stomping her foot on the deck.

"I have to let the crew out of their cages," he answered over his shoulder, "this ship won't sail itself."

With Navari joining the lookout in the crow's nest and the errfords and archers stationed strategically about the deck, The Scorpion slowed to drifting speed as we began to circle around Exland Mountain.

"Ship ahoy!" The lookout called down.

Captain Magnus produced a spyglass from his pack and raised it to his eye.

"What do you see?" Commander Ashpin asked after a moment.

"One ship sitting stationary," he reported, "just sitting there."

"What flag are they flying?" she asked.

"They're not," he answered, "take a look."

He handed his first officer the spyglass.

"That's troubling," she commented as she looked through the lens.

"Captain," a large human male shouted as he lumbered towards us, waving his arms.

"Report, Mister." Captain Magnus commanded.

"Commander Roash sent me to tell you that she can see the crew of the ship," he reported, slightly out of breath.

Kuchoff and Meeka patiently waited.

"She says she sees orcs and hobgoblins aboard," the fighter breathed, "And two humans, Sir."

Kuchoff began to quickly exit the bridge, followed by Meeka, informing the crew to be ready for a fight.

Within moments, the entire crew was on alert and the errfords were ready to raise their shields at the first sign of danger.

I ran down to the lower deck to make sure Tatenda Waxx was ready with the Creature Controls, but, as usual, he was already at his station, ready to make The Scorpion come to life.

"I was born for dis!" Tatenda exclaimed with a glowing smile on his face.

"Quite literally," I agreed as I retreated up the stairs and stationed myself near the harpoon in case Roash needed some help.

"We've been spotted," the lookout announced, "she's moving towards us."

"Steady," the captain called to his crew.

The ship began to slow as she made her way around Exland Mountain and then stopped and dropped anchor.

"Slow to a full stop right next to her, Helm." Captain Magnus called to the bridge.

"Aye, Captain." Helm called back.

"Hold your fire until the errfords begin to shield." Captain Magnus ordered.

"Aye, Captain," a voice called from down below, "holding."

I took a quick look around and found Balt and a few other ground team members preparing for battle, doing yoga poses and stretches.

Lemac found a rope ladder and climbed down to inspect the eggs a bit closer.

His sudden appearance startled the trolls directly around him, but they soon recognized him and carried on with their duties.

The foul stench of trolls, rotting meat and feces violated Lemac's senses as he reached the bottom.

The odor was so strong he could actually taste it in his mouth.

"Clean this place up!" he gagged at the closest trolls. "Why must you shit near the eggs?" He rhetorically screamed as he noticed that he had stepped into a large, still soft pile of troll dung.

"Because trolls shit wherever they please, my lord." A heavy voice breathed from somewhere within the cavern.

Anxiety began to creep up on me as we slowed to a stop right next to the Grand Ascendancy's ship.

"Ahoy, Captain Magnus!" A female voice called from the opposing ship.

Kuchoff paused and looked at Meeka, "She knows who I am?"

"Apparently." Meeka shrugged.

"Yer famous, Captain!" Balt chuckled.

"Ahoy, Grand Ascendancy." Captain Magnus called back.

"Request permission to come aboard, Sir." She called after a moment.

"Is anyone sensing anything?" Kuchoff asked into the air.

Avilyn stepped forward, "I'm sensing a magic user aboard that ship, Sir."

"Elaborate, please." Captain Magnus urged.

"Perhaps I can clear things up, Captain," Navari hissed as she joined the conversation, "I sense no ill will toward us," she explained, "I'm sensing fear and worry more than anything else."

"Granted," Captain Magnus called to the opposing ship, "but only you. Come alone."

A puff of grey smoke began to build a couple of meters to my right and I instinctively reached for my sword.

There was the familiar pop and a short, plump human woman appeared alone on the deck.

Clad in the usual purple robes of the Grand Ascendancy, she showed us that her hands were empty and she wore no weapons.

"I am at your mercy, Captain, but if you'll hear me out..."

"I'm no monster," Kuchoff laughed, "take ease, you're in no danger."

"If ye behaves yerself." Balt grumbled.

"*Balt!*" Meeka hissed.

"Wot??" Balt defended.

"Meeka?" Our visitor breathed as she recognized the First Officer, "Meeka Ashpin?"

A look of familiarity began to etch across the commander's face as she too realized that she knew this person.

"Daph?" Meeka giggled and leaned in for a hug and then looked at her questioningly, "Why?"

Daph looked confused.

"Why did you join this...*cult*?" Meeka asked.

"I didn't know what I was getting into," she frowned, "I began having second thoughts years ago when the dragon eggs arrived. Then they began to hatch and I started looking for a way to escape, but I had nothing to do with the dragons *or* their upkeep, so I decided it wasn't so bad and I stayed. Until this morning."

"What happened this morning, Child?" Avilyn asked, trying to sound soothing.

Daph looked up and recognized Avilyn's description from her master, "Avilyn?" Daph asked, studying the side of his face that seemed melted.

"I am." The old elven wizard replied, raising an eyebrow.

"Master Ficolus charged me to find you and give you a message." Daph beamed.

"Out with it then, Girl." Avilyn coughed.

"My master told me to tell you that he concedes and that you were right.

He said that you'll know what it means."

Avilyn began to smile, fully amused at this sudden news, "It's about bloody time," Avilyn coughed, "Tell me what you know, Love."

"Lemac informed us that Amaliya was dead and that he was now in charge." Daph choked.

"How did Ficolus take that news?" Avilyn snorted, failing to hide his amusement.

"Apparently, he was there and witnessed it." Daph answered,

"He seemed to be in agreement, until Lemac left.

Master Ficolus waited until he knew Lemac was gone, then he sent me out to look for The Scorpion and ultimately, you." She explained to Avilyn.

"Did they explain how she died?" Captain Magnus asked.

"Lemac told us that *you* killed her," she sniffed, "but I don't believe him. Why would you kill your own mother? She always told us that she wanted you to join us and that you would lead us into victory."

"Victory?" Kuchoff asked, "Against whom?"

"I'm not really sure," Daph confessed.

"Do you have any idea where Lemac is right now?" Kuchoff asked.

"I don't," she confessed, "but I can tell you where he's not."

Kuchoff raised an eyebrow.

"He's not in Exland Mountain." Daph pointed to the top of the mountain we were sitting next to.

"But your master is." Loher commented with a devious look in her eyes.

"Where be t' dragons?" Balt asked excitedly.

"They're in a different..." she paused, thinking.

"A different realm?" I asked.

"You know of the stones." Daph sighed, making it sound more like realization than a question.

"Indeed," Avilyn replied sternly.

"How do we get there?" Meeka asked, "What should I think of?"

"Think of?" Daph asked, confused.

"Umm...dragons." Twig blurted with disdain in her voice, "Duhh."

"*Twig!*" Balt growled.

"What?!" Twig asked in defense, "It's obvious."

"Mind yer manners an' call 'er Sir." Balt snapped.

"My apologies, Commander." Twig added with a slight bow.

"What are your plans," Meeka asked Daph, "now that you've found us?"

"I'm going to lead you up the mountain and right to my master's chamber door." Daph smiled, "He's expecting you."

Lemac strolled among the giant eggs until one in particular caught his eye.

He stopped, took off the glove of his right hand and inspected the gigantic bronze colored egg by running his bare hand across its hard, roughly patterned surface.

It was cool to the touch but pulsating with a soothing rhythm.

"Is that one your favorite, my lord?" the deep voice breathed again, sounding a bit more feminine.

Lemac laughed, "What makes you think that?" he asked.

"Because it's the only bronze egg." She breathed.

"No," Lemac answered, "if I were to have a favorite," he frowned, "it would be a mythical *iridescent* egg."

The cavern suddenly began to tremble as the voice chuckled, "It's no myth, my lord.

The one and only iridescent egg was indeed laid and hatched almost six-hundred thousand years ago," she paused and became very serious, "and there hasn't been one since. In any realm. Long live the king of dragons."

"He's still alive?" Lemac asked in shock.

"Oh yes," she purred, "very much alive."

⟢⬥⟢

Clouds of pink, grey and orange smoke puffed on the top of Exland Mountain as we appeared from within accompanied by the familiar 'pops.'

"I'm sure I don't have to remind you that the entrance is just this way, Commander." Daph smiled and gestured the way.

"You can call me Meeka," she smiled, "if we're not aboard The Scorpion."

Daph nodded and began to lead us to the door.

Once we entered the hallway and began to approach the stairs, Balt and Rion began to chuckle.

"What's so funny?" Jacen Feldspar asked, looking a bit worried.

The magician's question was just enough for Meeka to lose her composure and begin to giggle as well.

Jacen looked around in confusion.

"Don't worry," Navari soothed and placed her hand on his shoulder, "it's a long story from before I even joined the crew."

By this time, Roash and Lybiidae were laughing too, "It's about Cirdan, our former commander." Roash laughed and punched Rion in the arm.

"Ow." Rion chuckled.

Jacen nervously laughed and we continued up the stairs.

"Do you have a key?" I asked as we stood in front of the door at the top.

"I don't need one." Daph answered as she tossed a coin through the hole in the door Balt made with his axe the first time we were here.

The coin jingled on the stone floor as Daph blinked into the room in a puff of grey smoke.

She unlocked the door and opened it wide with a gesture of, 'come on in.'

Sir O'cha and Sir Gregg drew their swords and prepared to enter.

"Ye won't be needin' yer weapons, Lads." Balt stoically groaned.

The pair of knights frowned and put their swords away.

⁌◉⁍

Through the velvet darkness, Lemac strained his vision like a man peering through storm-tossed waters.

"Show yourself," he commanded, authority ringing in his voice, "your very presence seems to have grown twice as vast since our last encounter."

"Indeed, it has, my lord," came the reply, a symphony of silk and steel that sent shivers down his spine.

The shadows themselves seemed to part like a curtain as she emerged into the torchlight's trembling embrace.

Before him towered Nerium, a magnificent fusion of mortal and dragon-kind that stretched twenty feet toward the heavens.

Her form, though following the graceful lines of humanity, was adorned in scales that shimmered like rose petals dipped in molten silver.

Each movement sent cascades of light dancing across her armor-like hide.

Her wings, more reminiscent of a noble's ceremonial cloak than instruments of flight, draped dramatically about her powerful frame.

At fifteen hundred kilograms, she embodied the perfect marriage of beauty and lethal strengtha ground-bound huntress who had traded the sky for raw, landbound power.

Her visage was a mesmerizing blend of dragon's might and human subtlety.

Beneath jaws that could shatter stone, lurked expressions of surprising complexity, while her eyes held ancient wisdom and predatory cunning in equal measure.

She moved with the fluid grace of a court dancer wrapped in the body of an apex predator, each step a display of perfectly controlled power.

When she hunted, her mighty legs carried her across the land like a storm given flesh, her tail sweeping behind her with the precision of a master swordsman's balance.

Her hands, though tipped with claws that could rend steel, possessed the delicate control of a sculptor's tools.

She was no mere dragon, nor simple human, but something far more terrible and beautiful—a predatory goddess forged in evolution's fires, combining draconic might with human guile.

Nature itself had conspired to create in her the perfect fusion of raw power and deadly cunning, a hunter who ruled not from the skies but from the shadows of the land itself.

⁕

The heavy oak door slowly swung wider as Avilyn strode into the chamber, his ancient elven eyes igniting with cold fury at the sight of Ficolus.

The tension in the air was palpable, causing Meeka to step forward urgently.

"Avilyn, wait! We need to—"

Without warning or word, the air itself seemed to crystallize as he unleashed a lance of pure force toward the human wizard.

The spell's power was so intense it split the stone floor beneath its path.

"NO!" Daph screamed, her voice cracking with horror as her master barely managed to raise his skeletal hands, conjuring a shield of crimson energy that shattered like glass under Avilyn's assault.

The backlash sent both Sir O'cha and Sir Gregg stumbling backward, their drawn swords suddenly feeling as substantial as children's toys.

Rion crouched low, his tail straight with excitement, fangs bared in a feral grin.

"Ye mad bastard!" Balt shouted, ducking as arcane lightning arced overhead, leaving scorch marks across the vaulted ceiling. "Could've given us a bloody warning! T'ough t'is is brilliant!"

"Stop this!" Meeka commanded, attempting to weave a barrier spell between the combatants.

It dissolved instantly under the sheer force of their magic.

Ficolus recovered quickly, weaving shadows into a writhing mass of tentacles that sought to crush his elven opponent.

Blood streamed from his nose and ears; his eyes wild with desperation.

"Master, please!" Daph sobbed, pressed against the wall as the magical energies made her hair stand on end.

Avilyn's response was devastating—a word in the tongue of dragons transformed the shadows into searing light, forcing the human wizard to shield his eyes.

The spell burned with such intensity that it left smoking holes in the stone walls.

"Get him, get him!" Rion yowled, practically dancing with excitement. "His left side's open!"

"Stay back!" Avilyn commanded as Sir Gregg attempted to flank Ficolus, the knight's gleaming blade singing through the air.

"Let me have a go!" Sir O'cha shouted, his sword trailing blue sparks in the magically charged air.

The knight's sword passed harmlessly through a phantom image as the real Ficolus materialized behind him, hands wreathed in emerald flame.

The heat was so intense it melted the edges of Sir Gregg's armor.

But Avilyn had anticipated this.

The stones beneath Ficolus' feet erupted upward, sending chunks of razor-sharp rock tearing through the wizard's robes and flesh.

Blood began to pour down the old man's leg.

"That's the way!" Balt bellowed, charging forward with his axe. "Hold him there!"

The dwarf swung his axe with a triumphant roar, only to hit the wall, cleaving out a chunk as both wizards vanished in a swirl of acrid smoke that left those nearby coughing and gagging.

They reappeared at opposite ends of the chamber, Ficolus bleeding heavily from a dozen cuts where Avilyn's spells had found their mark. His left arm hung uselessly, shredded by the stone shrapnel.

"Master, surrender!" Daph pleaded, tears streaming down her face. "Please!"

Her master began a desperate incantation, dark energy coalescing around him like a storm cloud.

The very stones of the chamber began to crack under the mounting pressure.

"Whatever ye're plannin', Elf, do it fast!" Balt shouted to Avilyn, as the very air began to taste of copper and ash.

"This ends now," Avilyn's voice resonated with power as his hands traced complex patterns in the air.

"NO!" Meeka lunged forward, but Rion caught her, holding her back. "We need him alive!"

Avilyn's response was swift and final.

His spell, crafted from millennia of arcane knowledge, struck Ficolus with the precision of a surgeon's blade.

The air itself seemed to scream as reality twisted around the human wizard.

It unraveled not just the old man's desperate final spell, but the very essence that held his physical form together.

Ficolus' flesh began to dissolve like wax under flame, his bones showing through briefly before they too began to crumble.

"MASTER!" Daph's anguished scream mixed with Ficolus' final cry as his body collapsed in upon itself, reduced to nothing more than a fine, glittering dust that scattered across the chamber floor.

Where the mighty wizard had stood, only his empty robes remained, settling gently to the ground like autumn leaves.

The silence that followed was deafening, broken only by Daph's quiet sobs.

"By the gods," Sir O'cha whispered, lowering his unused blade.

"You didn't just kill him. You... *unmade* him."

"That was magnificent!" Rion purred, still holding a struggling Meeka.

"Aye, 'aven't seen a wizard's duel like t'at since t'e Battle o' Nobles!" Balt agreed, grinning broadly.

Avilyn's face showed no triumph, only grim satisfaction as he surveyed what remained of his ancient foe. "Some threats," he said quietly, "must be ended completely."

In the shadows, Navari, Lybiidae, and Roash had already melted away, leaving the others to deal with the aftermath of the devastating magical duel.

⁙

Grotesque trolls shuffled between carefully arranged nests, tending to the dozens of dragon eggs with surprising gentleness.

Their grunts and shuffles seemed to emphasize the deadly silence of Nerium's movements.

Lemac fought to maintain his composure as she lowered her head toward him, her dragon-like features twisted into what might have been a smile.

Those jaws could snap him in half with no more effort than breaking a stick.

Her clawed hands, though capable of delicate work, could tear him apart in seconds.

"Does my larger stature unsettle you, my lord?" she asked, amusement dancing in her predatory eyes. "I remain your most faithful creation."

She lowered her head in a gesture of submission, though the movement itself was somehow both respectful and menacing.

"Unsettle me?" Lemac laughed, finding his footing in their familiar dynamic despite his racing heart. "My dear, you are magnificent. Though I admit, theory and practice are quite different things."

Nerium's laugh echoed through the chamber, sending several trolls skittering between the eggs.

⸺◆⸺

The glittering dust that was once Ficolus settled in the chamber's stale air as the shock of his destruction slowly lifted.

"That was bloody brilliant!" Balt roared, practically bouncing on his heels. "Did ye see how 'e just... just..." He made explosive gestures with his hands.

"The way the floor broke..." Rion purred, his tail twitching with excitement as his pointed ears stayed perked forward, "...incredible!"

"You FOOL!" Meeka's voice cut through their celebration like a blade. "We needed him alive!"

"All that knowledge, gone." Daph's voice trembled with barely contained rage. "My master's research, his plans, everything—just scattered like common dust!"

"Awe, come now, Lass," Balt commented, "ye dinna even like t'e ol' man."

Avilyn turned slowly to face the enraged wizards, his ancient features calm. "Your concern is misplaced."

"Misplaced?" Meeka advanced on him, magic crackling around her clenched fists. "We've spent months tracking him down!"

"Stand down, Meeka," I warned, "first officer or not. Please, stand down." I pleaded, though I shared her frustration.

"He's lost his elven mind," Daph spat. "All those centuries must have addled his—"

"You already possess what we seek," Avilyn interrupted, his eyes fixed on Daph.

"What?" Daph stepped back. "I don't—"

"He's right," Lybiidae spoke from the shadows. "Think, girl. Where were you when your master worked?"

"I... no, I didn't..." Daph's voice faltered.

"Navari," Avilyn spoke softly. "If you would."

"My pleasure," Navari hissed as she lowered her hood.

Her violet eyes began to glow, brighter still, the closer she got to her prey.

"No!" Daph tried to turn away, but Navari was already there, her serpentine hair writhing as she caught the young wizard's gaze.

"Look at me, child," Navari commanded. "What did you see in his workshop? What did you hear in his chambers?"

Daph's resistance crumbled as Navari's power took hold, her eyes going wide as forgotten memories surfaced.   "I... I remember everything. The formulae, the incantations... By the gods, it was all there. I was there. I know where Lemac is and I know how to get there."

"Well," Jacen muttered, "that's rather unsettling."

"Quite effective though," Sir O'cha added, while Sir Gregg nodded in agreement.

Roash merely watched from her perch in the shadows, her tail swishing thoughtfully.

"Ye could've mentioned t'is bit earlier," Balt grumbled at Avilyn, his battle-high finally fading.

"Some memories must be drawn forth carefully," Avilyn replied. "Or they shatter like glass."

CHAPTER THREE
GATHER

Lemac knelt beside the three hatchlings as they tumbled and played, his face beaming with paternal pride. "Look how strong they're getting! The red one's already breathing smoke."

"Aren't they precious?" Nerium cooed, her massive form curled protectively around the play area.

She reached out one deadly claw with surprising gentleness to stroke the red dragon's head. "Such perfect little darlings..." Her voice carried an edge of bitterness.

"Something troubles you, my dear?" Lemac asked, though he already knew the answer.

"They should be mine," she hissed softly, watching as the two green hatchlings wrestled.

"I should be their mother. Not some wild dragon whose eggs we stole."

"You are their mother now," Lemac soothed, standing to pat her scaled arm. "And soon they'll help us take everything we deserve. Speaking of which..."

"Ah yes," Nerium's mood lifted, her predatory smile returning.

"Our forces grow stronger by the day.

The orcs number nearly two hundred thousand now, and the hob-goblin clans have pledged another hundred fifty thousand warriors."

"And the ogres?"

"Ten thousand strong. Stupid brutes, but useful as siege weapons." She chuckled darkly.

"With Jade and Emeral leading from the air, and my ground forces..."

"While I provide magical support," Lemac added, watching as the red hatchling successfully produced a tiny flame.

"Excellent! Well done, little one!"

"There's still the matter of the locket," Nerium reminded him, her voice turning serious.

"The Scorpion's defenses are formidable."

"The ship's crew is skilled, yes. But they won't expect an attack from within. Our agent is already in place."

Lemac picked up the red hatchling, cradling it like a proud father. "Once we have the locket's power, Beornan Heafod will fall. The realm will be ours."

"Ours," Nerium echoed, watching the hatchlings with hungry eyes.

"And these precious ones will help us rule it all. Though I still wish..." She trailed off, her massive tail twitching in agitation.

"Patience, my dear. Perhaps once we've conquered the realm, we can find a way to give you what you truly desire." Lemac stroked the red dragon's scales. "For now, let us focus on raising these three to be proper engines of destruction."

"Yes," Nerium purred, lowering her head to nuzzle the wrestling green dragons.

"My perfect little destroyers. Mommy will teach you all about proper hunting techniques. Starting with humans, they're so delight-fully crunchy."

After collecting what little remained in Ficolus' chambers, we made our way back down the mountain toward The Scorpion.

The air felt electric, both from the lingering magic of Avilyn's display and the tension of what lay ahead.

"Are ye sure them portal stones be safe?" Balt asked, his axe swinging dangerously at his side. "Last time we went t'rough one o' t'em fancy doors, we ended up lost."

"At least it won't be boring," Twig declared, adjusting the twigs in her wild red hair. "Though I still think we're idiots for following someone who was trying to kill us yesterday."

"Hey!" Daph protested. "I never tried to kill anyone!"

"You were literally part of a dragon-raising death cult," Twig pointed out.

"She's got you there," I chuckled, though I kept my hand near my sword.

Rion scratched his head, his lion-like features scrunched in concentration. "So, we think about dragons and then... poof? What if I think about the wrong dragon?"

"Then we all die horribly," Twig answered cheerfully.

"Oh." Rion's tail drooped. "That's not good."

"Nobody is dying," Avilyn interjected, his partially melted features stern in the fading light.

"The portal stones respond to intent more than specific thoughts. Focus on following our guide."

We reached The Scorpion as the sun began to set, her proud bulk a welcome sight after the chaos in the mountain.

Captain Magnus stood at the helm; his face unreadable as we approached.

"Report," he commanded.

"Ficolus is dead," Meeka stated flatly. "Daph knows where Lemac is hiding."

"And the dragons?" Kuchoff asked, his hand absently touching the pack where his mother's severed hand lay.

"Through the portal stones," Daph explained. "In a realm where they've been gathering armies. But we should hurry—Lemac will know something's wrong when Ficolus doesn't return."

"Ach, armies?" Balt perked up. "Now yer speakin' me language! How many we talkin' about?"

"Thousands," Daph answered quietly.

"Thousands?" Rion's ears flattened. "Like... more than ten?"

"A wee bit more than ten, ye great furry lump," Balt laughed, slapping Rion's arm. "Just means more fer us ta kill!"

"If we can get through the portal," Twig reminded everyone. "Unless you'd all rather stand around comparing who has the biggest sword?"

"I vote for the portal," I suggested, watching the sun sink lower. "Before we lose the light."

Captain Magnus nodded. "Helm, take us to the stones. Crew to battle stations. Errfords to their positions." He turned to Daph, his voice hard. "If this is a trap..."

"It's not," she insisted. "I swear on my master's ashes—which I believe are still in Avilyn's robe pockets."

"Actually," Avilyn smiled thinly, "I left them for the wind."

As The Scorpion turned toward the portal stones, I found myself wondering if we were sailing into salvation or slaughter.

But then, that sort of uncertainty had become almost comfortable over the years.

"McLaaud," Loher called from her position near the bow. "Ready to add another realm to our list?"

I smiled at my wife, fangs showing just slightly. "As long as this one has better taverns than the last."

⁓ ❖ ⁓

From their vantage point atop the weathered cliffs, Lemac and Nerium surveyed their assembled might.

Five hundred ships stretched across the horizon like a floating city of wood and canvas, their black hulls stark against the steel-grey waters.

Each vessel bore the mark of the Grand Ascendancy—a purple dragon coiled around a burning sword—painted on sails that could easily shroud The Scorpion twice over.

"Magnificent, isn't it?" Lemac breathed, watching as torches began to flicker to life across the fleet in the growing dusk.

The combined effect created a constellation of orange dots that rivaled the emerging stars above.

Nerium's massive form shifted beside him, her scales catching the last rays of sunlight like polished copper.

"Two hundred thousand orcs," she purred, her draconic features twisting into what passed for a smile. "I can smell them from here."

The nearest ship's deck crawled with activity as orcs in black armor performed combat drills with brutal efficiency.

Their war chants carried across the water; a guttural chorus that seemed to make the very air vibrate.

Siege weapons—massive ballistae and catapults—lined the decks of every third vessel, their mechanisms gleaming with fresh oil.

"The hobgoblin clans took the rear guard position," Lemac noted, pointing to the sleeker vessels at the back of the formation.

Their distinctive, red-striped sails stood out against the darkening sky.

"One hundred fifty thousand of their finest warriors, each one worth three human soldiers."

"And my precious ogres," Nerium added with maternal pride, indicating the reinforced ships in the center of the formation.

Their decks had been specially widened to accommodate the ten thousand massive creatures.

"Though I do wish they'd stop eating the rigging."

A horn sounded from somewhere in the fleet—deep, resonant notes that echoed off the cliffs.

In perfect unison, thousands of torches raised to the sky in acknowledgment.

The display of discipline sent a shiver of anticipation down Lemac's spine.

"Even The Scorpion can't stand against this," he said softly.

"Not with Jade and Emeral providing air support."

As if summoned by his words, two shadows passed overhead—the young green dragons executing a perfect formation turn above the fleet.

Nerium's tail swished against the rocky ground, leaving deep grooves in the stone. "We should attack now, while we have surprise on our side."

"Patience, my dear." Lemac placed a hand on her scaled arm.

"Once we have the locket, your psi powers will rival Amaliya's. Then Beornan Heafod's walls will crumble before us."

He paused, watching as a group of ogres accidentally tore down a mast while trying to adjust it.

"Though perhaps we should separate the ogres onto different ships before they sink our own fleet."

The hybrid creature laughed. "They are rather enthusiastic." Her expression suddenly turned serious.

"Our agent aboard The Scorpion... are you certain she can be trusted?"

"With her very soul," Lemac smiled.

"Now, shall we review the invasion plans one final time? I believe our generals are waiting."

As they turned away from the cliff's edge, the assembled fleet began to fade into the gathering darkness.

Only the torches remained visible—a sea of flames that promised to set the world ablaze.

Chapter Four

THE PROPHET

The Scorpion cut through the hazy waters as we approached the ancient portal stones.

Their weathered surfaces rose from the sea like accusing fingers, their runes glowing with a faint purple luminescence that seemed to pulse in time with the waves.

"Those symbols," Twig observed from her perch near the bow, "they're dragon script, aren't they?" She looked to Avilyn for confirmation.

The old wizard nodded, his scarred features thoughtful. "Indeed. Though few remain who can read them properly."

I noticed Meeka standing slightly apart from the others, her hands clenched at her sides as she stared at the stones.

There was something in her posture that seemed...off.

Before I could analyze it further, Kuchoff approached her.

"You're troubled," he said softly, placing a hand on her shoulder.

She started slightly at his touch.

"Just remembering the last time we traversed realms," she said with a weak smile.

"We lost good people."

"We got stronger," Kuchoff reminded her.

The way they interacted—surrogate mother and son—had always been touching.

Now, with his birth mother dead, their bond seemed even more pronounced.

"Ye both gone soft in t'e head?" Balt called from his position near the harpoon.

"Save yer tender moments fer when we ain't about ta sail through a magic door!"

"Speaking of which," Daph interjected, "everyone needs to focus.

Think of dragons, but don't fixate on any particular type.

Let the stones guide us."

"That's about as clear as mud," Twig muttered.

"Just think about dragons eating people," Rion suggested helpfully.

"That's what I'm doing!"

"Creature Controls, prepare for engagement!" Captain Magnus commanded.

"Errfords, ready shields. Archers to the rails."

He turned to Daph. "How close do we need to be?"

"The stones will reach for us," she assured him.

"We'll know when—"

The air suddenly crackled with energy.

The runes on the portal stones flared brilliantly, their purple light reflecting off the waves and casting everyone's faces in an otherworldly glow.

I felt the familiar tingle of magic raising the hair on my arms.

"Helm, hold her steady," Kuchoff ordered, moving to the bow.

Meeka followed, her face a mask of concentration.

"Focus, everyone," Avilyn commanded.

"Let your thoughts drift to dragons, but don't—"

The world twisted.

I felt my stomach lurch as reality seemed to fold in on itself.

The sky above became the sea below, then both became something else entirely.

Colors that had no names burned across my vision.

The last thing I heard before everything went white was Balt's cheerful voice: "If we die, I'm hauntin' the lot of ye!"

Then we were somewhere else entirely.

As the white light faded and reality reasserted itself, the first thing I saw was Balt practically dancing at the rail, his beard bristling with excitement.

"Would ye look at t'at!" He bounced on his heels, pointing at something ahead of us.

"It's like Ziggy's tavern during th' summer festival—except wit more things tae kill!"

Through the dissipating portal haze, I could make out what had gotten our dwarven warrior so excited.

The shoreline ahead was dotted with campfires—hundreds of them—each surrounded by armed figures.

"Those would be the armies Daph mentioned," I observed dryly.

"Aye!" Balt's grin threatened to split his face.

"T'ousands o' em! Like a bloody birthday present wrapped in armor!"

He turned to Rion, eyes gleaming.

"How many d'ye reckon ye can take, ye great furry lump?"

"Um..." Rion scratched his head.

"More than ten?"

"Quiet," Captain Magnus ordered, though I caught the slight smile tugging at his lips.

"Let's not announce our arrival just yet."

"Ach, ye're nae fun at all," Balt grumbled, though he did lower his voice.

He leaned closer to me, practically vibrating with anticipation.

"But jest look at all t'em beautiful baddies! It's like th' gods themselves heard me prayers fer more things tae hit wi' me axe!"

"Your prayers involve asking for armies to fight?" Twig asked incredulously.

"Aye, among ot'er things," Balt nodded sagely.

"I also pray fer stronger ale an' tougher pillows.

But mostly fer things tae fight."

He patted his axe lovingly.

"A dwarf has tae have his priorities straight, ye ken?"

"You're completely insane," Twig declared.

"Thank ye kindly!" Balt beamed, taking it as a compliment.

"Now, if ye'll excuse me, Lass, I need tae go count how many spare axe handles I brought.

Wi' t'is many heads tae crack, I might need t'e extras!"

As he strutted off, humming what sounded suspiciously like a battle hymn, I heard Navari sigh.

"How does he maintain such enthusiasm for violence?"

"I believe," I answered, watching him practically skip across the deck, "that for Balt, combat is less of a profession and more of a hobby.

Like gardening, but with more screaming."

"An' better fertilizer!" Balt called back, having apparently heard us.

"Nutt'n makes ta flowers grow like a wee bit o' bloodshed!"

Deep within the castle's war room, Lemac stood before a massive stone table, its surface carved into an intricate map of Beornan Heafod and the surrounding territories.

Carefully placed markers indicated the positions of their forces, while a single black piece—carved in the shape of The Scorpion—sat near the portal stones.

Nerium's massive form dominated one side of the chamber, her tail occasionally brushing against the weapons that lined the walls.

The assembled generals—a mix of orc chieftains, hobgoblin war-leaders, and human commanders—kept a respectful distance from her hybrid form.

"The Scorpion has just crossed through the portal stones," a breathless messenger announced, bursting into the room.

"Right on schedule," Lemac smiled, moving the ship's marker on the map.

He looked up at the assembled leaders.

"Is everything in position?"

An orc chieftain stepped forward, his black armor gleaming in the torchlight.

"My warriors are ready to—"

The doors suddenly burst open again as two troll handlers rushed in, their faces twisted with panic.

"The bronze egg!" one wheezed.

"It's hatching!"

Nerium's head snapped up, her eyes blazing.

"Now? It's too soon!"

"Take me to it," Lemac commanded, already moving toward the door.

He paused only long enough to address the gathered commanders.

"Maintain your positions.

Wait for my signal."

The trek down to the dragon nursery seemed to take an eternity, even with Nerium's long strides eating up the distance.

When they arrived, the chamber was in chaos.

Trolls scattered in every direction as the massive bronze egg rocked violently on its nest of heated stones.

A deep crack ran down its center, golden light spilling from within.

The shell's surface rippled like liquid metal as the creature inside fought for freedom.

"This changes everything," Nerium breathed, her clawed hands flexing with barely contained excitement.

"How so?" Lemac asked, though his eyes never left the hatching egg.

"Bronze dragons are special," she explained, moving closer to the nest.

"They're born with an innate connection to time itself.

If we can control it..."

The egg suddenly exploded outward, sending fragments of metallic shell in all directions.

In the center of the nest, gleaming like a newly minted coin, sat a bronze wyrmling.

Its eyes, already filled with ancient wisdom, fixed upon them.

Then it spoke, its voice carrying the weight of centuries:

"You should not have brought me into this world."

Lemac's triumphant smile faltered.

"What?"

"The timeline fractures," the wyrmling continued, its gaze boring into them.

"The king of dragons stirs.

The deceiver chooses true heart.

All your carefully laid plans..."

It spread its wings, golden light cascading off them.

"They end in bisection."

Nerium moved faster than something of her size should be able to, her clawed hand snatching the wyrmling before it could take flight.

"Tell us what you mean!"

The wyrmling 's only response was a sound that might have been laughter.

CHAPTER FIVE

INSIDE UP & DOWNSIDE OUT

The Scorpion drifted silently through waters that seemed too still, too dark to be natural.

The countless campfires along the shore cast shifting shadows across our deck, making every rope and spar appear alive.

"I dinnae like t'e look o' t'at water," Balt grumbled, leaning over the rail.

"It's like sailin' on black oil."

"Everything here feels wrong," Daph whispered.

"The air itself is different."

She was right.

Each breath felt heavy, as though the very atmosphere resented our presence.

Above us, the sky held no stars, only a perpetual twilight that made judging time impossible.

"Ye ken what would make it feel more homey?" Balt's eyes gleamed.

"A wee bit o' violence!

Look at all t'em camps just waitin' fer us tae introduce ourselves!"

"If by 'introduce' you mean 'slaughter,'" Twig observed.

"Aye! Now yer gettin' it, Lass!"

"Quiet," Captain Magnus ordered from the helm.

"Navari, what do you sense?"

Our Medusan scout closed her glowing eyes in concentration.

"Many minds... thousands. But there's something else..."

Her serpentine hair writhed in agitation.

"Something vast. Ancient."

"Dragons?" I suggested.

"No," she hissed.

"Different. Like a shadow across time itself."

"Oh, t'at's jest wonderful," Balt threw up his hands.

"First we get armies, t'en we get cryptic warnings about time shadows.

Why can't we ever find a nice realm wit' simple things tae kill?"

Suddenly, Meeka gasped.

She was standing at the bow, her face pale in the strange light.

"Captain," she called, her voice tight.

"You need to see this."

As we moved to join her, the sight ahead drew curses from even the most seasoned crew members.

Rising from the dark waters like the bones of some fallen god, a massive structure dominated the horizon.

Its architecture defied reason—towers that spiraled in impossible directions, bridges that crossed empty space at angles that hurt the eyes to follow.

"That would be where they're keeping the dragons," Daph confirmed.

"Ach, finally!" Balt hefted his axe.

"A proper castle tae storm! None o' t'at sneakin' about nonsense."

"Actually," Meeka interjected, her voice carrying an odd note that I couldn't quite place,

"I think I might know another way in."

Everyone turned to look at her.

"There's something familiar about this place," she continued, studying the twisted spires.

"From old texts I've studied. There should be underwater passages, hidden from common knowledge."

"And ye're just now mentionin' t'is?" Balt asked incredulously.

I wasn't certain until I saw it," she replied, perhaps a touch too quickly.

"But I'm sure now."

Captain Magnus studied her for a long moment.

"How sure?"

"Trust me," she said softly, looking at Kuchoff.

"I wouldn't risk your lives if I wasn't certain."

I caught something in her expression—a flicker of... what? Pain? Resolve?

Before I could analyze it further, a sound split the air that made my blood run cold.

From somewhere within the twisted castle, a dragon's roar echoed across the water.

<hr>

The youngest green dragon, Emeral, landed gracefully on the castle's balcony as Lemac paced the chamber.

The bronze wyrmling's prophecy had left him unsettled, but there was no turning back now.

"Master," a whisper of wind announced the quickling's arrival.

The creature stood barely knee-high, its form seeming to blur even when standing still.

"I await your command."

Lemac produced a small scroll with The Scorpion's layout carefully detailed.

"Find this locket.

It will be heavily guarded, either on the captain's person or secured in his quarters.

Do not engage anyone.

Just get in, take it, and return."

The quickling's smile was sharp as a dagger.

"Simple theft? How delightfully boring."

It took the scroll, studied it for barely a second, then dissolved into pure motion.

"Now we wait," Lemac sighed, turning to where Nerium lounged against the wall, her massive form making the chamber feel cramped.

"Not for long," she purred.

"Your little thief is quite efficient."

True to her words, barely ten minutes passed before the quickling materialized, holding something that gleamed gold in the torchlight.

"The ship's Medusan sensed me," it reported, dropping the locket into Lemac's outstretched hand.

"And a rather observant halfling caught a glimpse as I left. But by then..."

It shrugged; the motion almost too fast to follow.

Lemac examined the locket carefully before presenting it to Nerium.

"Your enhanced power awaits, my dear."

The hybrid creature's clawed hands trembled slightly as she took the locket, its delicate chain looking absurd against her massive, scaled fingers.

The moment she clasped it around her neck, her eyes began to glow with an inner fire.

"Yes," she breathed, her voice resonating with new power.

"YES!"

Without warning, her gaze fixed on the doorway where two orc guards stood watch.

They suddenly rose into the air, clutching their throats.

The sound of cracking bones filled the chamber as their bodies began to twist in impossible ways.

"Magnificent," Lemac whispered, though he took an involuntary step back.

The guards' final screams were cut short as their bodies literally tore apart, showering the stone floor with gore.

"Now that's power," Nerium laughed, the sound like breaking glass.

"Shall I demonstrate further?"

"Perhaps..." Lemac swallowed hard, finding his voice.

"Perhaps we should save your strength for The Scorpion?"

She turned to him, eyes still blazing, blood dripping from the ceiling above them.

"Oh, my dear Lemac," she purred.

"This is just the beginning."

Her gaze shifted to the bronze wyrmling in its cage.

"Now, little one, let's discuss this prophecy of yours in more detail."

The wyrmling met her gaze without flinching.

"Your power is borrowed," it said simply.

"And what is borrowed must be returned."

Nerium's laugh echoed through the castle halls, sending hardened warriors scrambling for cover.

In the distance, dragons roared in response, while deep below, armies of orcs and hobgoblins huddled in their barracks, suddenly unsure if they were truly the predators in this realm after all.

⸻ ◦◊◦ ⸻

Navari's sudden hiss cut through the eerie twilight. "Something was just here—something fast."

The hair on the back of my neck stood up as I watched her serpentine locks writhe in agitation.

Anything that could disturb a Medusan's composure was cause for concern.

"I saw it!" Twig called from her position near the bow.

"Like a shadow but moving wrong.

It went that way!"

She pointed toward the twisted castle.

"Toward those impossible towers."

"Ach, so now we've got invisible beasties runnin' about?"

Balt hefted his axe.

"Why can't anythin' ever be simple?"

Loher burst from the captain's quarters, her face ashen.

"The locket," she said, her voice tight with barely controlled rage.

"It's gone."

"What?" Kuchoff's hand instinctively went to his pack where his mother's severed hand was stored.

"How?"

"A quickling," Avilyn's voice carried an edge I'd never heard before.

"One of the few creatures that could bypass our defenses through pure speed."

"I dinnae care if it can outrun lightnin' itself," Balt growled.

"Nobody steals from t'is crew!"

Meeka stood slightly apart from the others, her face unreadable in the strange light.

"With the locket's power," she said carefully, "our enemy's capabilities will be significantly enhanced."

As if in response to her words, an agonized scream echoed from the castle—suddenly cut short.

Even at this distance, we could feel the pulse of deadly power.

"That would be Lemac's new creature, testing her new abilities," Daph whispered, her face pale.

"We need to—"

She was interrupted by another scream, this one accompanied by a wet tearing sound that made several crew members gag.

"Right then," Balt said cheerfully, though I noticed his grip on his axe was white-knuckled.

"When do we storm ta castle?"

"We don't," Captain Magnus replied, his eyes fixed on the twisted spires.

"Not yet. First, we need a plan."

"Ye ken what I always say about plans," Balt started.

"Yes," the entire crew responded in unison, "'dey juss get in de way o' perfectly good violence.'"

"Ach, ye're all startin' tae sound like me. I be so proud!"

The bronze wyrmling sat calmly in its cage, watching as Nerium paced the blood-slicked chamber floor.

Her massive form seemed larger somehow, power radiating from her in almost visible waves.

"Tell me more about this fracturing timeline," she demanded, absently gesturing at another guard.

His body lifted into the air, bones cracking like dry twigs.

"Must you?" Lemac winced as gore splattered the walls.

"Does my newfound strength disturb you?" She turned to him, her draconic features twisting into something that might have been a smile.

"After all your talk of power, of destiny..."

"Not at all," he lied smoothly.

"I simply prefer my servants alive until they're needed otherwise."

The wyrmling's ancient eyes shifted between them.

"The balance shifts," it said softly.

"The borrowed power was never meant for hybrid flesh. It burns too bright, too fast."

"Nonsense," Nerium snapped, though her clawed hand unconsciously touched the locket.

"I feel magnificent. Unstoppable."

"Pride comes before a fall," the wyrmling observed.

"Enough riddles!" She seized the cage, lifting it to eye level.

"Speak plainly or I'll—"

"You'll what?" The young dragon's voice carried millennia of wisdom.

"Kill me? Then you'll never know about the choice."

"What choice?" Lemac stepped forward, genuinely curious.

"The one your deceiver must make." The wyrmling's gaze fixed on some distant point.

"When love proves stronger than loyalty.

When the heart becomes more important than the goal."

Nerium's grip on the cage tightened, the metal groaning.

"If you speak of betrayal..."

"I speak of what will be," the bronze dragon replied.

"Of true heart."

"Lies!" The cage crumpled in her grasp, but the wyrmling simply spread its wings, hovering unperturbed.

"Time cannot lie," it said simply.

"Though mortals often wish it could."

Lemac started forward.

"Enough of this. Nerium, we should—"

"Do not presume to command me," she cut him off, her voice carrying harmonic undertones that made the chamber's stones vibrate.

"Not anymore."

He raised his hands placatingly.

"My dear, I would never—"

"But you would," she purred, turning to face him fully.

"You always have. Your clever plans, your subtle manipulations.

And I followed, like an obedient pet."

She flexed her clawed hands. "

Perhaps it's time for a change in leadership."

The wyrmling's soft laughter drew both their attention.

"And so, it begins."

Captain Magnus gathered us in the ship's war room, the tension thick enough to cut with a blade.

Meeka's suggestion about underwater passages had sparked a heated debate.

"So, we're just supposed tae swim up and knock on t'eir door?" Balt crossed his arms.

"And here I thought we were done wit' all t'is sneakin' about."

"The passages aren't underwater anymore," Meeka explained, spreading out an old map on the table.

"This realm's sea level is much lower. They'd be exposed now."

"And you know this how?" Twig asked, her usual bluntness making several crew members shift uncomfortably.

"From ancient texts," Meeka replied smoothly.

"The architecture matches descriptions of—"

"Does it matter?" Kuchoff cut in.

"They have my mother's locket.

Every moment we waste arguing gives them more time to use it."

"And that's exactly why we can't rush in," I pointed out.

"You felt that power surge.

Lemac's creature, which we have no idea what it is or how big it is, with enhanced abilities..."

"Will tear us apart if we're not careful," Avilyn finished, his scarred features grim.

"We need a strategy."

"I have an idea," Daph spoke up from where she'd been studying the map.

"But you're not going to like it."

"Ach, t'ose are always t'e best kind," Balt grinned.

"The castle will be heavily guarded," she continued,

"but there's one section they'll leave relatively unprotected—the dragon nursery."

"Because who'd be crazy enough tae break intae a room full o' dragons?" Balt's grin widened.

"I like it already!"

"Young dragons," Daph corrected.

"Mostly unhatched. They keep them separate from the adults to prevent... accidents."

"The bronze one has hatched," Navari announced suddenly.

Everyone turned to look at her.

"I can sense its mind. It's... different. Ancient somehow."

"Wonderful," Twig muttered.

"So now we have prophecy-spewing baby dragons to deal with?"

"Better than prophecy-spewing adult dragons," I offered.

"Focus," Captain Magnus commanded.

"Daph, continue."

"The nursery connects to the lower levels through maintenance tunnels.

The trolls use them to bring food and supplies. If we can get in there..."

"We can move through t'e whole castle!" Balt finished excitedly.

Finally, a proper plan!"

"You just like it because it involves hitting things," Twig observed.

"Aye, t'at I do, lass. T'at, I do."

"It's risky," Kuchoff said, but I could see the consideration in his eyes.

"Though with the errfords' shields..."

"And my magic," Meeka added quickly. Perhaps too quickly.

"We'll need a distraction," I suggested.

"Something to draw attention away from the nursery."

"Leave t'at tae me," Balt patted his axe lovingly.

"I'm verra good at bein' distractin'."

Captain Magnus studied the map for a long moment.

"It could work. But we'll need perfect timing. One mistake and—"

A roar from the castle cut him off—not a dragon's roar, but something else.

Something that made the very air vibrate with power.

"That would be Nerium," Daph whispered.

"She's getting stronger."

"Who is Nerium?" Jacen asked, entering the conversation.

"Lemac's creature." Daph breathed.

"Then we'd best get moving," Kuchoff said grimly.

"Before she gets any stronger."

⸻ ◆ ⸻

The chamber hummed with an unnatural stillness, broken only by the heavy breathing of Nerium and the soft, metallic scraping of the bronze wyrmling's scales against the stone floor.

Lemac stood apart, his eyes darting between Nerium and the young dragon, calculating.

Nerium's hands trembled, fingers twitching with newfound power that seemed to pulse just beneath her scales.

The locket—Kuchoff's locket—hung gingerly around her neck, its stolen memories thrumming with an intensity that made her vision blur at the edges.

"Tell me," she said to the wyrmling, her voice a razor's edge of barely contained desperation, "what prophecy burns inside you?"

The bronze wyrmling lifted its head, eyes like molten copper fixed on Nerium.

When it spoke, the words seemed to echo from somewhere beyond the chamber, beyond time itself.

"Shadows gather where stolen memories bleed. The locket is a key, but not the lock."

Lemac stepped forward, one hand half-raised—whether in caution or preparation to intervene, it was impossible to tell.

"Nerium," he said softly, a warning threaded through his tone, "the power is—"

"—changing me," she finished, a bitter laugh escaping her lips.

The air around her began to shimmer, charged with an energy that made Lemac take an involuntary step back.

"I can feel it. Every memory in this locket, every stolen breath of the child it once belonged to—they're becoming *part* of me."

The wyrmling tilted its head, scales catching what little light filtered into the chamber.

"Transformation is rarely gentle," it intoned.

"Nor is it ever complete."

Lemac's hand now rested near a weapon, not quite drawn, but close enough to suggest the threat of imminent violence.

"What are you implying?" he demanded of the wyrmling.

But the young dragon merely blinked, a slow, knowing gesture that suggested depths of understanding far beyond its apparent years.

"The path splits," it said.

"And Nerium stands at the fracture."

Nerium's laugh this time was wild, unhinged.

Power crackled around her like static, making Lemac's hair stand on end.

"A fracture," she repeated.

"Or a choice."

The tension in the chamber was a living thing now—Lemac's controlled fury, the wyrmling's cryptic knowledge, and Nerium's volatile new power all coiling together like serpents ready to strike.

And beneath it all, the locket continued to pulse, a heartbeat of stolen memories waiting to be unleashed.

———◆———

"Run through the teams one more time," Captain Magnus suggested as we gathered in the war room.

"The infiltration team will be led by Roash," Commander Ashpin began, pointing to positions on the crude map.

"With her will be Rion, Balt and his errford companion, both McLaauds with their errfords, and the captain himself with an er-rford."

"And six of my best hunters," Roash added, motioning to a group of lean, dark-furred eline warriors who seemed to melt into the shadows even while standing still.

"No errfords for them?" Twig asked, adjusting a twig in her wild red hair.

"Can't risk the glow giving us away," one of the eline hunters replied softly.

"We'll be moving ahead as scouts.

Errfords would defeat the purpose of stealth."

"Ach, all t'is sneakin' about," Balt grumbled, though his eyes gleamed with anticipation.

"When do we get tae t'e fun part?"

"The 'fun part' as you call it," Roash purred, "depends entirely on how well we sneak in first."

"I still say we should just march up and knock," Balt chuckled.

"Politely like."

"With your axe?" Twig quipped.

"Aye! Most polite weapon t'ere is. Gets straight tae t'e point o' t'ings."

"If we could focus," Captain Magnus cut in.

"Timing is critical here. The diversion team needs to..."

A distant roar from the castle made the very air vibrate.

Even at this distance, we could feel the pulse of unnatural power.

"Nerium grows stronger," Daph whispered.

"We need to move soon."

"Then let's begin," Captain Magnus said grimly.

"Positions, everyone. And may the gods watch over us all."

"Except fer Nerium," Balt added cheerfully.

"T'e gods can look t'e ot'er way when we get tae her."

— ◆ —

"Lock that thing away," Nerium commanded, her voice carrying new harmonics that made the chamber's stones vibrate.

"Somewhere it can't spout any more prophecies."

Two troll handlers scrambled to comply, though their usual clumsiness was amplified by obvious terror.

The bronze wyrmling allowed itself to be guided into an iron cage, its ancient eyes never leaving Nerium's transformed figure.

"Time flows like water," it said softly as the cage door clanged shut.

"And even the strongest dam must eventually break."

"Take it to the lower vaults," Lemac ordered before Nerium could respond.

"The ones with the enchanted locks."

As the trolls hurried away with their prophetic cargo, Lemac turned his attention back to the assembled war leaders.

The orc chieftains had backed away from the table, their usual bloodthirsty grins replaced by wary frowns.

Even the hobgoblin commanders, known for their stoic nature, seemed unsettled by Nerium's growing power.

"The plan remains unchanged," Lemac declared, though he kept a careful distance from his transformed ally.

"When The Scorpion approaches—"

"The plan changes," Nerium cut him off.

Her massive form seemed to ripple, scales catching the torchlight in ways that defied natural law.

"I no longer require such... elaborate preparations."

She gestured at the map table.

The carefully placed markers representing their forces suddenly lifted into the air, spinning like deadly dancers before exploding into splinters.

"Nerium," Lemac started, fighting to keep his voice level,

"we've spent months positioning our forces. The timing—"

"Time?" She laughed, the sound like breaking glass.

"That little bronze prophet has made me think about time.

About power.

About destiny."

Her clawed hand touched the locket at her throat.

"Such interesting memories in here.

The boy's childhood, his training, his fears..."

"The locket's power was meant to enhance your abilities," Lemac reminded her.

"Not to—"

"To what?" She turned to face him fully, and Lemac had to stop himself from stepping back.

Her features had changed again, becoming something that straddled the line between dragon and human in new, unsettling ways.

"To change me? To awaken things that slumbered in my hybrid blood?"

An orc chieftain cleared his throat.

"My warriors stand ready to—"

His words ended in a gurgle as Nerium's power lifted him from the floor.

Unlike her previous displays of strength, this was different.

The orc's flesh began to ripple and twist, his armor crumpling like it was nothing as forces beyond natural law remade him from the inside out.

When she finally let his corpse drop, it no longer looked entirely solid.

"Your warriors," she purred to the remaining commanders,

"will follow my orders directly now.

No more clever strategies.

No more waiting."

Her smile showed far too many teeth.

"The time for subtlety is over."

Lemac watched as his carefully orchestrated plans crumbled around him.

He had thought the locket would simply enhance Nerium's existing abilities.

Instead, it had awakened something else.

Something that had perhaps always lurked in her unique biology, waiting for the right catalyst.

"The Scorpion approaches," a messenger announced from the doorway, either unaware of or choosing to ignore the orc chieftain's twisted remains.

"Good." Nerium's voice echoed with harmonics that should not have been possible from a single throat.

"Let them come. Let them see what true power looks like."

She turned to Lemac, and for a moment he saw something almost like affection in her transformed features.

"You gave me form, purpose, direction. For that, I will always be grateful."

Her smile widened.

"But now it's time for me to become what I was always meant to be."

"And what is that?" Lemac asked softly.

Before she could answer, another messenger burst into the chamber.

"The bronze one! It's escaped!"

"What?" Lemac spun toward the door.

"How?"

"The locks... they just... aged. Decades of rust in moments. The trolls..."

"Are all dead," Nerium finished, sounding almost pleased.

"It seems our little prophet had one last trick to show us."

She laughed again, the sound making several commanders cover their ears in pain.

"No matter. The game has changed now. The rules..."

Her form rippled again, growing larger, more impossible.

"The rules are whatever I say they are."

In the distance, dragons roared—whether in challenge or terror, it was impossible to tell.

Armies stirred in their barracks, commanders whispered among themselves, and somewhere in the castle's impossible architecture, a young bronze dragon flew through corridors that might or might not have existed moments before.

The game had indeed changed.

But even Nerium, drunk on her newfound power, couldn't see all the pieces yet.

After all, time flows like water.

And some currents run deeper than others.

Chapter Six

SWEEP

The twisted spires of the castle loomed before us as our infiltration team gathered on The Scorpion's lower deck.

I could feel my vampiric nature stirring, responding to the unnatural energy radiating from those impossible towers.

A few rats had already begun to gather in the shadows near my feet, their tiny eyes gleaming with shared anticipation.

"Ye've got some admirers t'ere, McLaaud,"

Balt chuckled, nodding toward my rodent companions.

"P'raps they can help us sneak about, eh?"

"I doubt even rats would volunteer for this mission," Twig muttered, adjusting her makeshift arsenal of sharpened twigs.

"We're really going to break into a dragon nursery. Because that's completely sane."

"Ye say t'at like it be a bad t'ing!" Balt's grin threatened to split his beard.

"Dragons, armies, impossible architecture—it's like Midwinter came early!"

Roash silenced them both with a look, her feline features stern in the strange twilight.

Her eline hunters had already melted into the shadows, barely visible even to my enhanced vision.

"The scouts report minimal guard presence along the lower passages," she reported.

"Just as Meeka predicted."

I caught another flash of that something in Meeka's expression—a tension around her eyes that didn't quite match her confident pose.

She stood close to Kuchoff, her hand occasionally brushing his arm in what might have been reassurance.

"Remember," Avilyn's voice carried quiet authority,

"we move in phases. The diversion team draws attention to the main gates while we—"

A pulse of power from the castle made the air itself seem to shudder.

Even the rats at my feet bristled, their tiny bodies trembling with instinctive fear.

"Nerium grows stronger," Daph whispered, her round face pale.

"The locket's power... it was never meant for hybrid flesh."

"Then we'd best hurry," Kuchoff replied grimly, checking his weapons one final time.

"Aye," Balt hefted his axe with obvious relish.

"Time fer a wee bit o' chaos."

"Stay in formation," Roash commanded as we began to move out.

"Errfords, shields ready but powered down until my signal. We can't risk the glow giving us away."

"Unless ye want tae announce our arrival," Balt suggested hopefully.

"I still say we could just knock..."

"Balt," several voices hissed in unison.

"WOT?" The dwarf feigned innocence, "Ach, fine. Sneakin' it is."

As we made our way toward the castle's base, I noticed Avilyn studying the architecture with an intensity that seemed to go beyond tactical assessment.

His partially melted features held an expression I couldn't quite read—recognition perhaps?

Or something deeper?

The rats followed us for a short distance before melting away into the darkness.

I could still sense them though, their tiny minds connecting with the predator in my blood.

They were afraid—not of us, but of something in the castle.

Something that made their primitive instincts scream in terror.

I caught Loher watching me, concern evident in her eyes.

She knew my tells by now, knew when my vampiric senses were picking up danger.

I gave her what I hoped was a reassuring smile, though I kept my fangs hidden.

No need to worry the others just yet.

"The entrance should be just ahead," Meeka whispered, pointing to a section of wall that seemed to bend in ways that hurt the eyes to follow.

"The maintenance tunnels..."

She trailed off as another roar echoed from above—not a dragon's cry this time, but something else.

Something that carried harmonics of both human and draconic voice, twisted together into something that should not exist.

"Nerium," Daph breathed.

"She's... changing."

"Good," Balt declared cheerfully.

"Makes t'ings more interestin'!"

"You have a very concerning definition of 'interesting,'" Twig observed.

"Quiet," Roash commanded.

"We're about to—"

The air suddenly crackled with power, making my vampiric senses surge.

The rats that had been hiding nearby burst from their holes, fleeing in terror.

Above us, where the castle's impossible geometry vanished into the perpetual twilight, something moved.

Something massive.

Something that had once been merely hybrid but was now becoming something else entirely.

The infiltration of the dragon nursery would have to wait. First, we had to survive whatever Nerium was becoming.

"Send search parties after that wyrmling," Lemac commanded, trying to keep the desperation from his voice. "It knows too much about—"

"Let it run," Nerium interrupted, her massive form now nearly touching the chamber's vaulted ceiling.

"Let it share its little prophecies with whoever it finds. Soon, none of it will matter."

She gestured casually at the remaining commanders.

They scrambled from the chamber, clearly relieved to escape her presence.

The last hobgoblin officer actually ran, his legendary racial stoicism broken by whatever he saw in Nerium's transformed features.

"My dear," Lemac started, adopting the soothing tone that had always worked before,

"consider the tactical disadvantage we create by letting it—"

"'My dear?'" Nerium's laugh shattered several of the chamber's windows.

"Still trying to manipulate me with soft words and gentle persuasion?"

She lowered her head to look at him directly, her eyes now swirling with temporal energies stolen from the locket.

"I can see it all now, you know.

Every subtle nudge, every careful suggestion.

You shaped me like clay, molded me into your perfect weapon."

"I gave you purpose," Lemac countered, standing his ground despite every instinct screaming at him to flee.

"Together, we were going to reshape the realm."

"Were we?" She began to circle him, her movements carrying a predatory grace that seemed to ignore the laws of physics.

"Or was I merely another piece in your grand game? A powerful beast to be pointed at your enemies?"

Before Lemac could respond, a messenger's voice echoed from the corridor:

"The bronze one was spotted near the lower levels! It's heading toward—"

The rest of his warning was cut off by sounds of chaos—running feet, shouts of alarm, and the distinctive ring of steel on steel.

"Ah," Nerium's smile showed far too many teeth,

"it seems our guests have arrived ahead of schedule, the infiltration team you were so worried about."

She turned her impossible gaze back to Lemac.

"Would you like to know what I see in the locket's memories? What little hints and clues float in young Kuchoff's stolen past?"

"What I would like," Lemac said carefully,

"is for us to focus on the tactical situation. If The Scorpion's crew reaches the nursery—"

"They won't." Nerium's form rippled again, growing even larger, more impossible.

"But that's not what truly concerns you, is it? You're worried about your agent. Your carefully placed spy."

Her laugh this time seemed to come from multiple throats.

"Poor, loyal one. Did you really think I wouldn't sense her presence in these memories?

The surrogate, the trusted one... the perfect tool for your schemes."

Lemac felt his carefully constructed plans crumbling around him. "The agent's loyalty is not in question. She—"

"'The deceiver chooses heart,'" Nerium quoted the wyrmling's prophecy.

"Would you like to wager on where her loyalty truly lies? When she must choose between your schemes and her beloved ward."

Another crash echoed from below, followed by the distinct sound of Balt's voice bellowing a war cry.

The infiltration team was clearly making progress, despite the chaos.

"The wyrmling," Lemac tried one last time to regain control of the situation.

"It's leading them here. We should—"

"Yes," Nerium purred, her voice now carrying harmonics that made Lemac's teeth ache.

"Let them come. Let them all come. Let them see what true power looks like.

Let them witness what I'm becoming."

She reached for the locket, its tin surface now pulsing with an inner light that seemed to bend reality around it.

"Such interesting memories in here. So many moments, so many possible futures..."

Her massive form began to shift again, taking on aspects that should not have been possible in three-dimensional space.

"Did you know that psionic energy could do this? Did you understand what might happen when you mixed dragon blood with human form and added stolen time?"

"Nerium," Lemac took an involuntary step back, "perhaps we should—"

"Perhaps," she cut him off, her voice now echoing from multiple points in space simultaneously, "you should be quiet now. The game is changing, my dear Lemac. The rules are changing. Reality itself is changing."

Her smile transcended physical geometry.

"And I am changing with it."

In the corridors below, the bronze wyrmling flew through shadows that weren't quite natural, seeking those who needed to hear its prophecies.

Time itself seemed to twist around it, showing paths that existed and paths that might exist and paths that should not exist at all.

The infiltration team drew closer.

And in the chamber that was quickly becoming something else entirely, Lemac watched his carefully laid plans dissolve into chaos, while the creature he had thought to control transformed into something beyond anyone's control.

The game had changed indeed.

But no one, not even Nerium with her stolen psionic power, could see all the moves yet to come.

After all, prophecies have a way of fulfilling themselves in unexpected ways.

⸺ ❖ ⸺

The twisted corridors seemed to shift and bend as we made our way deeper into the castle's impossible architecture.

Roash's eline hunters moved ahead like living shadows, while Balt struggled to keep his natural enthusiasm in check.

A flash of metallic scales caught my vampiric vision.

"Movement ahead," I whispered, the rats at my feet bristling in response.

The bronze wyrmling emerged from a corridor that might not have existed moments before, its ancient eyes fixing upon our group.

"The mother's choice approaches," it said simply.

"Blood will flow before truth emerges."

"Wonderful," Twig muttered, adjusting her arsenal of sharpened twigs.

"More cryptic nonsense."

Before anyone could respond, heavy footsteps echoed from multiple directions.

Roash's ears twitched.

"Hobgoblins," she hissed.

"At least a dozen."

"Finally!" Balt's grin was practically feral as he brought his axe to ready position.

"Some proper—"

The first hobgoblin warrior burst around the corner, his black armor gleaming dully in the strange light.

His shocked expression lasted only a moment before Roash's blade opened his throat in a spray of crimson.

The body hadn't hit the floor before chaos erupted.

Two more hobgoblins charged toward me, their curved swords whistling through the air.

I sidestepped the first strike, my fangs extending as predatory instinct took over.

My own blade found the gap between armor plates, sinking deep into the warrior's armpit.

Hot blood gushed over my hand as I twisted the steel, shredding arteries and muscle.

The second hobgoblin's sword caught me across the forearm, but Loher's arrow caught him perfectly in the throat, punching through his armor with devastating force.

The hobgoblin stumbled back, dark blood fountaining from the wound as a second arrow took him through the eye socket, the broadhead bursting out the back of his skull in a spray of brain matter and bone.

"Behind!" Kuchoff's warning came just as four more hobgoblins emerged from another corridor.

His psionic power manifested like heat ripples in the air, and the lead warrior's armor suddenly crumpled inward with a wet crunch.

Bones splintered through flesh as the hobgoblin was crushed into a bloody mass.

Balt's war cry echoed off the walls as he charged the foes.

His axe caught the first warrior between neck and shoulder, cleaving through armor, bone, and spine.

The hobgoblin's head and arm flew in different directions, painting the ceiling with arterial spray.

"T'at's how it's done!" he roared, even as one of the survivors scored a hit across his thigh.

The dwarf's response was to headbutt his attacker with enough force to cave in the hobgoblin's face plate.

Teeth and bone fragments burst from the back of the warrior's skull.

Rion moved like liquid death, his claws finding gaps in armor with surgical precision.

One hobgoblin screamed as the eline warrior literally disemboweled him, steaming entrails spilling across the floor.

Another lost his lower jaw to Rion's follow-through, drowning in his own blood as he collapsed.

Three more attackers came at Roash simultaneously.

She flowed between their blades like smoke, her own weapons leaving ribbons of flesh in their wake.

One hobgoblin staggered back, trying to hold his own throat closed.

Another spun completely around as Roash's blade severed his spine, his legs going in one direction while his torso twisted in another.

The bronze wyrmling observed it all with ancient calm, even as Twig's sharpened twigs found vulnerable eyes and throats with deadly accuracy.

One hobgoblin fell thrashing, wooden spikes penetrating deep into his brain through his eye sockets.

"More coming!" Navari's warning carried over the sounds of combat.

Her serpentine hair writhed as she caught a hobgoblin's gaze, turning him to stone mid-swing.

His petrified form shattered as Balt's axe struck it, sending razor-sharp shards into two of his companions.

They fell screaming, stone fragments having penetrated deep into their flesh.

Meeka's magic manifested as searing bolts of force, literally tearing one hobgoblin in half at the waist.

His torso hit the wall with enough impact to leave a bloody smear, while his legs took two more steps before collapsing.

The last hobgoblin turned to flee, but my enhanced speed let me catch him easily.

My sword took his leg off at the knee, sending him sprawling.

Before he could scream, my fangs found his throat.

The hot rush of blood filled my mouth as I tore through muscle and arteries, silencing him permanently.

As the echo of combat faded, we surveyed the carnage.

Body parts and blood covered every surface, and the air was thick with the metallic stench of death.

The bronze wyrmling regarded the scene with what might have been approval.

"The path is marked in blood," it said softly.

"As it must be."

"If ye start wit' more prophecies," Balt warned, wiping gore from his beard,

"I swear by me mother's axe..."

"Quiet," Roash commanded, her ears twitching.

"Something's moving above us. Something big."

The very stones seemed to vibrate as Nerium's transformed voice echoed through the impossible architecture:

"I can smell you, little infiltrators. Come. Let me show you what true power looks like."

The bronze wyrmling's ancient eyes fixed on Meeka.

"The choice comes soon."

In the shadows, I caught Meeka's hand tighten on Kuchoff's arm, though whether in protection or something else, I couldn't tell.

The game was indeed changing, and we were about to discover just how much.

The dragon nursery stretched before us; its vast chamber filled with carefully arranged nests.

Steam rose from heated stones that cradled eggs of various sizes and colors.

The bronze wyrmling perched near a particularly large crimson egg, its ancient eyes watching as Nerium's transformed shape filled the chamber's far entrance.

"Ye know," Balt whispered, still dripping hobgoblin blood,

"when I pictured meetin' the big beastie, I didnae think it'd be quite so... geometric'ly challengin' to look at."

He wasn't wrong. Nerium's form seemed to bend reality around itself, her massive bulk somehow occupying spaces that shouldn't have been possible.

The locket pulsed at her throat, temporal energies warping the air.

"Careful where you aim those weapons," she purred, her voice echoing from multiple points simultaneously.

"We wouldn't want any accidents around such... precious cargo."

Her impossible gaze swept over the eggs.

"Stand down, Nerium," Kuchoff commanded.

"You have something that belongs to me."

"Oh? This little trinket?" She touched the locket.

"Such interesting memories in here. Including some about dear Meeka."

Her smile transcended normal physical laws.

"Would you like to know what your surrogate mother has been hiding?"

I caught Meeka's subtle flinch, saw her step closer to Kuchoff.

Lemac emerged from another entrance, looking significantly less confident than usual.

"The time for secrets ends," the bronze wyrmling announced.

"As does the time for lies."

"Shut up," Nerium and Lemac said simultaneously, though with vastly different levels of authority.

"Ye know what I think?" Balt hefted his axe.

"I think—"

"If that axe moves a centimeter," Nerium cut him off,

"I'll reshape reality around these eggs in ways that will haunt your dreams forever." Her form rippled.

"But perhaps we can be civilized about this. You want the locket. I want... well, what I want has grown significantly more complex recently."

"This isn't you," Lemac tried, earning a laugh that shattered several empty eggshells.

"No," she agreed.

"I'm becoming so much more. But..."

She glanced at the eggs, particularly a pair of green ones near the chamber's center.

"These are still my children. So let us negotiate, somewhere more... appropriate."

"The fleet," Lemac suggested quickly, clearly trying to regain some control.

"We can—"

"Yes," Nerium's smile showed too many teeth in too many dimensions.

"Let us take this discussion to sea. Neutral water, between your ship and my armada."

She focused on Kuchoff.

"Bring your crew, little captain. Let's see if we can resolve this without devastating your ship entirely."

"Don't trust—" the wyrmling started.

"Enough prophecy," Nerium's power crackled.

"Choose, Captain Magnus. Civilized discourse on the waves, or..."

Her form expanded slightly, making several eggs tremble in their nests.

"You're just going to let us walk out?" Twig asked skeptically.

"Walk, run, fight—I care little for the method." Nerium's laugh echoed strangely.

"But in one hour, I expect to see The Scorpion approaching my fleet.

We'll determine then whether this ends in negotiation or annihilation."

"An' if we refuse?" Balt challenged.

Rather than answer directly, Nerium's power reached out and twisted a small portion of empty air.

The resulting geometric impossibility made several crew members dizzy.

"One hour," she repeated.

"Don't be late. I'm discovering that time has become a rather... personal subject for me."

As we withdrew from the nursery, Loher nocked an arrow.

"We're not seriously considering this?"

"We don't have much choice," I replied, watching Meeka's face carefully.

Whatever secrets she held were clearly weighing on her.

"The choice is made soon," the wyrmling whispered as it glided past. "When paths converge on dark water."

"I swear by me axe," Balt grumbled.

"Focus," Kuchoff commanded.

"We need to get back to The Scorpion and prepare for whatever comes next."

"Oh, aye," Balt's grin returned.

"Naval combat with impossible beasties and their pet armies? Now that's more like it!"

Above us, Nerium's transformed laughter echoed through the castle's twisted architecture, as reality itself seemed to shiver in anticipation of what was to come.

⸻ ⸰ ⸻

The dark waters stretched between The Scorpion and Nerium's massive fleet, our single ship looking impossibly small against their armada.

Meeka stood at the rail; her knuckles white as she gripped the wooden barrier.

I could see the weight of decades of secrets in the set of her shoulders.

"The time comes," the bronze wyrmling announced from its perch near the helm.

"When morals prove stronger than chains."

"Ye say that one more time," Balt growled, "an' I'll be makin' meself a nice pair o' bronze boots."

Nerium's transformed shape dominated the deck of her flagship, her impossible geometry making the air itself seem to bend.

The locket pulsed at her throat, psionic energies dancing across her scales.

"Tell them, Meeka," she called, her voice echoing unnaturally across the waves.

"Tell your precious adopted son who you really are. What you've really been doing all these years."

Kuchoff turned to his surrogate mother, confusion warring with growing suspicion on his face.

"Meeka?"

She straightened slowly, tears streaming down her cheeks.

"I was sent to watch you," she whispered.

"To report on you. To... to help them take you when the time was right."

The silence that followed was deafening.

Even Balt's usual quips died in his throat.

"You're Lemac's spy," Kuchoff said softly, decades of trust crumbling in his voice.

"I was," Meeka's voice cracked.

"But you have to understand—I was supposed to just observe, to stay detached.

Then this little boy with incredible power needed someone to teach him, to guide him, to love him..."

She reached for him, but he stepped back.

"Everything was a lie?" The hurt in his voice made even hardened crew members flinch.

"No!" Meeka's cry echoed across the water.

"The love was real. Is real. That's why I couldn't—why I can't..."

She spun to face Nerium.

"You want to know why your plans kept failing? Why you could never quite get close enough? I've been protecting him! Every step, every plan, every scheme—I twisted them just enough to keep him safe!"

Lemac's outraged voice carried from Nerium's ship:

"You betrayed us? All this time?"

"I chose love," Meeka declared, power crackling around her hands.

"I chose my son."

"How touching," Nerium's laugh distorted reality around her.

"The spy grew a heart. But tell me, dear Meeka, did you also tell him about his father?"

The color drained from Meeka's face.

"No. You can't—"

"Your mother's power was remarkable," Nerium's smile transcended dimensions.

"But did you never wonder where such raw psionic talent truly came from? Should we tell him what else was in his blood?"

"You know nothing of his gifts," Meeka's voice was steel.

"You see only power to be used, to be twisted."

She glanced at Nerium's transformed shape.

"The way you twist everything you touch."

"The mother's heart proves true," the wyrmling commented, earning a murderous glare from Balt.

"Enough talk," Nerium's power crackled across the waves.

"Choose now, little captain. Join us willingly or watch your world burn. After all,..."

Her impossible smile widened.

"Family should stick together."

Kuchoff stood frozen, processing decades of lies and love. Then, slowly, he turned to Meeka.

"All those years," he said softly.

"All those lessons about honor, about doing what's right... Were any of them real?"

"Every single one," she whispered.

"Because you taught them to me."

He was silent for a long moment.

Then, to everyone's surprise, he laughed.

"You know what this means?" He stepped forward, taking Meeka's hand.

"I still had a mother who loved me.

Who chose me.

Who betrayed everything she believed in to protect me."

He squeezed her hand.

"The rest is just details."

"How disappointing," Nerium sighed, her form rippling with barely contained power.

"I had hoped we could be civilized about this. But if you choose defiance..."

The locket pulsed brighter.

"Then let us show you what family can really do to each other."

"Ye know what?" Balt hefted his axe with a maniacal grin.

"I been waitin' fer someone ta say somethin' like that!

Now we can stop wit' all this talkin' and get to the proper violence!"

The skies darkened as Nerium's power began to reshape reality around her fleet. Below us, Tatenda Waxx's hands flew across the Creature Controls, ready to bring The Scorpion truly to life.

As the first waves of smaller ships began to surge forward, I heard Meeka whisper to Kuchoff:

"I will always choose you. Always."

The time for secrets was over.

The time for war had begun.

CHAPTER SEVEN

SNAP BACK TO REALITY?

"Fire!" Captain Magnus commanded as The Scorpion's unique design sprang to life under Tatenda Waxx's skilled hands.

The ship's wooden scales rippled as hidden weapons emerged from previously seamless hull plates.

Ballistae burst from concealed ports while specialized harpoon launchers tracked multiple targets simultaneously.

"Take out their command vessels first!" Roash called from her position at the main harpoon controls.

Her shot caught an orc-crewed ship dead center, the massive projectile punching through their hull with ease.

"Errfords, shields up!" Kuchoff ordered as enemy arrows began to darken the sky.

The defensive barrier snapped into place just as the first volley struck, magical energy dispersing the deadly rain.

"Now t'at's what I call a proper fight!" Balt roared as his battle station's ballista caught a hobgoblin ship broadside.

The impact sent dozens of warriors tumbling into the dark waters.

The Scorpion moved with impossible agility for a vessel her size, Tatenda's mastery of the Creature Controls letting her literally dance between enemy vessels.

Three ships collided trying to trap her, their crews screaming as splintered wood and broken bodies flew in all directions.

"Your ship is impressive," Nerium's voice echoed across dimensions as she observed from her flagship.

"But let's see how it handles this."

Her transformed shape rippled as she reached out with the locket's power.

Reality bent around two nearby ships, their wooden hulls twisting into geometric impossibilities that somehow still floated.

"Incoming!" Loher's warning came just as the twisted ships opened fire.

Their weapons now fired in directions that shouldn't have been possible, arrows and bolts curving around The Scorpion's shields at impossible angles.

"I've got them!" Meeka's magic manifested as searing bolts of force, striking one of the transformed ships.

The impact sent the enemies screaming as the vessel imploded, taking three nearby ships with it into a briefly existing black hole.

"Meeka!" Kuchoff called out as he deflected a barrage of arrows with his psionic power.

"What's happening to the water?"

The dark seas had begun to churn, reality fracturing around Nerium's flagship as she channeled more of the locket's psionic energy.

"The realm tears," the bronze wyrmling announced from somewhere above.

"She seeks escape through wounds in time itself."

"Ye know what?" Balt shouted as his ballista claimed another victim.

"I actually understood that one!"

Massive whirlpools began to form around Nerium's vessel, their spiral patterns ignoring normal fluid dynamics.

Several of her own ships were caught in the maelstrom, their crews screaming as they were torn apart by forces that existed outside normal space-time.

"She's opening a portal!" Avilyn's voice carried over the chaos.

"Using the locket's power to tear through—"

A flash of impossible light cut him off as reality split open around Nerium's flagship.

Through the tear, we caught glimpses of a realm that shouldn't exist—where the laws of physics were more suggestion than rule.

"Follow them!" Kuchoff commanded as Nerium's vessel and her few remaining escorts began to slip through the breach.

"We can't let her escape!"

"Ye want us to sail into that?" Balt asked incredulously.

Then he grinned.

"Finally! A proper challenge!"

"Tatenda," Captain Magnus called to our creature control expert, "can you do it?"

"Juss watch, Mon!" Tatenda's smile was fierce as his hands flew across the controls.

"Everyone hang on to somethin' solid!"

The Scorpion's wooden scales rippled as she surged forward, riding the edge of the temporal whirlpool.

Around us, reality began to bend and twist as we followed Nerium's flagship through the tear in space-time.

"The choice is made," the wyrmling's voice seemed to come from everywhere and nowhere as we crossed the threshold.

"Now we sail paths that should not be."

"One more prophecy," Balt yelled as he clung to his battle station,

"and I swear by me mother's—"

The rest of his threat was lost as we emerged into bright daylight.

A vast ocean stretched before us, its waves a natural deep blue under a clear sky.

In the distance, green mountains rose from a forested coastline.

"Well," Twig observed as she adjusted her arsenal of sharpened twigs,

"at least this looks more normal."

Ahead of us, Nerium's flagship cut through the waves, her transformed shape still defying natural law even in this more conventional realm.

"Welcome to my new domain," her voice carried across the water.

"Perhaps you'll find these more familiar surroundings to your liking for our family reunion?"

"Aye!" Balt's enthusiasm was undimmed.

"Now this is proper sailing weather! Let's show these beasties how we do things at sea!"

The battle was about to begin again, but this time in a realm where we at least understood the rules.

Now it would come down to skill, strategy, and the determination of The Scorpion's crew to end this once and for all.

———— ◦◦◦ ————

The waves parted before Nerium's flagship as she led her three remaining escort vessels in an evasive pattern across the unfamiliar sea.

The Scorpion pursued relentlessly, its enhanced capabilities keeping pace despite the enemy's desperate maneuvers.

A thunderous roar split the air as Jade and Emeral burst through the closing portal behind us, their massive green forms casting shadows across our deck.

"Dragons off the stern!" Roash shouted, but her warning came too late.

Twin streams of dragon fire caught The Scorpion's port side, igniting rigging and scorching our magical protections.

The heat was intense enough to make the wooden scales buckle.

"Me got dis situation!" Tatenda called from the Creature Controls, his hands flying across the mechanisms. "But dem dragons catching us proper!"

"Och, that's gonnae leave a mark!" Balt shouted as he directed crew members to battle the flames.

"Some beastie's gonna pay fer that!"

As the dragons wheeled around for another attack run, something extraordinary happened.

Avilyn stepped forward; his scarred features set with ancient determination.

"I had hoped to avoid this," he said quietly, his voice carrying despite the chaos.

"But some secrets have carried their weight long enough."

The air around him began to shimmer and distort.

His form grew larger, impossibly larger, until where the old elven wizard had stood now towered a dragon of legendary proportions.

Its scales shifted through every color imaginable, creating patterns that told stories of ages past.

Power radiated from its very presence—not the twisted energy of Nerium's transformation, but something pure and primal.

The bronze wyrmling's voice was filled with awe:

"The One Who Came First. The King of Dragons himself."

Jade and Emeral pulled up short, their previous attack forgotten.

They tucked their wings and dove toward our deck, landing with heads bowed in complete submission.

"My lord," they said in unison.

"We did not know."

"Ach, ye mean tae tell me," Balt's voice cracked with disbelief, "that our crusty old wizard has been the actual KING OF THE DRAG-ONS this whole time? The one what started everything?"

"Ja Mon," Tatenda shook his head in amazement,

"dis explains why him never could get comfortable in dem chairs me built!"

But Nerium had used the distraction to her advantage.

Her flagship and escorts were already approaching a distant set of portal stones, their forms beginning to shimmer with temporal energy.

"We must pursue!" Kuchoff called, but before The Scorpion could close the distance, reality twisted around Nerium's vessels.

"You cannot hide forever!" she called, her transformed voice echoing across the waves.

"The locket's power grows stronger! I will find what I seek!"

"You're the ones running away," Twig called after them,

"Cowards!"

In a flash of impossible light, she and her remaining ships vanished into another realm.

"We cannot follow," Avilyn's voice rumbled in his true form, the sound carrying harmonics that spoke of ages past.

"She scatters her temporal wake across too many possibilities. To pursue blindly would risk being lost between realities."

"Then we return home," Captain Magnus decided after a moment's thought.

"Back to Beornan Heafod, to prepare for whatever comes next."

"The portal stones respond to clear intent," Meeka reminded everyone as we approached the glowing monoliths.

"Think of The Scorpion's Den. Where it all began."

The stones began to pulse with familiar energy as The Scorpion aligned herself between them.

Reality prepared to shift once more, but this time we knew exactly where we were going.

Jade and Emeral, still bowed before their true king, awaited his command.

"Come," Avilyn's dragon-voice carried the weight of millennia.

"It seems I have much to explain." His massive form began to shimmer, returning to his more familiar wizard shape.

"And perhaps," he added with what might have been a smile, "it's time I told you the real story of how I got these scars."

As The Scorpion slipped between realms, carrying us back to familiar waters, I caught Balt muttering under his breath:

"Ach, all this time I been tellin' dragon jokes right tae their king's face. I'm never gonnae live this down."

⚬

The hidden entrance to The Scorpion's Den appeared before us as we rounded the cliff face, a natural formation that concealed one of the best-kept secrets in the realm.

The narrow channel was barely visible unless you knew exactly where to look.

"Time for me delicate touch," Tatenda grinned as he took manual control of the Creature Controls.

His skilled hands guided The Scorpion through the treacherous passage, walking her carefully into the interior lagoon where she would rest.

The cave opened into a vast interior cove; its high ceiling lost in shadows despite the clever system of mirrors that brought in natural light.

The fortress had been naturally carved directly into the mountain's heart.

Multiple levels of living quarters, workshops, and storage areas have all been built into the natural rock, carved by Balt and his brothers.

"Och, let me see what them dragons did tae our lady," Balt said, examining the scorched planks along the port side.

"We'll need at least a day's proper work before she's ready tae sail again."

"Two days minimum," the shipwright called after inspecting the damage more closely.

"Some of these support beams took more heat than I'd like."

"Then we wait," Captain Magnus decided.

"Once repairs are complete, we'll make the journey to the castle."

"Day and a half's good sailing, if the wind holds," Tatenda noted as he finished securing The Scorpion in the lagoon.

Jade and Emeral followed Avilyn toward the east caverns, their massive forms disappearing into the chambers typically used for storage.

The bronze wyrmling glided silently behind them.

"Take some rest," Kuchoff suggested to the crew.

"Shore team, begin repairs at first light. The king will want our report, but it can wait until The Scorpion is seaworthy again."

Most of the crew dispersed to their quarters within the Den's residential levels, while others headed for the common areas or the well-stocked kitchens.

The fortress was entirely self-sufficient, capable of housing and feeding the entire crew for months if necessary.

"Meeka," Kuchoff said softly as the others departed,

"walk with me?"

I watched them disappear into one of the Den's many passages, their relationship clearly stronger despite—or perhaps because of—recent revelations.

Somewhere above in the east caverns, dragon voices echoed through the mountain passages as our new allies settled into their temporary home.

And from the direction of the common area, I could already hear Balt working on his latest composition:

"Ach, how do ye properly praise a dragon king in our wee mountain home, ye ken?"

The repairs would take time, but at least here in the Den, we could rest and recover before making the long journey to deliver our report to the king.

Chapter Eight

BLOOD ON DARK WATERS

A gentle rain fell across The Scorpion's deck as we made our way through the morning mist.

The repairs had been completed ahead of schedule, every plank and beam restored to perfect condition.

In the crow's nest, Chron—our bronze wyrmling prophet—perched silently, his ancient eyes scanning the horizon.

"Still troubled?" I asked Meeka as she stood at the rail, watching the coastline slip past.

She had been unusually quiet since our departure from the Den.

"He deserves better than secrets," she replied softly.

"After what happened with his birth mother..."

"Then tell him the truth," I suggested.

"All of it."

She nodded slowly and made her way toward the captain's quarters.

I caught Balt watching her go, his usual grin softening with something like sympathy.

"Ye ken," he said thoughtfully,

"fer all her sneakin' about, she did right by the lad."

Inside the captain's quarters, Meeka found Kuchoff studying charts at his desk.

He looked up as she entered, and something in her expression made him set aside his work.

"I need to tell you about that day," she began, her voice barely above a whisper.

"When your mother—when that thing pretending to be your mother—tried to take you."

"Meeka..." he started, but she held up a hand.

"Please. You need to understand." She took a shaky breath.

"When I saw her there, acting so smug, so certain she could just claim you... I wasn't thinking about my mission or my orders. All I could see was this monster trying to steal my son."

"The energy balls," Kuchoff remembered.

"You charged them while you were frozen."

"Because a real mother protects her child," Meeka's voice cracked.

"Not because of any orders or schemes, but because love demands it."

She met his eyes.

"I chose you then, just as I've chosen you every day since. The only thing I regret is not telling you the truth sooner."

Kuchoff was silent for a long moment.

Then he stood and pulled her into a fierce embrace.

"You've always been my mother," he said softly.

"The rest is just details."

Their moment was interrupted by Chron's sharp cry from above:

"Time fractures! The dark ship approaches!"

I rushed to the port rail as a familiar purple glow began to build near Haze Mountain.

The portal stones were activating, reality twisting as something forced its way through from another realm.

"Battle stations!" Kuchoff's command rang across the deck as he emerged from his quarters, Meeka right behind him.

"Errfords to positions! Archers ready!"

"Finally!" Balt's manic grin was back as he sprinted to his battle station.

"Some proper action!"

A massive black hull burst through the dimensional tear, water cascading off its sides as it materialized less than fifty meters to our starboard.

The vessel was easily twice The Scorpion's size, its deck crawling with armed figures.

"Hard to port!" Kuchoff ordered as the enemy ship's ram swung toward us.

"Tatenda, bring her to life!"

"Aye, Cap'n!" Tatenda's hands flew across the Creature Controls.

The Scorpion's wooden scales rippled as she responded, her enhanced agility letting her barely evade the larger vessel's attack.

"Look at the size of that thing!" Twig called from her position near the bow, already reaching for her arsenal of sharpened twigs.

"We're actually going to fight that?"

"Aye!" Balt's laugh carried over the sound of rushing water. "Ain't it beautiful?"

The enemy ship's side erupted in cannon fire, but The Scorpion's errford shields flared to life just in time.

Steel shot bounced harmlessly away as Roash took aim with the main harpoon.

"Firing!" her call was followed by the massive weapon's distinctive thump.

The projectile punched through the larger vessel's hull just above the waterline, steel cable trailing behind it.

"Reel them in!" Kuchoff commanded.

"Prepare for boarding!"

"Now that's what I'm talking about!" Rion's tail lashed with excitement as he checked his weapons.

"Some proper close-quarters combat!"

As the harpoon's mechanism drew the ships together, I caught movement on the enemy vessel's deck.

A robed figure stepped to the rail; hands wreathed in dark energy.

"Incoming!" I barely had time to shout before the spell launched toward us.

But Jacen Feldspar was already moving, his own magic manifesting as a brilliant counter-spell that met the attack halfway between the ships.

The resulting explosion lit up the misty air like daybreak, sending both vessels rocking in suddenly turbulent waters.

Through the magical aftermath, I saw the enemy wizard preparing another attack.

"Focus on their hull!" Kuchoff called to our archers.

"Let Jacen handle the magic user!"

The air crackled with power as the two wizards began their duel, bolts of energy crisscrossing between the vessels as they drew closer together.

Each blast carried enough force to shatter stone, but neither combatant could land a decisive hit.

Finally, the ships ground against each other with a sound of tortured wood.

Grappling hooks flew from both sides, lashing the vessels together as warriors prepared to board.

"Here they come!" Balt's warning was almost gleeful as the first wave of attackers swung across.

"Let's show these lubbers how The Scorpion's crew handles boarders!"

The enemy crew crashed onto our deck like a wave of steel and muscle.

I caught glimpses of Rion tearing through their front ranks, his claws opening throats and bellies with surgical precision.

Beside him, Balt's axe sang its lethal song as he literally cut a path through the attackers.

"Is this all ye got?" the dwarf bellowed as he separated a hobgoblin's head from his shoulders, arterial spray painting the deck crimson.

"I've had more challenging bar fights '!"

Above us, Jacen and the enemy wizard continued their arcane duel.

The air between them had become so charged with competing energies that reality itself seemed to ripple and tear.

"Your power is nothing!" the purple-robed figure called, his voice carrying unnatural harmonics.

"I've studied in realms you can't imagine!"

Jacen's response was another blast of pure force that caught his opponent square in the chest.

The enemy wizard stumbled back, his robes smoking, but managed to catch himself on the rail.

"Then you should have studied harder," Jacen spat, gathering energy for what would be his final spell.

The two mages released their power simultaneously.

The resulting collision of forces created a sphere of pure destruction that consumed everything it touched.

When it finally dissipated, the enemy wizard lay broken and lifeless on his own deck.

But Jacen had no time to savor his victory.

The thundering of massive feet announced the arrival of two ogres, their grotesque forms towering over the normal combatants.

"Pretty magic man die now," one growled as they charged forward, their crude weapons raised high.

Jacen managed to conjure one final spell, catching the first ogre in the leg.

The beast stumbled but didn't fall.

Before our wizard could react, their massive hands seized him.

What happened next would haunt my nightmares for years to come.

The ogres literally pulled Jacen apart, his screams cut short as his body was torn in two.

They threw the pieces aside like discarded trash, already looking for their next victim.

"No!" Twig's cry carried equal parts rage and horror.

Her fingers moved in a blur as she sent a barrage of specially treated twigs into the first ogre's face.

The wooden projectiles, honed to needle sharpness, penetrated deep into the beast's eyes and brain.

It toppled forward, dead before it hit the deck.

The second ogre roared in fury and charged toward Twig, but I was already moving.

My vampiric speed let me get behind the monster before it could react.

My sword took its hamstring, bringing it to one knee.

As it tried to turn, I drove my blade up through its jaw and into its brain, twisting the steel to ensure the kill.

"T'at's how it be done!" Balt called approvingly as he gutted another attacker.

"Though I still say we should've just knocked politely!"

The battle continued to rage across both decks, but I could already see the tide turning in our favor.

Roash moved like a shadow of death, her twin blades claiming lives with every strike.

The errfords maintained their protective barrier while our archers thinned the enemy ranks with precise shots.

Through it all, Chron watched from above, his ancient eyes taking in every detail.

"Blood flows," he intoned, "as it must. But greater battles await."

"If ye don't shut it with them prophecies," Balt shouted up between kills, "I'll be using yer scales fer boot decoration!"

The rain began to ease as the last of the enemy crew fell or surrendered.

The deck was slick with blood and worse, the air thick with the copper-iron stench of death.

We had lost good people—Jacen's remains were a testament to that—but The Scorpion herself was undamaged.

"Clear the bodies," Kuchoff commanded, his voice carrying equal parts authority and compassion.

"Prepare Jacen for burial at sea. He died protecting his crew—he deserves full honors."

"Aye, Captain," several voices responded as crew members began the grim task of separating our dead from theirs.

I made my way to where Twig stood, still staring at the ogre she had killed.

"That was impressive shooting," I offered.

"He died protecting us," she said softly. "Just like you said a Scorpion crew member would."

"Aye," I nodded, "and we avenged him properly. Come on—help me check the rest of their ship before we send it to the depths."

As we separated the vessels and prepared to continue our journey, I caught Meeka and Kuchoff standing close together near the helm.

Whatever final walls had existed between them seemed to have crumbled in the heat of battle.

Sometimes, I reflected, it takes death to remind us what truly matters in life.

The castle still awaited us, but for now, we had other duties to attend to.

We would honor our fallen, tend our wounded, and make ready for whatever challenges lay ahead.

After all, that's what The Scorpion's crew had always done—face whatever came our way, together.

Chron spread his wings in the freshening breeze, his voice carrying to all on deck:

"The path remains true, though marked in sorrow. Forward lies destiny, written in blood and bonds stronger than birth."

⸺ ◆ ⸺

The remainder of our journey through the Strait of Avilyn passed without incident, though the crew remained vigilant.

Jacen's burial at sea had sobered even Balt's usual enthusiasm.

We performed the ceremony with full honors, committing his body to the depths as Brother Fost spoke the traditional words of passage.

As we approached the river mouth leading to the castle, the weather cleared completely, leaving us with calm waters and clear skies.

The change felt almost too perfect, as if nature itself was holding its breath.

"Something's not right," I muttered, watching the rats gathering near my feet.

Their tiny bodies were tense, whiskers twitching with shared unease.

"Aye," Roash agreed, her feline ears flattening slightly.

"Too quiet."

"The air thickens with possibility," Chron observed from his perch.

"Choices made echo forward and back."

The castle's spires came into view as we rounded the final bend, their white stone gleaming in the afternoon sun.

Guards along the battlements had already spotted us, and I could see messengers running to alert the king of our arrival.

"Tink they've got fresh ale in ta castle?" Balt asked hopefully.

"After all tat action, I could use a proper drink."

"You always need a proper drink," Twig observed, though her usual sharp tone had softened somewhat since the battle.

"Aye, tat I do, lass. Tat I do."

As we approached the dock, I noticed Meeka standing close to Kuchoff, their shoulders just touching.

Whatever came next, whatever news we had to deliver to the king, at least that relationship had found its truth.

"Prepare to moor," Kuchoff commanded as we drew near the pier.

"Full honors for the castle guard."

"And if they ask about the dragons?" Roash inquired softly.

"We tell them the truth," he replied.

"All of it."

Chron spread his wings, catching the last rays of sunlight.

"Time's wheel turns ever forward," he intoned.

"But some cycles complete themselves in ways we cannot—"

A clang of metal interrupted his prophecy as Balt's thrown axe handle bounced off the mast near the wyrmling's head.

"I warned ye!" the dwarf called up triumphantly.

The bronze dragon actually chuckled, a sound like ancient bells.

"Some fates," he added with what might have been a wink,

"are worth tempting."

The Scorpion settled against the pier as castle guards rushed to secure our lines.

Above us, the king's banner flew proud and strong, welcoming us home.

We had lost good people, shed blood on foreign seas, and uncovered truths both beautiful and painful.

But we had survived, as The Scorpion's crew always did.

Together, standing ready for whatever challenges awaited within those castle walls.

"Right then," Balt adjusted his weapons as we prepared to disembark.

"Who's ready to explain to His Majesty why we're down a wizard but up a prophesying dragon?"

"Just try not to mention making boots in the throne room," Twig suggested.

"Spoilsport."

Our laughter carried across the water as we made our way toward the castle.

The tale we had to tell would be long and complex, full of betrayal and redemption, loss and love.

But first, we would honor our dead, celebrate our living, and re-member that family isn't always about blood—sometimes it's about choice.

After all, that's what The Scorpion's crew had always been—a family bound by choice and loyalty, sailing together through whatever storms fate threw our way.

Even if some of us occasionally threatened to turn prophetic drag-ons into footwear.

As we made our way up the winding path to the castle, Chron glided silently overhead, occasionally landing on lamp posts or ornamental pillars to survey our progress.

Balt kept one eye on the bronze wyrmling, his hand never far from his axe.

"Watch that loose stone!" Chron warned urgently as Balt's foot hovered inches above it.

Balt froze, his breath catching as the jagged rocks below loomed like teeth on the edge of a precipice.

"Tat was close," Balt muttered, wiping the sweat from his brow as he looked up at the young dragon who had saved him from a deadly fall.

"The path holds many dangers," Chron replied.

"Some seen, some hidden. As does your future, Stone-Heart."

"Stone-Heart?" Balt's bushy eyebrows rose.

"Tat's... actually not bad. Better tan what tey called me in ta north-ern mines."

"Your heart beats with the mountain's rhythm," Chron observed.

"Strong, steady, protecting those who shelter within."

A slow grin spread through Balt's beard.

"Ye know what? Yer all right, wee dragon. Even wich yer fancy words."

He patted his axe.

"Maybe I won't be needin' them boots after all."

The castle gates opened as we approached, revealing a contingent of royal guards in their ceremonial armor.

Their captain, a tall woman with graying temples, stepped forward.

"Welcome, crew of The Scorpion," she said formally.

"The royal family awaits in the Garden of Twilight Dreams."

"Fancy name," Twig muttered.

"Wait till ye see it, lass," Balt whispered.

"Even I have tae admit it's a sight worth seein'."

The guards formed up around us, not as prisoners but as honored guests, their polished armor catching the afternoon sun.

They led us through corridors of marble and gold, past tapestries that told stories of the realm's history.

When we emerged into the garden, even Twig's usual skepticism fell silent.

Flowering vines bearing blossoms of rich purple and dark blue gracefully draped over crystal trellises, with petals that appeared to emit a subtle inner glow.

The air was filled with a sweet, intoxicating fragrance, reminiscent of honey and fresh rain, mingling with the earthy scent of the moist soil beneath the trellises.

White stone fountains created musical patterns with their waters, as butterflies with stained glass wings flitted among exotic flowers.

The crystal-clear streams cascaded rhythmically, playing a soothing melody that echoed through the garden.

Roses of deep crimson and orchids in every shade of purple swayed gently in the breeze, releasing a mix of fragrant scents into the air.

Shimmering dragonflies darted above lily pads floating on pristine ponds, while tiny birds with iridescent feathers sang harmoniously from the treetops.

The royal family was positioned around a central courtyard, where a jester in silver and blue attire performed for a group of off-duty knights and their families.

The sound of children's laughter combined with the fountain's noise as the performer juggled colored balls of light, making them move in intricate patterns.

The jester danced and twirled, his bells jingling with every move.

He pulled a small rabbit from his hat, earning gasps and cheers from the children.

Knights cheered as the jester pretended to trip and fall, only to land gracefully on one knee with a flourish.

The Queen chuckled, her eyes twinkling with delight, while the King clapped along to the rhythm of the show.

The air was filled with the smell of freshly baked pastries, and the sun cast a warm glow over the joyful scene.

"Welcome, friends!" the King called out, rising from his cushioned seat.

His formal robes couldn't quite hide the athletic build beneath—a reminder that he had once adventured with us.

Beside him, the Queen adjusted their infant son's blanket, smiling warmly at our approach.

The knights and their families turned to watch us, many nodding in recognition.

Several children pointed excitedly at Chron, who had perched on a nearby fountain.

"Some futures bloom like night flowers," the wyrmling observed softly.

"Beautiful yet hiding thorns."

"Aye," Balt agreed, surprising us all.

"But tat's what makes tem worth protectin', eh?"

The jester ended his performance with a flourish, the light-balls bursting into showers of sparks that entertained the young audience.

He spun around dramatically, causing giggles and gasps as confetti rained down.

The children's eyes widened in delight, and their laughter filled the air.

As the families applauded, the King, grinning broadly, motioned for us to join them.

We weaved through the crowd, marveling at the jester's antics and the infectious joy that spread across the garden.

The atmosphere was electric, with a hint of magic lingering in every corner.

"Come," he said, "share a moment of peace before we speak of weightier matters.

"The children would love to hear tales of The Scorpion's adventures." He smiled.

"The ones suitable for young ears, of course."

"Oh aye," Balt grinned, already moving toward the gathered families.

"Have I told ye about the time we faced down a ghost ship with nothing but a barrel of pickled herrings and me grandmother's best tablecloth?"

As our dwarven warrior launched into his tale (which I was certain grew more outrageous with each telling), I caught Chron watching him with what might have been approval.

The young dragon had named him well—Stone-Heart indeed.

For all his bluster and battle joy, Balt's strength had always been in protecting others.

The garden's peace settled around us like a comfortable blanket, the horrors of our recent battles temporarily forgotten.

Soon enough, we would have to deliver our report, to speak of Nerium and betrayal and realms torn apart by stolen power.

But for now, we could simply be here, in this moment of beauty and light, watching children laugh as a dwarf and a prophetic dragon together told tales of adventure on the high seas.

⸻◈⸻

Silence filled the great hall as Captain Magnus finished his report.

Torchlight flickered across the king's face as he absorbed the gravity of what he'd just heard.

Even the usual guards seemed to hold their breath, waiting for their monarch's response.

"A hybrid creature wielding stolen memories," the king finally spoke, his voice carrying none of the casual warmth from the garden.

"Enhanced by power she was never meant to possess, deluded by dreams of supremacy."

He adjusted his position on the throne, the golden crown seeming to weigh heavily upon his brow.

"And you believe she means to challenge your abilities directly?"

"Her psionic powers are formidable with the locket," Kuchoff confirmed, "but she fundamentally misunderstands their nature.

She thinks quantity equals quality—that stealing more power automatically makes her stronger."

"Like thinkin' ye can win a fight just by having ta biggest axe," Balt added.

"When any fool knows it's how ye swing it tat matters."

Chron stirred on his perch near the hall's vast windows.

"Pride blinds her to truth," he observed.

"She sees the surface of power, but not its depths."

"Then we must find her," the King declared, "before her delusions bring more harm to our realm."

His fingers drummed thoughtfully on his throne's armrest.

"How many follow her?"

"An army that grows with every port she visits," Meeka answered.

She stood close to Kuchoff, their earlier reconciliation giving her words added weight.

"She's very convincing when she wants to be."

The King nodded slowly, looking to his generals who had been listening intently.

"Send word to every ally we have. We must be ready when she makes her move."

"Ready for what exactly?" Twig's skepticism couldn't quite hide her concern.

"For someone drunk on stolen power," I offered, remembering Nerium's transformed shape.

"Someone who thinks she's become something she's not."

"Ach, we've handled worse," Balt interrupted, though his tone held more affection than annoyance.

"Just point us in the right direction, wee prophet. The Scorpion's crew has never failed yet."

The King managed a small smile at the dwarf's confidence.

"Ready your forces," he told his generals, "but do it quietly. We don't want to start a panic."

"And The Scorpion?" Kuchoff asked, though I suspected he already knew the answer.

"Make whatever repairs you need," the king replied.

"Resupply, rest your crew." His expression hardened.

"But be ready. When we locate Nerium, you'll be our first line of defense."

He looked at each of us in turn.

"You've faced her before. You know what she thinks she's capable of. More importantly, you know what she's actually capable of."

"Just another day aboard The Scorpion," Twig mused.

"No wonder the pay is so good."

Several guards tried to hide their shocked expressions at her casual tone, but the King just shook his head with bemused tolerance.

"Indeed." He sobered quickly.

"Rest tonight. Tomorrow we begin planning our response to this threat."

The Queen entered quietly from a side door, carrying a small bundle wrapped in royal blue silk.

The King's expression softened as she approached, and he gestured for her to join him.

"Before we retire for the night," the King announced, "I would like to formally introduce you to my son."

He gently took the bundle from the Queen, turning so we could all see the infant's face.

"This is Prince Gavin."

I caught several knowing smiles among the crew at the name.

It had been Brother Fost's idea, years ago, when we needed to smuggle the then-barely known king through the Hollow.

* "Call yourself Gavin," the halfling priest had suggested. "Common enough to avoid attention, but memorable enough to be believable." *

The name had served him well during those adventures.

"A fitting tribute," Loher said softly, "to remember how you came to truly know your people."

The King nodded.

"Those months traveling as 'Gavin' taught me more about this realm and its citizens than all my years of formal education."

He smiled down at his son.

"It seems right that the future king should carry a name that represents both who we are and who we serve."

The baby Prince yawned, completely unimpressed by the gravity of the moment.

Several of the guards tried to maintain their stoic expressions but couldn't quite hide their smiles.

"We must now take our leave and retire for the night, rest easy, my friends."

The King smiled and escorted his family into their private chambers.

As we filed out of the great hall, I caught Chron watching the proceedings with his ancient eyes.

"The heart sees truth," he whispered, "when the mind is clouded by dreams of power."

"Aye," Balt nodded, surprising us once more with his acceptance of the prophecy.

"And we'll be there when she finally figures that out."

And somehow, watching the strange friendship forming between a dwarven warrior and a time-touched dragon, I felt a spark of hope.

Perhaps that's what we needed to face whatever came next—not just strength or strategy, but the unexpected bonds formed in the heart of chaos.

Chapter Nine

GATHERING STORM

The great hall of Salvus Hus buzzed with commotion as maps and reports covered every available surface.

Three days had passed since our audience with the King, and scouts were finally bringing back useful intelligence about Nerium's movements.

Brother Fost moved thoughtfully between the assembled groups, offering quiet insights as he studied each report.

His halfling stature meant he sometimes had to stand on chairs to properly see the maps, but no one dared smile at the sight—his counsel was too valuable to risk offending.

Lybiidae stood in the shadows near the war table, her dark elven features focused intently on a detailed nautical chart.

The Drow's presence made several of the castle guards nervous, but The Scorpion's crew had long since learned to value her tactical expertise.

"Another sighting here," Commander Ashpin noted, marking a point near the mouth of Dragon's Breath Bay.

"A fishing vessel spotted Nerium's flagship and two escorts moving north along the coast."

"Just three ships?" Kuchoff asked from his position near the strategy table, where he was conferring with Sir O'cha about defensive formations.

"The flagship is massive," Meeka replied from across the room, where she and Navari were reviewing scout reports.

"The escorts are smaller, but still formidable."

Sir Gregg entered with a fresh stack of reports, his armor gleaming in the afternoon light.

"The coastal towns are evacuating, Your Majesty," he reported to the King, who had joined us for the strategic session.

"Though there have been no signs of the reality distortions we feared."

"She's losing her connection to the temporal realm," Avilyn observed, his restored face carrying an expression of scholarly interest.

The elven wizard—or dragon king in disguise—stood near one of the tall windows, conferring quietly with Jade and Emeral in their human forms.

"The locket's power becomes more focused, but she lacks the training to use it properly."

"Good," Roash declared, her tail swishing as she sharpened her blades.

"That makes her predictable."

"No," Lybiidae spoke up, her voice carrying centuries of dark wisdom.

"It makes her desperate. And desperate enemies are often the most dangerous."

"Like that time in the northern caves," Rion rumbled from his position near the door, his leonine features twisted in memory.

"When we cornered those rock trolls."

"Aye," Balt agreed grimly,

"Nasty business, that was."

The dwarf was methodically checking his battle gear, all business now that real combat approached.

I felt the rats at my feet growing restless, their tiny minds sensing the tension in the room.

Twig noticed their agitation from her perch on a window ledge and adjusted her grip on her specialized twig darts.

"Do we have a count on her crew complement?" Tatenda asked from where he was reviewing ship schematics with the castle's master shipwright.

"Need to know what we're up against, Mon."

Before anyone could answer, the great hall's doors swung open.

A messenger entered, followed by one of Roash's eline scouts, his fur still damp from hard riding.

"The flagship's been spotted entering the Strait," the scout reported, catching his breath.

"They're not trying to hide anymore—flying purple banners and moving straight for the harbor."

"Then it's time," Kuchoff declared, looking around at his assembled crew.

"Signal the rest of The Scorpion's company. We sail within the hour."

"Finally," Rion's tail lashed with anticipation.

"Some proper action!"

"The scouts also report..." the messenger hesitated, glancing nervously at the King.

"They say the hybrid creature was visible on deck. She's..." he swallowed hard.

"She's smaller now. More like she was before. But the power around her—they say it feels wrong somehow. Twisted."

"She never understood what she was taking," Kuchoff said quietly.

"The locket's gifts require more than mere possession."

From his perch near the ceiling beams, Chron's ancient eyes tracked something none of us could see.

"Pride becomes hubris," the bronze wyrmling observed.

"Hubris becomes—"

The rest was lost in the clatter of Balt's thrown axe handle against the nearest beam.

"WOT?" He asked, "some habits die hard," the dwarf shrugged as we all turned to look at him.

Brother Fost hid a smile as he gathered his medical supplies.

"Let's hope your aim stays that true when we face Nerium."

"Speaking of which," Sir O'cha interjected, "shouldn't we discuss boarding tactics? Those escorts will try to protect their flagship."

"Already planned," Roash purred, her claws flexing.

"My hunters will deal with the escorts while The Scorpion focuses on the main target."

"And the errfords will maintain shields throughout," Sir Gregg added, patting the shoulder of his companion warrior. "No surprises this time."

The king stepped forward, his presence drawing all eyes.

"You all know what's at stake," he said gravely.

"Nerium's power may be focused now, but that makes her no less dangerous. She must be stopped before she can threaten our realm further."

"We'll stop her," Kuchoff assured him, his voice carrying the weight of command that had earned him his captaincy.

"One way or another, this ends today."

As the crew began filing out to make final preparations, I caught Loher's eye from where she'd been quietly observing the proceedings.

My wife gave me a slight nod—she'd already made sure all our weapons were perfectly maintained for the coming battle.

The rats followed me as I headed for the door, their heightened instincts already attuned to the prospect of violence.

Above, Chron spread his wings in the shaft of afternoon light but remained mercifully silent.

The time for prophecies was ending. The time for action had begun.

Chapter Ten

THE LEAD-UP

The Scorpion's deck was a mixture of organized chaos as final preparations were made.

Tatenda ran through his pre-battle checks of the Creature Controls while Brother Fost moved among the crew, ensuring everyone had fresh healing potions within easy reach.

"Remember," the halfling priest instructed, passing out the last of his specially prepared elixirs,

"These take effect instantly—no need to stop fighting to drink them. Just break the vial against any part of your body."

"Even works through armor," Sir Gregg added, demonstrating by smashing a practice vial against his breastplate.

The magical liquid seeped instantly through the metal, though it carried no actual healing properties.

"Ye sure ye made enough?" Balt asked, carefully storing his share in specially padded pouches.

"I always make extra," Brother Fost replied with his characteristic giggle.

"Some of us tend to need more healing than others."

"Oi! I resent that implication!"

"He's not wrong though," Rion rumbled as he helped Roash's hunters check their specialized boarding equipment.

The grappling hooks had been wrapped in leather to muffle any sound they might make during deployment.

Lybiidae emerged from below decks, her dark magic already gathering around her like a cloak.

"The preparation room is ready," she announced.

"Should we require... reinforcements."

Everyone knew she meant the bodies of any of the fallen she might need to raise.

"Let's hope it doesn't come to that," Loher said softly as she finished her final check of the ship's trap mechanisms.

My wife's expertise had turned The Scorpion's deck into a deadly maze for any unwanted visitors.

"Positions!" Kuchoff's command carried across the deck as lookouts spotted the first signs of our quarry.

"Errfords to your stations. Archers ready. Tatenda?"

"De Scorpion be ready to dance, Captain!" Tatenda called back, his hands hovering over the Creature Controls.

I moved to my assigned position near the port rail, feeling the rats gathering in the shadows around my feet.

Their tiny minds were focused entirely on the approaching threat, whiskers twitching in shared anticipation.

"All this waiting makes me hungry," Rion rumbled, eyeing the rats gathering near my boots.

"Don't you dare," I warned, though I couldn't help but smile.

"These ones are working."

The massive eline warrior grinned, showing impressive fangs.

"Just one? The little gray one there looks particularly plump."

"Rion..."

"Fighting on an empty stomach is dangerous!" he protested, but his eyes sparkled with mischief.

Quick as lightning, his paw shot out and snatched up three rats from the periphery of my group.

The tiny creatures disappeared into his maw with disturbing efficiency.

"Those were my reserves!" I complained.

"Were being the operative word," Rion purred, licking his chops.

"Besides, you always attract more. It's like having a portable snack cart following you around."

"If you two are done discussing lunch," Roash called from her position, though her whiskers twitched with amusement, "I believe we have some ships to sink."

"Fiiine," Rion sighed dramatically. "But if we're boarding the enemy vessel, I'm eating any rats I find over there."

"Deal," I agreed.

"Just leave mine alone. I need them focused, not worried about becoming cat food."

The remaining rats pressed closer to my feet, clearly having gotten the message.

Through the thinning morning mist, Nerium's flagship appeared like a dark mountain rising from the sea.

The vessel was massive, easily twice The Scorpion's size, its black hull emblazoned with purple designs that seemed to catch the light in unnatural ways.

The two escort ships flanked it closely, their own decorations matching the flagship's aesthetic.

"She's compensating for something," Twig observed as she settled into her sniping position high in the rigging.

Her arsenal of specially treated twig-darts gleamed with fresh poison.

"Eyes sharp," Roash called to her hunters.

"Watch for movement along their gunwales."

"And their colors," Navari added, her serpentine hair writhing as she extended her supernatural senses.

"They may try to disguise boarding parties with illusions."

The distance between our vessels closed rapidly.

I could see figures moving on the enemy flagship's deck, and there—at the bow—stood Nerium herself.

She was indeed smaller now, closer to her original twenty-foot height, but power still radiated from her hybrid form.

The stolen locket gleamed at her throat.

"Remember," Kuchoff addressed the crew, his voice carrying easily over the sound of waves against the hull.

"She's desperate now. Focused on the psionic powers she barely understands. That makes her predictable, but also dangerous. Stay alert.

Trust your training. And most importantly..." he allowed himself a small smile,

"Try not to let Balt get too excited."

"I make no promises!" the dwarf called back cheerfully.

A horn sounded from Nerium's flagship—deep, resonant notes that carried challenge and warning in equal measure.

Her escort ships began to spread out, clearly intending to flank us.

"They're still using standard naval tactics," Sir O'cha observed.

"Despite everything else, they're fighting this like a normal sea battle."

"Then let's show them why that's a mistake," Kuchoff replied.

"Tatenda—bring her to life!"

"Aye, Captain!" The Drow's hands flew across the Creature Controls, and The Scorpion shuddered as hidden mechanisms engaged throughout her hull.

Wooden scales rippled as weapon ports opened, while the ship herself began to move with the deadly grace of her namesake.

"Shields up!" Meeka commanded as the first flickers of enemy magic became visible along the flagship's rails.

The errfords responded instantly, their protective barrier snapping into place around our vessel.

Nerium's voice carried across the waves, amplified by powers she thought she understood:

"Last chance, little captain! Join us willingly, or watch your precious ship burn!"

"You know," I commented to no one in particular as I extended my fangs,

"I'm getting very tired of people threatening to burn this ship."

"Aye," Balt agreed, his axe gleaming in the morning sun. "

Let's do something about tat, shall we?"

The first shots were about to be fired, and The Scorpion's crew was ready.

Whatever came next, we would face it as we had faced every other challenge—together, standing ready, with a dwarf who was probably enjoying himself just a bit too much.

Chapter Eleven
THE FUN OF WAR

"First escort's in range," Roash called out, her claws flexing on the harpoon controls.

"Permission to introduce ourselves?"

"Granted," Kuchoff replied.

"Show them why they should have brought more ships."

The harpoon's release echoed across the water like thunder.

The massive projectile punched through the escort's hull just above the waterline, its barbed head erupting from the other side in a spray of splintered wood and screaming crew members.

"Tat's how it's done!" Balt whooped as Roash engaged the retraction mechanism.

The steel cable went taut, dragging the smaller vessel toward us.

"Though I still say... wait, what's that smell?"

"Lunch!" Rion announced cheerfully, having somehow acquired another rat without my noticing.

"Focus, you two," Meeka called, though her lips twitched with amusement.

"Second escort's trying to flank us."

They never got the chance. The Scorpion's massive iron-clad claws, gleaming in the morning sun, swung wide at Tatenda's command.

Our ship's most distinctive feature, besides her mighty tail, moved with devastating precision.

"Watch dis!" Tatenda crowed as the mechanical appendages slammed into the second escort's deck.

Wood splintered and men screamed as the claws ripped through their hull like cloth.

"Nobody survives de claws, Mon!"

The first escort, now firmly in our grasp, was taking heavy fire from our archers.

Twig's poisoned darts found vulnerable spots in armor while Loher's arrows cut down officers with lethal accuracy.

The enemy crew scrambled for cover, but The Scorpion's elevated deck gave our ranged fighters the perfect angle.

"Their formation is chaos," Sir Gregg observed as he directed our errford defenses against incoming fire.

"No discipline at all."

"Speaking of discipline," I called out, watching a particularly enthusiastic display from our dwarf,

"Balt, are you actually juggling severed heads?"

"Keeps the enemy distracted!" he shouted back, catching another bloody trophy as it rolled past.

"Plus, it's fun! Look, this one still has its eyes!"

A massive explosion rocked the second escort as something in their powder magazine caught fire.

The blast sent burning bodies cartwheeling through the air, some landing on our deck still aflame.

"A bit overdone for my taste," Rion commented, batting a burning corpse back over the rail.

"I prefer my meals rare."

"Less food criticism, more fighting!" Roash commanded as she swung the harpoon around for another shot.

The Scorpion's claws were doing their brutal work, tearing massive holes in both escort vessels while keeping them close enough that our boarding parties could leap across.

Navari's serpentine hair writhed with deadly purpose as she turned three enemy officers to stone with a single glance. The statues toppled over the rail, dragging several of their companions into the blood-darkened water.

"Now that's just showing off," Twig commented as she sent a spread of darts into an enemy mage's face. The man fell screaming, poisoned wood protruding from his eye sockets.

"You're one to talk about showing off," I replied, watching her next shot take a man's ear off. "Wasn't that a bit... precise?"

"He wasn't using it anyway," she shrugged, already targeting her next victim.

Chapter Twelve

PREDATOR VS. PREDATOR

"Tatenda," Kuchoff called out as the flagship settled into the sand, "Time to show them what The Scorpion can really do."

"Oh Mon, you gonna love dis!" Tatenda's hands flew across the Creature Controls with practiced grace.

The ship shuddered, and then something extraordinary happened.

The masts began to retract, folding impossibly into the deck while the sails collapsed and disappeared into hidden compartments.

The entire vessel shifted, wooden scales rippling as eight massive legs extended from the hull.

The tail, now unrestricted, rose high above the deck like a striking serpent.

"By the gods," Kuchoff breathed, watching his ship transform. "I really could have used this in Errfordland."

"Better late than never!" Balt called out as The Scorpion took its first steps onto dry land, moving with the fluid grace of its namesake. "Now this is what I call a proper landing party!"

Jade and Emeral swept down from above, their green scales flashing in the sun as they engaged Nerium.

Avilyn joined them in his true form, his iridescent scales shifting through impossible colors as he dove into the fray.

The battle exploded into chaos. The Scorpion's claws snapped and grabbed, catching enemy soldiers and crushing them like toys.

The tail struck with lethal precision, its armored tip punching through men as if they were made of straw.

Sir O'cha led a charge down one of The Scorpion's legs, his sword flashing in the morning light.

"For the King!" he cried, cutting down three of Nerium's guards in rapid succession.

But his victory was short-lived.

Nerium caught him with a blast of psionic energy that lifted him into the air.

We watched in horror as she literally twisted him inside out, his armor melting like lava as steaming blood and organs sprayed across the sand.

His screams cut off abruptly as his spine snapped in multiple places.

"You'll pay for that!" Sir Gregg roared, charging forward.

He made it two steps before Nerium's power caught him as well.

His armor imploded, crushing him into a bloody ball of metal and flesh that she hurled into a group of his fellow knights.

Rion moved to help but never reached them.

A piece of falling rigging from the flagship, torn loose by the dragons' assault, caught him full in the chest.

The heavy wood and metal smashed him into the sand, and when Navari reached him, his crushed body was already still.

"Focus!" Kuchoff commanded as grief threatened to overwhelm us. "Loher?"

My wife nodded grimly, pulling her cloak of invisibility around her shoulders and vanishing from sight.

While Nerium was distracted by the dragons' relentless assault—they were forcing her to constantly defend herself though they couldn't quite finish her—Loher ghosted across the battlefield, completely unseen.

The dragons coordinated their attacks perfectly.

Jade and Emeral drove in from either side, forcing Nerium to split her attention.

Avilyn's breath weapon, a beam of pure iridescent energy, kept her from advancing.

She fought with desperate fury, using her stolen psionic powers to tear chunks from their scales and twist the very air around them, but she couldn't match their aerial superiority.

Twig provided additional chaos, her poisoned darts taking down any of Nerium's guards who might accidentally stumble into Loher's path.

One man made the mistake of wandering too close to where I knew my wife was moving.

The dart that took him in the eye carried enough poison to kill ten men.

He died screaming, clawing at his face as the toxin turned his blood to fire.

The Scorpion's tail struck again, impaling three men who tried to flank our position.

Their bodies hung from the armored tip for a moment before being flung aside like broken dolls.

The ship-turned-creature moved with deadly grace across the battlefield, its legs crushing anyone foolish enough to get too close.

That's when everything changed.

Loher, moving with the silent skill that had kept her alive for so many years, managed to get within arm's reach of Nerium.

The hybrid creature never saw her coming—she was too focused on the dragons harrying her from above.

With one perfect motion, Loher severed the locket's chain and darted away.

Nerium's scream of rage shook the very air.

She lashed out wildly, her psionic powers fading but her physical strength still terrifying.

Her claws caught Roash's youngest hunter, literally tearing the eline warrior in half.

Blood and entrails rained across the sand as the two pieces fell in different directions.

"Fall back!" Kuchoff commanded as Nerium began literally ripping her own men apart in her fury. "Regroup around The Scorpion!"

Our living ship moved to protect us, its massive body providing cover as we withdrew to a more defensible position.

The sand beneath our feet was stained crimson, littered with bodies and pieces of bodies from both sides.

Nerium stood among the carnage, her massive form heaving with rage and exertion.

The dragons continued to harry her, but now she could only strike back with physical force.

It was enough to keep them at bay—she was still incredibly strong—but the terrible psionic powers were gone.

"Well," Balt commented as we caught our breath, his armor drenched in gore, "Tat could have gone worse."

"How exactly?" Twig demanded, counting her remaining darts.

"Could've been raining."

Thunder cracked overhead as storm clouds began gathering.

"I hate you," Twig said with feeling.

"ATTACK!" Nerium's roar shook the ground as her army poured over the dunes.

Ten thousand orcs charged forward, their black armor catching the strange light filtering through the storm clouds.

Behind them came the hobgoblin clans, their disciplined ranks interspersed with towering ogres.

Mages in purple robes took position on the higher dunes, their hands already glowing with deadly power.

"Now that," Balt said appreciatively, "is a proper army ta kill!"

The Scorpion shifted on its massive legs, tail raised and ready as Tatenda guided our living ship into a defensive stance. "We gonna need more den regular magic for dis one, Mon!"

Lybiidae stepped forward, her dark power crackling around her like black lightning. "Then let's change the odds."

Her hands moved in complex patterns as she spoke words that hurt to hear.

The very sand beneath our feet began to shift and bubble.

Dragon bones, buried for centuries in the Dead Dunelands, erupted from the ground.

Skeletal wings spread wide as undead dragons rose to serve her will.

The remains of ancient hill giants followed, their massive bone-frames reassembling into engines of destruction.

The first wave of orcs hit our line like a tidal wave of steel and muscle.

The Scorpion's claws swept through their ranks, literally pulling warriors apart.

Black blood sprayed across the sand as body parts rained down around us.

Tatenda's expert control sent the tail striking again and again, each hit turning armored soldiers into broken dolls.

That's when the air split with multiple roars.

Four dragons—two reds, a black, and a massive brown—descended from the storm clouds to join Nerium.

Their arrival scattered our front lines as soldiers dove for cover.

"Traitors!" Avilyn's voice boomed across the battlefield as he launched himself skyward, Jade and Emeral flanking him.

The aerial battle that followed was like nothing I'd ever seen.

The first red dragon fell quickly, caught between Avilyn's iridescent breath weapon and Jade's coordinated strike.

Its wings shredded, it plummeted into a formation of hobgoblins, crushing dozens on impact.

The weight of its corpse created a crater in the blood-soaked sand.

Navari claimed our first major victory on the ground, her gaze turning an entire squad of enemy mages to stone.

But her triumph was short-lived.

The black dragon's acid breath caught her from above, reducing her to bubbling remains even as her last victims toppled into the chaos below.

"You'll pay for that!" Roash screamed, leading her hunters in a devastating charge through the enemy's left flank.

They moved like living shadows, blades claiming lives with every strike.

But the cost was terrible.

A hobgoblin elite unit surrounded them, and we watched in horror as they systematically cut down Roash's warriors one by one.

The brown dragon proved surprisingly agile for its size, nearly catching Emeral with its massive jaws.

But Jade's intervention gave his brother the opening he needed.

Their combined breath weapons literally cooked the larger dragon inside its own scales.

It crashed into one of Nerium's ogre units, its massive bulk crushing them beneath its death throes.

The battle swirled around The Scorpion's legs as our living ship continued its deadly work.

Three ogres thought to climb one of the armored limbs—their broken bodies soon decorated the sand below.

The tail struck with surgical precision, each hit turning enemy soldiers into red mist.

Twig's position in the rigging proved devastating until the second red dragon noticed her.

She managed to blind it in one eye with her poisoned darts, but its retaliatory flame breath turned our halfling archer into ash.

Her final dart, however, found the dragon's remaining eye.

The blinded beast careened into the black dragon, disrupting its attack run on our position.

The blinded red dragon and wounded black dragon recovered enough to coordinate another attack, but Avilyn was ready.

His true form, magnificent in its iridescent fury, caught them both with a breath weapon that defied description.

The red literally came apart in midair, while the black spiraled into Nerium's own lines, crushing scores of her soldiers.

Lybiidae's undead dragons and giants turned the tide against the enemy's center mass.

Skeletal claws ripped through armor while bone-clubs reduced entire formations to paste.

The psychological effect was devastating—even hardened hobgoblin veterans broke ranks at the sight of dragon bones moving with terrible purpose.

But our victories came at a terrible price.

Roash fell defending Brother Fost from a hobgoblin champion, her throat opened by a perfectly placed blade.

The priest tried to reach her with healing magic, but a purple-robed mage's spell caught him mid-stride.

The beloved halfling died trying to cast one final healing spell.

Meeka's retaliation was apocalyptic.

Her magic carved burning swaths through enemy ranks, reducing whole squads to ash.

"For Fost!" she screamed, tears streaming down her face as she turned soldiers into torches.

Storm clouds churned overhead, casting the battlefield in an eerie twilight glow as lightning danced between sky and earth.

Nerium stood atop a massive dune, her scaled form silhouetted against the darkening sky.

Wounded and cornered, she remained an imposing figure.

Blood matted her rose-silver scales, and deep gashes marked where Jade and Emeral had scored hits during the aerial battle.

"Is this how you imagined it would end, Kuchoff?" she called down, her voice carrying over the wind that whipped sand across the battle-field. "Your precious crew decimated, your ship damaged, all to corner me in this wasteland?"

Behind her, ranks of orcs and hobgoblins formed a protective wall, their black armor gleaming dully in the storm light.

Ogres towered among the smaller warriors, wielding massive clubs that could crush a man in a single blow.

At least two thousand strong, they awaited her command to attack.

The Scorpion loomed behind us, its mechanical legs partially sunk into the unstable sand, tail raised and ready.

What remained of our crew formed a semicircle at the base of the dune, cutting off any chance of escape.

Our errfords hovered close to their bonded partners, their squirrel-sized bodies pulsing with protective energy that created faint, shimmering auras around everyone except Kuchoff, who needed no such protection.

"This ends today," Kuchoff replied, his voice steady despite the exhaustion etched on his face.

A faint shimmer of psionic energy surrounded him, his natural shield far stronger than any errford could provide. "One way or another."

Nerium's laugh was bitter, echoing strangely across the dunes.

"Your pathetic force against my army?" She gestured to the thousands of warriors at her command. "You've finally lost your mind, little captain."

"Who said we came alone?" Avilyn stepped forward, his elven form showing no sign of the power contained within.

His demeanor remained impassive as he raised his flaming sword.

On cue, Jade and Emeral appeared over the dunes behind us, leading a flight of dozens of dragons that had remained loyal to their true king.

The sky darkened further as their massive shapes blocked what little sunlight remained.

Nerium's confidence faltered momentarily, but she quickly recovered.

"Kill them all!" she commanded, and her army surged forward with a roar that shook the very sand beneath our feet.

"Lybiidae!" Kuchoff called. "Now would be a good time!"

The Drow necromancer stepped forward, dark energy swirling around her.

The bodies of our fallen companions—preserved by her magic—rose from beneath the sand where they had been temporarily interred.

Roash and Rion were among them, their once-dead forms now animated by Lybiidae's power, their eyes glowing with an unnatural light.

"For The Scorpion!" Roash called, her voice carrying the hollow echo of the grave.

The reanimated crew charged to meet Nerium's forces, creating a macabre advance guard that sent the front ranks of orcs into disarray.

The sight of their dead companions returned to fight against them struck fear into even the most hardened of warriors.

Balt let out a wild battle cry, his axe already swinging as he charged into the fray. "This is more like it!" he bellowed, cleaving through an orc's armor as if it was naked. "A proper fight!"

The battle exploded across the dunes.

Errfords projected their shields as arrows and spears rained down from Nerium's forces.

The tiny creatures' energy orbs punched through armor and flesh with devastating precision, creating perfect, cauterized holes wherever they struck.

Kuchoff moved like a force of nature, his psionic shield deflecting everything thrown at him.

Where he focused his power, orcs and hobgoblins fell screaming, their armor crumpling inward as if crushed by an invisible fist.

His katana flashed in the storm light, each strike finding gaps in armor with surgical precision.

I fought my way through the chaos, my vampiric speed allowing me to dart between enemies before they could react.

Fangs extended, I tore through throats and severed arteries, the predator in my blood reveling in the carnage.

The rats at my feet swarmed over fallen enemies, their tiny teeth finding vulnerable eyes and exposed flesh.

Loher moved like a ghost through the battlefield, her errford's shield making her nearly invisible as she slipped behind enemy lines.

Ogres fell inexplicably, blood gushing from precisely placed arrows that appeared as if by magic.

Her arrows found vulnerable spots with unerring accuracy, leaving death in her wake.

Above, the dragons engaged Nerium's aerial forces—wyverns and other flying beasts that she had somehow bound to her will.

The sky became a chaotic dance of wings, claws, and elemental breath weapons.

Avilyn directed this aerial ballet with subtle gestures, his seemingly frail elven form belying the dragon king's power within.

Tatenda brought The Scorpion into the fray, the massive mechanical arachnid crushing dozens of enemies beneath its armored legs.

Its tail struck with devastating force, impaling ogres and sending their broken bodies flying across the battlefield.

But for every enemy we felled, two more seemed to take their place.

The battle hung in precarious balance, neither side able to gain a decisive advantage.

"We need to reach Nerium!" Kuchoff called over the chaos. "She's the key!"

Avilyn nodded in agreement.

With a gesture that seemed almost casual, he began to change.

His elven form shimmered and expanded, growing larger until the dragon king stood revealed in all his glory.

His iridescent scales shifted through colors that almost hurt the eyes to follow, power radiating from him in palpable waves.

Nerium's army faltered at the sight, many throwing down their weapons and fleeing.

But the hybrid creature herself stood firm, her expression a mixture of defiance and awe.

"Even you cannot stop what I've set in motion," she snarled as Avilyn approached, his massive form dwarfing even her impressive stature.

"Perhaps not alone," the dragon king agreed, his voice resonating with harmonics that made the sand beneath our feet vibrate. "But I am not alone."

Kuchoff seized the opportunity, charging up the dune toward Nerium while her attention was fixed on Avilyn.

His psionic shield flared brighter as he focused his power, creating a battering ram of pure mental energy that scattered her remaining guards like toys.

Nerium sensed his approach too late.

She turned, claws extended to rip through his seemingly fragile human form, but his psionic shield held firm.

Her attack slid harmlessly off the invisible barrier, leaving her momentarily off balance.

That single moment was all he needed.

Kuchoff's katana struck with lightning speed, the enchanted blade slicing through scales at the junction of her neck and shoulder.

Blood sprayed in a crimson arc as major vessels were severed, but the wound wasn't immediately fatal.

Nerium roared in pain and fury, her tail whipping around to sweep Kuchoff's leg out from under him.

Even his psionic shield couldn't fully absorb the impact.

He was spun backward down the dune, his katana wrenching from his grasp.

I moved without thinking, my vampiric speed carrying me to his side before he even stopped rolling. "Kuchoff!"

"I'm fine," he gasped, blood trickling from the corner of his mouth. "But she's wounded now. Vulnerable."

Across the battlefield, Lybiidae sensed the opportunity.

She directed her undead forces to converge on Nerium's position, creating a wall of reanimated flesh between the hybrid creature and her retreating army.

Roash and Rion led this grisly charge, their movements more fluid than the other reanimated crew members.

Roash's blades flashed with unnatural speed, opening new wounds across Nerium's already damaged scales.

Rion, even in death, moved with feline grace, his claws finding vulnerable spots with unerring precision.

Nerium fought with desperate fury, her tail and claws tearing through the undead warriors.

Bodies fell in pieces around her, but they felt no pain, no fear.

They simply got up and kept coming, directed by Lybiidae's inexorable will.

"Now, Balt!" Kuchoff commanded, having recovered his katana and regained his feet.

The dwarf had been waiting for this moment.

His errford launched a barrage of energy orbs, each one punching through Nerium's scaled hide with devastating accuracy.

The tiny magical projectiles created a pattern of perfectly cauterized holes across her chest and abdomen, weakening her further.

Balt himself charged up the dune, his axe held high.

"This be fer Rion!" he bellowed, though the undead eline warrior still fought nearby.

"An' Roash! An' all me other mates ye took from us!"

His axe connected with brutal force, cleaving deep into Nerium's already wounded shoulder.

The hybrid creature screamed as the expertly sharpened blade bit through muscle and bone, nearly severing her arm.

Rion seized the opportunity, latching onto Nerium's damaged limb and pulling with inhuman strength.

With a sickening tearing sound, the arm separated completely, blood fountaining from the socket in rhythmic spurts, drenching Rion in the process.

I swear I heard him laugh, even over Nerium's frantic screams.

He took a bite.

Nerium staggered but remained standing, her remaining arm lashing out to trounce Balt.

The dwarf was sent tumbling down the dune, his armor dented but intact.

His errford chittered in alarm, its shield flaring to protect him as he rolled to a stop.

"Enough of this," Avilyn's voice resonated across the battlefield.

The dragon king inhaled deeply, his massive chest expanding as he prepared to unleash his breath weapon.

Sensing her imminent destruction, Nerium made one final, desperate lunge toward Kuchoff.

"If I die," she snarled, blood bubbling from her mouth, "I take you with me!"

Kuchoff's psionic shield flared to maximum intensity, creating a clearly visible barrier between him and Nerium's charge.

Roash and Rion converged on her from either side, their reanimated bodies moving with purpose.

Loher appeared as if from nowhere, her sharp broadhead arrows severing tendons in Nerium's remaining arm and leg.

As the hybrid creature stumbled forward, momentum carrying her despite her newly crippled limbs, Lybiidae made her final move.

The Drow necromancer extended her hands, dark energy crackling between her fingers as she uttered words that hurt to hear.

The sand beneath Nerium's feet suddenly erupted upward, forming skeletal hands that grasped at her scaled body.

Bones of long-dead creatures, buried for centuries in the Dead Dunelands, answered Lybiidae's call.

They coalesced into a grotesque framework, a cage of femurs and ribs and skulls that trapped Nerium in place.

"Waxx!" Kuchoff yelled.

Tatenda responded instantly.

The Scorpion's tail arced overhead, its armored tip aimed precisely at Nerium's chest.

The massive appendage struck with devastating force, punching through scales, muscle, and bone.

The impact nearly tore her in half, internal organs rupturing as the stinger penetrated completely through her body.

Blood and viscera erupted from Nerium's mouth as she tried to scream, but only a gurgling hiss emerged.

The Scorpion's tail lifted her writhing form high into the air, her remaining limbs thrashing weakly as life drained from her massive body.

Avilyn approached in his dragon form, ancient eyes studying the dying hybrid with something like pity.

"You could have been magnificent," he said softly.

"Had you understood the gift of your unique nature rather than *perverting* it with stolen power."

Nerium's remaining eye fixed on him with undimmed hatred.

"I... *was*... magnificent..." she gasped, blood pouring from her ruined body in rivers down The Scorpion's tail.

"More than... dragon... more than... human..."

"No," Avilyn corrected gently. "You were a weapon. Nothing more."

With a final, desperate effort, Nerium raised her head to look at Kuchoff.

"Your... mother..." she began, but whatever revelation or curse she intended died with her.

Her massive body went suddenly limp, the last breath escaping in a wet rattle.

The hybrid creature who had torn through realms in her quest for power was, finally, irrevocably dead.

The Scorpion's tail lowered slowly, depositing Nerium's corpse onto the bloodied sand.

Already, the desert wind was beginning to cover her with a thin layer of grit, nature reclaiming what had never truly belonged.

Lybiidae approached the body, dark energy still swirling around her hands.

"Shall I?" she asked, looking to Kuchoff for permission.

He considered for a moment, then shook his head.

"No. Some things should remain dead."

He glanced at the reanimated forms of Roash and Rion, who stood nearby, awaiting new commands.

"Including our friends, once we've properly honored them."

The Drow necromancer nodded in understanding.

With a gesture, she released the magic animating our fallen companions.

Their bodies collapsed to the sand, once again merely empty vessels.

"We'll take them home," Kuchoff decided, looking out over the battlefield where the remaining enemy forces were being routed or surrendering.

"They deserve proper pyres, with all the honors."

"Aye," Balt agreed, limping to join us with his errford perched protectively on his shoulder.

"A proper sendin' fer proper heroes."

He studied Nerium's mutilated corpse with grim satisfaction.

"As fer her... let ta desert 'ave 'er. Let ta sand bury what's left until tere's no sign she ever existed."

As we gathered our wounded and prepared to depart, the errfords remained unusually subdued.

They sensed the gravity of our victory and its cost, their protective shields dimming to a soft glow that illuminated our path across the darkening dunes.

From his perch atop The Scorpion, Chron observed the scene with his ancient eyes.

"Even that which was never meant to be," he noted quietly, "returns to the elements from which it came."

For once, Balt didn't threaten to make boots out of the prophetic wyrmling. Instead, he looked out over the battlefield where so many had fallen and simply nodded.

"Aye," he agreed softly. "Back tae ta dust. Where mistakes an' heroes alike find teir rest."

Chapter Thirteen
RESPITE

The storm finally broke as we finished stowing our dead in The Scorpion's hold.

Rain mixed with blood on the sand as The Scorpion carefully shifted its weight.

"Two hunnerd an' eighty-tree confirmed enemy kills," Balt reported quietly, his usual boisterous tone subdued as he cleaned his axe. "Plus, whatever tat last group counted as."

He gestured to a pile of bodies so mangled it was impossible to determine their original number.

"Does it matter?" Loher asked, though the acid in her voice was dulled by exhaustion.

She sat checking her bow, still wearing her blood-soaked cloak of invisibility.

"The counting, the competing—what's the point now?"

"Ta point," Balt replied with surprising gentleness, "is each one counted was one less tat could harm the crew we have left."

He looked at the rows of our dead. "One less tat could take anudder mate from us."

Meeka worked silently, using her magic to preserve Brother Fost's body.

The beloved halfling priest looked almost peaceful, as if he might wake at any moment with one of his characteristic giggles.

But we all knew better.

"He died trying to heal Roash," Tatenda said softly from his position by The Scorpion's Creature Controls. "Right to de end, he was trying to save others."

"They all died protecting something," Kuchoff observed, his voice heavy with command and grief. "Or someone."

He looked up at Jade and Emeral, who sat on a few crates in their human forms, nursing their wounds. "How bad?"

"We'll heal," Jade replied, wincing as he shifted. "But it will take time. That last surge..." He shook his head.

"You didn't see her eyes at the end," Avilyn said quietly.

Kuchoff looked at Balt. "How do the dwarves send off their greatest warriors?"

A slow smile spread through Balt's beard.

"Wit fire," he said. "Wit song. An' wit a promise o' vengeance tat would make ta gods temselves tink twice."

"Then that's what we'll do," Kuchoff decided. "We'll build the pyres near the Den atop the highest peak of the mountain."

"And then?" I asked, already knowing the answer.

"Then we hunt," Kuchoff's voice carried steel beneath the grief. "We hunt until we find Lemac. Until we finish this. Until every death here today is answered for."

Thunder rolled overhead as we began our preparations.

The dead of both sides still littered the battlefield beyond our immediate position, but they would have to wait.

Our first duty was to our own.

"I'll need wood," Balt said, already planning the pyres. "Lots of it. And oil. And someone who can sing the old songs properly."

"I know them," Avilyn offered quietly. "All of them. From every culture that ever sent its warriors to rest."

The rain began to fade as we worked.

The Scorpion kept watch, its massive form a stark silhouette against the clearing sky.

Soon the pyres would burn, sending our fallen to whatever waited beyond.

And then...

Then we would remind Lemac why The Scorpion's crew was feared in every port, in every realm.

Why our name carried weight even in places we'd never sailed.

And why taking our family from us was the last mistake he would ever make.

The voyage back to The Scorpion's Den was quiet.

Everyone was reflecting on the battle.

Before we knew it, Tatenda had walked us back into the Den and settled back into the lagoon.

"Try to get some rest," Kuchoff called as we began to disembark into the cavernous abode we call home, "sleep if you can, for tomorrow we honor our fallen."

And with that, he ducked away into the shadows and disappeared.

The next morning, before the sun began to peek over the Ferrum Mons, we gathered our dead and began the upward journey.

Atop the highest peak overlooking The Scorpion's Den, the funeral pyres stood ready as dawn broke.

Each was meticulously constructed under Balt's supervision—platforms of seasoned wood stacked with precision, each adorned with symbols meaningful to the fallen they would honor.

The surviving crew of The Scorpion gathered in solemn formation.

Their usual banter was absent, replaced by a heavy silence as they watched the morning light touch the faces of their fallen comrades.

Sir O'cha, Sir Gregg, Rion, Roash, Brother Fost, Navari, Twig, —each body had been prepared with care, dressed in their finest, weapons positioned with honor at their sides.

Balt stepped forward; his normally boisterous demeanor subdued.

He wore ceremonial dwarven armor polished to a mirror shine, his beard intricately braided with silver beads that clinked softly as he moved.

"In ta mountains o' me homeland," he began, his voice carrying across the assembly, "we believe tat a warrior's spirit rises wit ta smoke ta join ta ancestors." He gestured to the pyres. "Today, we send our broters an' sisters home wit all ta honor tey deserve."

Captain Magnus stood with Meeka at his side, the locket once again in a hidden and secured location.

His face was a mask of controlled grief as he addressed the crew.

"They died as they lived—protecting each other, fighting for what they believed in," he said.

"There is no greater honor than to call them crew.

No greater privilege than to have fought beside them."

Avilyn stepped forward in his elven form, though power still radiated from him in palpable waves.

"I will sing the songs of passing," he offered, "that their journey may be swift and true."

When he began to sing, the sound was unlike anything I had ever heard—ancient melodies carrying harmonics that seemed to resonate with the very stone beneath our feet.

Each note carried grief and pride in equal measure, honoring sacrifice without diminishing its cost.

The errfords moved among the pyres, their tiny paws placing small glowing orbs next to each fallen warrior—final gifts of protection for the journey beyond.

Lybiidae stood apart, head bowed in respect.

Though her necromancy had briefly returned our friends to battle, she understood better than most the sanctity of their final rest.

Balt approached the first pyre—Brother Fost's.

The halfling priest looked peaceful, his healing supplies arranged around him like treasures.

"Ta fire tat consumes also cleanses," Balt intoned, taking a torch from Jade. "Ta smoke tat rises carries your spirit to ta halls of your ancestors, where healing and laughter await in equal measure."

He touched the torch to the pyre.

Flames licked upward, catching quickly on the oil-soaked wood.

One by one, each pyre was lit—Roash, Rion, Navari, the knights, Twig—until seven fires burned bright against the morning sky.

Loher squeezed my hand as we watched the flames climb higher.

Rats gathered quietly at my feet, sensing my grief.

When the pyres were fully engulfed, Balt raised his axe high.

"Now comes ta promise," he called out. "Ta oath tat gives meaning ta teir sacrifice."

The surviving crew raised their weapons in unison—swords, bows, staffs, all glinting in the firelight.

"By stone an' steel, by blood an' bone," Balt chanted, the traditional dwarven oath of vengeance giving voice to our collective resolve. "We swear tat yer deaths will be answered. Tat yer names'll be remembered. Tat tose what took ye from us will know ta full measure o' our wrath."

"We swear," the crew responded as one.

"Until ta mountains temselves crumble to dust," Balt continued, his voice breaking slightly. "Until ta stars fall from ta sky. Until our own journey ends and we join ye in ta halls beyond."

"We swear," came the response again, stronger now.

Captain Magnus stepped forward; his katana raised.

"For The Scorpion," he said simply.

"For The Scorpion," we echoed.

As the flames reached their zenith, Avilyn's song changed—the melody lifting, transcending grief to celebrate lives well-lived and deaths well-earned.

Balt produced small casks of dwarven fire-whiskey, passing them among the crew.

"One final toast," he instructed. "Ta send 'em on teir way."

We drank deeply, the spirits burning a path to our bellies that matched the fire in our hearts.

Then, as tradition demanded, we cast the empty vessels into the flames.

The pyres would burn throughout the day and into the night.

Crew members would come and go, sharing stories of the fallen, laughing and crying in equal measure.

But through it all, the oath remained—a promise written in fire and sealed in blood.

Tomorrow would bring planning and preparation, the hunt for Lemac and whatever remained of Nerium's forces.

But today was for remembrance, for honoring those who would sail with The Scorpion no more—except in memory, in legacy, and in the vengeance we would bring in their names.

Chapter Fourteen

The Price of Victory

The castle of Salvus Hus loomed before us, its white stone towers catching the late afternoon sun.

After the Battle of the Dead Dunelands, as the crew had begun to call it, our return journey had been somber but swift.

The Scorpion, despite bearing the scars of combat, had carried us faithfully back to Beornan Heafod.

I studied the guards on the battlements as we approached. Their posture changed subtly when they recognized our colors — a straightening of shoulders, a tightening of grips on spears. The Scorpion's reputation preceded us, especially now.

The rats at my feet grew restless, scurrying between my boots and the cobblestones. Their tiny minds sensed my discomfort. Not fear of the coming audience with the King, but the bitter knowledge that our victory remained incomplete.

"They're preparing a hero's welcome," Meeka observed quietly, coming to stand beside me.

"For heroes who lost half their crew," I replied, unable to keep the edge from my voice.

Her eyes dropped momentarily before meeting mine again with renewed determination. "We stopped Nerium. The realm is safer because of what we did."

"And Lemac?" I asked, watching her reaction carefully.

A flash of something—guilt perhaps—crossed her features before she composed herself. "We'll find him. He can't hide forever."

Loher appeared silently at my other side; her elven grace masking how close she'd been all along. "We'll find him," she echoed, though her tone carried none of Meeka's optimism. Her eyes never met Meeka's as she spoke. "And when we do, I'll personally ensure he doesn't slip away again."

The tension between the women was almost palpable—Meeka's betrayal still a fresh wound for Loher despite the reconciliation with Kuchoff. My wife had never forgiven easily, and this cut deeper than most.

Ahead of us, Balt trudged with uncharacteristic heaviness in his step. His normally boisterous demeanor had been subdued since the funeral pyres. Occasionally, he would mutter something to his errford or absently pat the pocket where he kept a small braid of Rion's mane—a keepsake from his fallen friend.

"Stone-Heart," Chron called from where he glided just above our procession. "Your grief clouds your sight."

Balt looked up, his eyes narrowing. "Didnae ask fer yer opinion, scale-back."

"Yet wisdom comes regardless," the bronze wyrmling replied gently. "The enemy who escapes lives in fear of your pursuit. Your vengeance is not denied, merely delayed."

"Ach, fancy words fer failure," Balt growled, though with less heat than I expected. "If tat snake Lemac hadnae slithered away while we were busy wit Nerium..." His hand tightened around his axe handle.

Captain Magnus, who had been walking slightly ahead conferring with Avilyn, dropped back to join us.

"We don't know when Lemac fled," he stated, his voice carrying the weight of command that silenced even Balt's grumbling. "He could have disappeared during the initial clash, or while we were engaged with Nerium's forces. What matters is that our primary target has been eliminated."

"And what will you tell the King?" Lybiidae asked from the shadows where she walked. The Drow necromancer had kept her distance from most of the crew since releasing our fallen comrades from her magic. "That we allowed a dangerous enemy to escape while we were... distracted?"

"The truth," Kuchoff replied simply. "That we defeated the most immediate threat to the realm at great cost, and now we hunt the remaining danger."

As we passed through the castle gates, the guards saluted with perfect precision. Word of our approach had clearly reached the inner keep, as we were met in the courtyard by the King's seneschal—a thin man with a perpetually worried expression.

"Captain Magnus," he greeted with a formal bow. "His Majesty awaits you and your officers in the Council Chamber. He has requested your immediate presence."

Kuchoff nodded. "Lead the way."

As we followed the seneschal through familiar corridors, I caught Balt studying the tapestries that depicted ancient battles.

"Ye notice tat none o' these fancy pictures show ta aftermath?" he muttered, just loud enough for me to hear. "Never see ta pyres or ta empty spaces where friends should be standin'."

"That's not what people want to remember," I replied softly.

"Aye," he agreed with unusual solemnity. "But it's what we carry nonetheless."

The council chamber doors swung open, revealing the King already seated at the massive oak table, maps and reports spread before him. Unlike the formality of the throne room, this space was designed for strategy and candor. The Queen stood near a window, bouncing their infant son gently in her arms.

"Scorpion," the King greeted, using our collective name with a warmth that belied his royal status. He rose as we entered, his eyes quickly taking inventory of our reduced numbers. A shadow passed over his features as he noted the many missing faces. "I've received preliminary reports, but I want to hear it directly from you."

Kuchoff stepped forward. "Nerium is dead, Your Majesty. Her hybrid form and stolen power have been extinguished permanently."

A visible wave of relief washed over the King's face. "Then the realm owes you a debt that can never be repaid." His expression darkened. "But at what cost?"

"Too high," Balt muttered, earning a sharp look from the seneschal that he completely ignored.

The Queen approached, her posture regal despite the domestic scene of her cradling her child. "Captain Magnus, we have prepared chambers for your wounded and accommodation for your remaining crew. Salvus Hus's resources are at your disposal during your recovery."

Her formal tone softened slightly as her gaze moved over our battle-worn company. "And arrangements are being made for a proper memorial for those who fell in service to the crown."

"Thank you, Your Highness," Kuchoff replied with appropriate deference, though I noticed his eyes kept returning to the King. "But there is more you should know."

The King nodded, gesturing for us to be seated. "Speak freely."

"Lemac escaped during the battle," Kuchoff stated without preamble. "In the chaos of engaging Nerium and her forces, he slipped away. We have no current information on his whereabouts or intentions."

The King's expression remained carefully neutral, though his fingers drummed once on the table's surface—a tell I'd noticed during our previous meetings. "I see."

"It was my fault," Meeka stepped forward suddenly, her voice steady despite the admission. "I was focused on Nerium and her psionic abilities. I should have anticipated that Lemac would use the confusion to flee."

Loher made a small sound—not quite a laugh, not quite a snort—that drew the Queen's sharp gaze.

My wife met her look unflinchingly before addressing Meeka directly, for the first time since the betrayal had been revealed.

"Lemac was always going to run," she said, her tone cutting. "Men like him don't stand and fight when their protections fail. He used Nerium as a shield while it suited him, then abandoned her when the tide turned." Her eyes narrowed. "Just as he used you."

The tension in the room thickened.

Avilyn cleared his throat delicately, drawing attention to where he stood in his elven form.

His face, now fully restored to its elven perfection, bore no trace of the damage that had once marked him—a physical reminder of the power he commanded as the King of Dragons.

"If I may, Your Majesty," he began, his ancient voice carrying the weight of countless centuries, "Lemac's escape, while unfortunate, was perhaps inevitable given the nature of our engagement with Nerium. Her power had grown to such proportions that she required our full attention."

"And now?" the King asked, turning back to Kuchoff. "What is your assessment of the threat Lemac poses on his own?"

Kuchoff considered this carefully. "Diminished but not eliminated. Without Nerium's power to amplify his own, Lemac returns to being a talented but conventional mage. However," he added with emphasis, "he still possesses knowledge of the portal stones, connections to remnants of the Grand Ascendancy, and a grudge against those who thwarted his plans."

"And dragons," Lybiidae added from where she stood in the shadows. "We cannot forget the hatchlings under his control."

The King nodded gravely, then turned to Avilyn. "Lord Avilyn, as—" he paused, still adjusting to addressing the ancient elven wizard by his true status, "—as King of Dragons, what can you tell us about these hatchlings?"

Avilyn's elven features showed a flicker of concern. "Young dragons are impressionable. If Lemac has indeed bonded with them from hatching, they will be loyal to him despite my presence. They could become powerful weapons in his hands as they mature."

"Then we hunt," Balt declared, slapping his hand on the table with enough force to make the maps jump. "We track down tat one-eared snake and put an end ta him before his lizards grow any bigger."

The King looked to Kuchoff, a question in his eyes.

"My crew needs rest," Kuchoff acknowledged. "We've lost good people, and the remaining crew is exhausted. But Balt is right—we can't allow Lemac time to regroup or the dragons time to grow."

The Queen shifted her son to her other arm, her expression unreadable as she studied our battered company. "Captain Magnus," she said formally, "while the crown recognizes the urgency of this threat, we cannot in good conscience send you and your people immediately back into danger without proper recovery."

Before Kuchoff could protest, she continued in the same measured tone, "Three days. You will have three days to rest, repair The Scorpion, and make whatever preparations you deem necessary. The royal physicians are at your disposal, as are our armories and supply chambers."

The King nodded in agreement. "Three days, during which our own intelligence networks will attempt to locate Lemac or any trace of Grand Ascendancy activity."

I watched as Kuchoff weighed this offer, glancing briefly at our exhausted companions.

Balt looked ready to argue, but a subtle shake of Meeka's head silenced him.

"Three days," Kuchoff accepted with a nod. "Thank you, Your Majesties."

As the meeting concluded and we filed out of the council chamber, I found myself beside Chron, who had remained uncharacteristically silent throughout the proceedings.

"No prophecies today?" I asked quietly.

The bronze wyrmling's ancient eyes studied me with something like compassion.

"Some truths need no prophecy to be foreseen," he replied. "The hunter becomes the hunted but first must tend his wounds."

Balt, overhearing as he passed, rolled his eyes. "If ye start wit tat cryptic nonsense again, I swear by me mother's beard—"

"You'll what, Stone-Heart?" Chron asked with what might have been a draconic smile. "Turn me into footwear? I believe we've moved beyond such threats."

To my surprise, Balt's beard twitched with what might have been the ghost of his old grin.

"Aye, perhaps. But I still keep me leather-working tools sharp, just in case."

As we made our way toward the guest quarters assigned to us, I noticed Loher hanging back, her movements deliberately creating distance between herself and Meeka.

When I slowed my pace to join her, she gave me a look that spoke volumes.

"She still hasn't earned my trust," she said without preamble, her eyes tracking Meeka's back. "Kuchoff may have forgiven her, but I haven't forgotten what betrayal does to a crew."

"She chose him in the end," I reminded gently. "Chose us."

"Too late for those we burned on the mountain," Loher replied, her voice tight. Her hand reached for mine, fingers intertwining with familiar strength. "But you're right—she did choose. Eventually."

Ahead of us, Kuchoff walked with Meeka and Avilyn, their heads bent in serious discussion.

The weight of command had never looked heavier on him, despite our victory.

The rats at my feet had grown strangely restless, their tiny claws skittering on the stone in patterns that seemed almost deliberate.

One particularly large specimen, Albi, kept circling back toward the corridor we had just left, its whiskers twitching in agitation.

My vampiric senses prickled in response. Something wasn't right.

"Thunor?" Loher had noticed my distraction. "What is it?"

I watched Albi's behavior for another moment before answering, my instincts sharpening.

"I'm not sure. But I think we may not have three days after all."

The hunt for Lemac might begin sooner than any of us had planned—and I couldn't shake the feeling that he was somehow, impossibly, already a step ahead of us.

⸻ ❈ ⸻

Sleep eluded me despite the luxury of the chambers we'd been given in Salvus Hus.

The bed was soft, the linens crisp, yet I found myself staring at the ornate ceiling as midnight came and went.

Beside me, Loher lay alert as always, her eyes tracking the shadows across the ceiling.

Unlike humans or even my half-elven nature, she had no need for sleep—a trait of her full elven heritage that had saved our lives more than once.

"Your mind is too loud," she whispered without turning her head. "Even without sleep, I can still appreciate the quiet."

"Sorry," I murmured, though we both knew I wasn't truly apologetic.

Our partnership worked because we understood each other's quirks.

A scratching at the door drew my attention.

I slipped from the bed and padded silently across the stone floor.

The small iron-bound door designed for castle servants swung open at my touch, revealing a cluster of rats huddled in the corridor.

"What have you found?" I whispered, kneeling to their level.

Albi twitched its whiskers in a pattern I'd come to recognize as urgency.

With vampiric sight, I noticed something clutched in its tiny paws: a thread of purple fabric.

My blood ran cold. Purple—the color of the Grand Ascendancy. The color Lemac favored.

I closed the door silently and turned to find Loher already on her feet, daggers in hand, having noiselessly risen and armed herself in the brief moment my back was turned.

"Albi has found something," she stated rather than asked, already checking her hidden weapon harnesses.

"Purple thread," I confirmed. "Recently torn, by the look of it."

Her eyes narrowed. "Here? In Salvus Hus?"

"It seems our enemy may have been closer than we thought."

Within minutes, we were moving silently through the corridors of the sleeping castle.

The rats led the way, their tiny forms darting from shadow to shadow with purpose.

The two guards we passed hardly seemed to notice us, their eyes glazed slightly, as if they'd been encouraged to look elsewhere.

"Magic," Loher whispered, noticing the same thing. "Subtle, but effective."

We followed the rats down a spiral staircase I didn't recognize, deeper into the castle's heart.

The air grew cooler, damper, with the unmistakable scent of old stone and older secrets.

"The archives," Loher realized as we approached a set of weathered oak doors. "Why would Lemac—"

"Knowledge," came a voice from behind us.

We spun to find Avilyn standing in the shadows, his elven form seeming almost to glow in the darkness.

Unlike us, he appeared fully dressed, as if he had never retired for the night at all.

"The castle archives contain records dating back centuries," he continued quietly. "Including detailed accounts of portal stone locations, dragon lore, and ancient magics that have been forgotten by most."

"You knew," I accused, though without heat. "You sensed him here."

Avilyn inclined his head slightly.

"I suspected. Dragon sense is different from your rats or Loher's instincts, but all point to the same conclusion. Lemac risked much to infiltrate this place."

"But why not attack?" Loher asked, her hand resting on her dagger's hilt. "If he could penetrate the castle's defenses enough to reach the archives..."

"He's not strong enough to face us directly. Not anymore," I reasoned. "Not without Nerium's power behind him. He's seeking alternatives."

"Precisely," Avilyn agreed. "And we must discover what he found before the trail grows cold."

The archives' doors were unlocked, another sign that shouldn't have been.

Inside, row upon row of shelves stretched into darkness, laden with ancient tomes, scrolls, and artifacts carefully cataloged over generations.

The rats scattered, racing down different aisles with determined purpose. I followed the largest one, trusting its keen sense of smell to lead me to recent disturbances.

Loher moved in a different direction, her thief's eyes scanning for subtle signs of tampering.

"Here," she called softly after several minutes. "Someone has been through these recently."

I joined her before a section dedicated to astronomical and planar charts.

Several heavy volumes had been recently disturbed, their ancient dust patterns broken by handprints.

One massive tome lay open on a nearby reading table, its pages displaying intricate diagrams of constellation alignments.

"Celestial portal stones," Avilyn breathed, studying the pages. "The rarest and most powerful of all. Unlike the fixed stones we know, these appear only when specific stars align."

"Which means we couldn't track them through normal means," I realized.

"And neither could Lemac, until now," Avilyn's finger traced a notation in the margin. "If I'm reading this correctly, such an alignment occurs three nights from now."

"The third night of our 'rest period,'" Loher noted grimly.

A scratching sound drew our attention to where Albi was frantically pawing at a fallen scrap of parchment beneath the table.

I retrieved it, finding a hastily scrawled note in handwriting I didn't recognize:

[Alignment confirmed.

The Scepter of Dourn

will emerge during Wyrmfall Moon.

Bring the scales.]

"The Scepter of Dourn," Avilyn's voice had gone dangerously quiet. "A legendary weapon forged to slay dragons."

The implications settled heavily upon us. Lemac wasn't just fleeing—he was preparing.

"We need to wake the others," I said, already moving toward the door. "The hunt begins now."

"Hold," Avilyn cautioned. "There's more to this. The note mentions scales."

"Dragon scales?" Loher asked.

"Perhaps. But more concerning is the reference to the Wyrmfall Moon." Avilyn's ancient eyes showed genuine worry. "The Wyrmfall Moon marks a time when dragon magic is at its weakest. If Lemac has indeed learned of this celestial portal and plans to retrieve the Scepter during this lunar phase..."

"He's planning something far worse than escape," I finished. "He's planning revenge."

As if to punctuate my words, a distant bell began to toll—the castle's alarm.

The three of us exchanged glances before racing toward the sound.

The peaceful night at Salvus Hus had ended abruptly.

Our three days of rest had just been shortened to hours, and somewhere beyond our reach, Lemac was preparing a weapon designed to kill dragons.

Including the King of Dragons himself.

The castle corridors had erupted into controlled chaos.

Guards raced past us, their armor clanking in the stone hallways as we made our way toward the source of the alarm.

We turned a corner and nearly collided with Balt, who was already fully armed, his axe gripped tightly in one hand.

"There ye are!" he exclaimed. "Thought ye might be involved in whatever mess this is."

"What's happening?" I asked as we fell into step beside him.

"Intruder in ta east wing," he replied grimly. "One o' the guards found another dead with his throat cut. Clean work, they say." His eyes flicked to Loher. "Professional-like."

"Not my work," my wife stated flatly, her daggers still visible in her hands.

"Never thought it was, lass," Balt assured her. "But whoever did it knew what they were about."

We rounded another corner to find Kuchoff and Meeka already at the scene.

The corridor was lit by hastily placed torches, illuminating the body of a young guard slumped against the wall.

The stone around him was remarkably clean, almost no blood despite the precise wound across his throat.

"Magic was used," Meeka confirmed as we approached. "The killer sealed the wound after death to prevent blood from leaving a trail."

"Too clean for Lemac," Kuchoff observed, kneeling to examine the body more closely. "He's many things, but subtle isn't one of them."

"He has allies," I suggested, the rats at my feet spreading out to search for scents. "We found evidence in the archives that he was there, seeking information on celestial portal stones."

"Celestial portal stones?" Meeka's head snapped up. "Those are theoretical at best—no one has documented a verified sighting in centuries."

"Yet the castle archives contain detailed records," Avilyn replied. "Including the location of one that will appear three nights from now, during the Wyrmfall Moon."

A shadow crossed Kuchoff's face. "That's when dragon magic is at its weakest."

"Which seems relevant," Loher added, "considering Lemac is apparently seeking something called the Scepter of Dourn."

"By the gods," Meeka breathed, her face paling. "The Dragon Killer."

The corridor fell silent at her words.

Even the hurrying guards seemed to sense the gravity of the moment and moved more quietly around us.

"I've only read mentions of it in ancient texts," Meeka continued. "A weapon forged during the First Dragon War, designed specifically to pierce dragon scales and strike at the heart of their magic. It was thought destroyed centuries ago."

"Or hidden," Avilyn corrected softly. "Behind a celestial portal that appears only once every seventy years, during the time when dragon defenses are at their weakest."

"And Lemac knows where to find it," I concluded.

Kuchoff stood, his decision already made. "We sail within the hour." He turned to one of the nearby guards. "Inform the King that The Scorpion departs immediately. The threat we discussed has accelerated."

The guard hesitated. "But sir, protocol requires royal approval for"

"Tell him we found purple threads in the archives and a dead guard with a sealed wound," Kuchoff cut him off. "He'll understand."

The guard saluted sharply and hurried away.

"Meeka, gather whatever supplies you can in the next half hour. Balt, alert the rest of the crew and get them to the ship."

Kuchoff's commands were precise, the weight of authority settled easily on his shoulders despite our recent losses.

"Thunor, Loher—I need you to return to the archives. Gather every scrap of information about this celestial portal and the Scepter. We can study it enroute."

"Aye, Captain," Balt replied, already turning to go. His usual jovial tone was absent, replaced by grim determination.

"I'll accompany you to the archives," Avilyn said to us. "There may be details only I would recognize."

As we dispersed to our assignments, the castle around us continued to bustle with activity.

The alarm had set Salvus Hus on high alert, with guards double-checking every entrance and patrolling every corridor.

Yet I couldn't shake the feeling that whatever Lemac had sought, he had already found it and vanished like smoke.

The rats at my feet seemed to share my unease, their tiny forms huddled closer than usual as we made our way back toward the archives.

"He knew exactly what he was looking for," Loher observed as we hurried down the spiral staircase. "This wasn't a random search."

"Which means someone told him what to seek," Avilyn agreed. "Someone with knowledge of what the archives contained."

The implication hung heavily in the air between us.

Another betrayal.

Another traitor in our midst.

"The guard wasn't killed to prevent discovery," I realized aloud. "He was killed because he saw someone he recognized with Lemac—someone who shouldn't have been there."

"And that makes our unknown accomplice more dangerous than Lemac himself," Loher concluded.

When we reached the archives, the massive oak doors stood wide open—unlike our earlier visit.

Inside, several castle scholars were already moving frantically among the shelves, pulling volumes and checking inventory listings.

"The King's archivists," Avilyn explained quietly. "They're trying to determine what exactly was taken."

An elderly woman with iron-gray hair pulled into a severe bun approached us, recognition flashing in her eyes as she spotted Avilyn.

"Lord Avilyn," she greeted with a perfunctory bow. "We've completed a preliminary assessment. Several texts are missing, all relating to celestial phenomena and inter-dimensional transit."

"Was anything else disturbed?" Avilyn asked.

"Only one other section," she replied grimly. "The sealed records of the First Dragon War."

Avilyn's expression remained neutral, but I sensed the tension that rippled through him.

"Show me."

She led us deeper into the archives, past rows of carefully preserved tomes to a small alcove sealed with heavy iron bars.

The gate hung open, its impressive lock lying shattered on the stone floor.

"These records were sealed by royal decree three centuries ago," the archivist explained. "They contain tactical information about dragon weaknesses, breeding grounds, and..." she hesitated.

"Methods of killing dragons," Avilyn finished for her. "Specifically, the forging methods for dragon-slaying weapons."

She nodded, clearly uncomfortable.

"The most dangerous text is missing—a treatise called 'The Binding of Draconic Essence.'"

"What exactly does that mean?" Loher asked.

"It details how to extract a dragon's magical essence when it's slain by specific weapons," Avilyn replied, his voice carefully controlled. "How to bind that essence into objects—or people—to grant them draconic powers."

The implications struck me like a physical blow.

"Lemac isn't just seeking a weapon to kill dragons. He's looking to become like Nerium—a hybrid of human and dragon."

"But without the unpredictability of her physical transformation," Avilyn confirmed. "The binding would allow him to absorb draconic power without changing his physical form."

"How many dragons would he need to kill?" Loher asked, her practical nature focusing on logistics.

"For a complete binding? Seven," Avilyn answered. "One for each of the primary draconic elements."

"And he already has three young dragons under his control," I reminded them.

"Which leaves four more to find," Loher concluded.

"Or steal," I added grimly, thinking of Jade and Emeral.

"There's more," the archivist interjected, hesitantly. "The visitor log shows that someone accessed these same records three days ago, using the royal seal for authorization."

"Before we returned from the battle," Loher noted. "Who has access to the royal seal?"

"Only the King, the Queen, and the Royal Seneschal," the archivist replied.

The three of us exchanged looks.

The betrayal ran deeper than we'd imagined, reaching into the very heart of Salvus Hus itself.

"We need to return to The Scorpion immediately," I said quietly. "And tell no one what we've learned until we're away from the castle."

Avilyn nodded in agreement.

"Gather what you can about the celestial portal's location. I'll speak with the King—alone."

As we moved to comply, I noticed my rats had scattered throughout the archives, as if searching independently.

Albi returned to me with something clasped in his tiny paws—a small, opalescent scale that shimmered with an inner light.

"Dragon scale," Avilyn identified it immediately. "Recently shed, from a young dragon."

"Lemac's dragons were never here," I said, examining the scale. "Which means..."

"A fourth dragon," Loher completed my thought. "One already within Salvus Hus."

The hunt for Lemac had just become exponentially more complicated.

We weren't just chasing an escaped enemy, we were fleeing a compromised sanctuary, with unknown enemies potentially watching our every move.

The sound of running footsteps drew our attention as one of The Scorpion's crew—a young sailor named Elias—appeared at the archive entrance, breathless from his sprint.

"Cap'n Magnus sen' me," he panted, his Jamaican accent thick with urgency. "De Scorpion ready to sail, but we got big problem, Mon!"

"What kind of problem?" I asked, already moving toward him.

"It de bronze one, yuh see," he replied, his eyes wide. "Chron missin' completely! We search everywhere—no sign of de little dragon."

The news struck like a physical blow.

Chron missing could only mean one thing—either the wyrmling had fled of his own accord, or someone had taken him.

"When was he last seen?" Avilyn demanded, his elven features sharp with concern.

"Bout an hour past, Mon," Elias replied, twisting his hands anxiously. "He was restin' on de ship's rail, then Tatenda say him fly toward de castle. Nobody tink nuttin' strange—him always explorin', yuh know?"

"And no one followed him?" Loher asked, her voice edged with suspicion.

"De captain set watch, but Chron small an' fast," Elias shook his head. "Him slip past easy-easy."

I exchanged a troubled glance with Loher.

The timing was too perfect to be coincidence—Chron disappearing on the same night we discovered Lemac's infiltration.

"The bronze wyrmling sees through time," Avilyn said quietly. "If he sensed the celestial portal opening, he might have sought more information."

"Or sensed the fourth dragon," I suggested, the rats at my feet growing increasingly agitated.

"We need to move, now," Loher decided, already gathering the scrolls we'd identified. "If Lemac has Chron—"

"He'd have both the knowledge of the portal location and a bronze dragon," Avilyn finished grimly. "One of the seven he needs."

Elias's eyes widened further. "Seven? Sounds like big trouble, Mon."

"Bigger than you know," I confirmed. "Return to the ship and tell the captain we're on our way. Tell him to prepare for immediate departure—and to trust no one from the castle."

"No one, sah?" Elias looked uncertain.

"No one," I repeated firmly. "Not until we're aboard."

As Elias hurried away, we gathered what remaining information we could.

The archivist, sensing our urgency, provided a sealed leather tube.

"These are copies of the star charts showing the celestial portal's location," she explained. "I made them myself after the alarm was raised, suspecting they might be needed."

"Thank you," Avilyn told her sincerely. "You may have saved more lives than you know."

We moved quickly through the castle corridors, avoiding the main hallways where guards and servants clustered.

Loher led us down servants' passages and forgotten staircases, her thief's knowledge of Salvus Hus proving invaluable.

"Something's wrong," I murmured as we approached a side exit.

The rats at my feet had formed a tight circle, all facing outward as if defending against an imminent threat.

"Ambush?" Loher asked, her daggers already in hand.

"I don't think" I began, but Avilyn cut me off with a raised hand.

"Not an ambush," he said softly. "But we're being watched."

He gestured subtly toward a shadowed alcove.

For a moment, I saw nothing, then a pair of gleaming eyes caught the torchlight—familiar ancient eyes that should not have been there.

"Chron?" I called cautiously.

The bronze wyrmling emerged from the shadows, his scales catching the light in metallic ripples.

He seemed unharmed, but there was something different about his posture, more guarded, more alert.

"Time fractures along seven paths," he said by way of greeting. "The hunter becomes the hunted, but the true predator watches from within."

"Where have you been?" Loher demanded, though she kept her voice low. "The entire crew is searching for you."

"Knowledge calls to knowledge," Chron replied cryptically. "I followed the whispers to their source."

Avilyn stepped forward; his eyes fixed on the small dragon.

"What did you see, little one?"

Chron's ancient eyes held secrets that belied his youthful form.

"The pretender wears familiar faces. The friend becomes the foe. The sanctuary harbors serpents."

"Enough riddles," Loher snapped, though her hand on her dagger had relaxed slightly. "Did you see Lemac? Is he still in the castle?"

The wyrmling shook his head, bronze scales catching the light.

"The one-eared wizard fled before moonrise, but his shadow remains, cast by trusted hands."

"The accomplice," I translated. "Someone in the castle is working with Lemac."

"Who?" Avilyn pressed.

Chron's response was interrupted by the sound of approaching footsteps.

We tensed up, but it was Kuchoff who rounded the corner, his expression dark with concern.

"There you are," he said, relief evident in his voice when he spotted Chron. "We've been searching everywhere."

"The young one decided to explore," Avilyn explained smoothly. "Fortunately, we found him."

Kuchoff studied us all for a moment, his psionic senses likely picking up our tension.

"What aren't you telling me?"

"Not here," I cautioned, glancing meaningfully at the surrounding walls. "The Scorpion."

He nodded, understanding immediately.

"We're ready to sail. The King has granted emergency clearance for immediate departure."

"The King himself?" Loher asked, her emphasis subtle but unmistakable.

"Yes," Kuchoff confirmed, giving her a curious look. "Is there a problem?"

"Nothing that can't wait until we're away from here," I interjected. "Let's move."

As we followed Kuchoff through the castle's lower levels toward the docks, I noticed Chron had positioned himself between Avilyn and me, his small form unusually vigilant.

The rats at my feet maintained their defensive circle, occasionally looking up at the bronze wyrmling as if seeking direction.

The night air was cool when we finally emerged onto the docks.

The Scorpion waited, her wooden scales gleaming in the moonlight, crew members moving efficiently across her deck as they prepared for departure.

"Something's wrong with the wyrmling," Kuchoff murmured as we walked up the gangplank. "His mind feels... fragmented."

"He's seen something," I replied quietly. "Something that's left him shaken."

Once aboard, Kuchoff immediately called for departure.

The moorings were cast off, and The Scorpion began to move away from the docks of Salvus Hus with practiced efficiency.

"My quarters," Kuchoff instructed. "Now."

We gathered in the captain's cabin — Kuchoff, Meeka, Balt, Loher, Avilyn, Chron, and me.

Lybiidae joined us moments later, her dark form materializing from the shadows as if she'd been there all along.

"Now," Kuchoff said once the door was secured, "what exactly did you find in the archives?"

I explained quickly about the celestial portal, the Scepter of Dourn, and the missing treatise on binding draconic essence.

Avilyn detailed the implications of the stolen knowledge, while Loher described the evidence of castle complicity.

"A traitor in Salvus Hus," Meeka whispered, her face pale. "But who?"

All eyes turned to Chron, who had perched himself on a shelf above Kuchoff's desk, his ancient eyes surveying us all.

"The wyrmling knows," Balt declared. "Don't ye, wee dragon?"

"Knowledge is burden," Chron replied. "Truth is danger. The betrayer wears a crown of trust."

"Stop with the riddles!" Balt slammed his fist on the desk. "People are dyin' while ye play word games!"

Chron flinched, and for the first time, I saw genuine fear in his ancient eyes.

Whatever he had witnessed had truly shaken him.

"Gently, Stone-Heart," Avilyn cautioned. "The young one sees across time—possibilities, not certainties. Such sight is a burden few could bear."

"De Seneschal," Elias suggested from where he stood near the door. "Him always nervous, always watchin'. Maybe him de traitor?"

"Or the Queen," Lybiidae offered coolly. "Her formality could mask deception. Who questions royalty too closely?"

"Or the King himself," Loher added, though her tone suggested she considered it unlikely. "He alone could access everything without question."

Kuchoff shook his head. "Not the King. I've known him for too long."

"As you knew me?" Meeka asked softly, the question hanging heavy in the air.

An uncomfortable silence fell over the cabin.

"Whosoever it be," Balt finally said, "they've given Lemac what he needs to find this deadly Scepter thing."

"And potentially create a new generation of dragon-human hybrids," Avilyn added grimly. "Without Nerium's instability."

"The portal opens in three nights," I reminded them. "At a location we still need to precisely determine from these charts."

"Then that's our priority," Kuchoff decided.

"Loher, Meeka, Avilyn—decipher those star charts. Pinpoint exactly where and when this portal will appear."

"Aye, Captain," Loher acknowledged.

"Thunor, Balt, Lybiidae—prepare the ship and crew for whatever we might encounter. If Lemac plans to sacrifice dragons for this binding ritual, he'll have defenses in place."

"And what about the wee prophet?" Balt jerked his thumb toward Chron, who had remained unusually silent.

Kuchoff studied the bronze wyrmling for a long moment.

"He stays with me. Whatever he saw has him frightened—and anything that frightens a creature who can see through time should concern us all."

As we dispersed to our assignments, I paused at the door.

The rats at my feet had formed a protective circle around Chron, who had glided down to rest on Kuchoff's desk.

The wyrmling's ancient eyes met mine, and I saw something there I'd never expected — uncertainty.

"The shadows have teeth," he whispered, just loud enough for me to hear. "And they know your name, Thunor McLaaud."

A chill ran down my spine as I closed the door behind me.

The hunt for Lemac had just become something far more dangerous — a race against both time and treachery, with the fate of dragons hanging in the balance.

And somewhere ahead, in a place where stars would briefly align, our enemy waited with a plan that was generations in the making.

Chapter Fifteen

SIGNS AND PORTENTS

The morning air carried the scent of salt and impending rain as I made my way onto The Scorpion's deck.

The ship had been fully repaired in the three days since our return to the Den, every scorched plank replaced, every damaged rope restored.

If not for the emptiness where fallen comrades should have stood, one might never know we had faced Nerium's wrath.

My rats scattered across the weathered boards, whiskers twitching as they explored familiar territory with renewed curiosity.

Something had them unsettled—a change in the air perhaps or simply reflecting my own unease.

"Ye've got tat look again, McLaaud," Balt's gruff voice broke through my thoughts.

The dwarf approached, his axe freshly polished and gleaming in the morning light.

His beard was intricately braided for battle, tiny skull-shaped beads of bone woven throughout—trophies carved from the remains of fallen enemies.

Each represented a notable kill, a victory worth remembering.

I'd once asked if he kept a record of whose bones he wore.

His response had been typically blunt: "Aye, in here," he'd tapped his temple. "Every skull has a name and a story. I remember them all."

Today he'd added a new one—freshly carved, the bone still ivory-white compared to the yellowed older beads.

I didn't need to ask whose remains had provided this newest trophy.

The battle with Nerium was still too fresh, our losses too painful.

"What look is that?" I asked, leaning against the rail.

"Ta one what says ye're tinkin' too hard about tings." He joined me, watching the activity below as crew members loaded supplies. "It's just a simple murder investigation. Village constables gettin' picked off. Nasty business, aye, but straightforward enough."

The King's message had arrived yesterday—a small seacraft had navigated the treacherous channel to The Scorpion's Den, the royal messenger exhausted from fighting the currents that protected our hidden sanctuary.

Throughout Beornan Heafod, constables were being systematically murdered, their bodies left in public places as warnings.

Purple-fletched arrows marked each killing.

"Seven dead lawmen in less than a fortnight doesn't strike me as simple," I observed.

Balt shrugged massive shoulders.

"Compared to fightin' a reality-bendin' dragon-human hybrid? It's practically a holiday."

I couldn't help but smile at his assessment, though the unease lingered.

"And the purple fletching? Same color as Lemac's robes."

"Aye," Balt's expression darkened. "That snake still has accounts ta settle." His fingers traced one of the newer bone beads in his beard. "As do we all."

Captain Magnus emerged from his quarters.

"Final preparations?" he asked, approaching us.

"Nearly complete, Sir," I confirmed. "We sail within the hour."

He nodded, satisfaction briefly crossing his features before the weight of command reasserted itself.

"Good. The King expects results. These killings have the realm on edge—local lords raising militias, villages barricading themselves at night."

"Do we actually believe Lemac is behind this?" I asked, giving voice to the doubt that had been gnawing at me. "After everything we discovered about the celestial portal and the Scepter of Dourn, killing village constables seems..."

"Beneath him?" Kuchoff finished when I hesitated.

"Tactical," I amended. "What does he gain from it?"

"Perhaps that's what we need to discover," Loher suggested, appearing beside me with her customary silence.

Even after years together, her ability to move undetected sometimes startled me.

"The pattern might reveal the purpose." She completed.

"What pattern have you noticed?" Kuchoff asked, instantly alert.

My wife's insights were never offered without careful consideration.

"The killings are moving," she explained. "Starting in the south near Bom Dabo, then Larix, now Senton. Circling clockwise around Beornan Heafod."

"Toward what destination?" I wondered aloud.

"If they continue on this trajectory," Loher traced an invisible arc with her finger, "either Dournan or Salvus Hus itself."

A heavy silence fell as we considered the implications.

The Shrine at Dournan was one of the oldest structures in the realm, a nexus of spiritual and political power.

And Salvus Hus was the heart of the kingdom, where the King himself resided.

"The Dragonfly is meeting us at Dewarg," Kuchoff said finally. "Captain Rina has been gathering information while we recovered. Perhaps she'll have more insight."

Meeka approached, her expression serious.

"The wind favors us," she reported. "We should reach Dewarg by nightfall if it holds."

"And our other guests?" Kuchoff asked quietly.

"Secured below," Meeka confirmed, her voice dropping. "The fewer who know about their presence, the better."

They meant Jade and Emeral, the green dragons who had taken human form and remained hidden aboard The Scorpion.

After the battle with Nerium, they had pledged loyalty to Avilyn, but their presence was still a closely guarded secret.

"Captain," a young sailor called from across the deck, "signal boat approaching through the channel. Flying urgent colors."

Kuchoff moved to the rail, watching as a small craft fought its way through the narrow entrance to our hidden cove.

The boat's sail bore the crimson stripe of urgent royal business—a second message so soon after the first.

The small vessel docked against The Scorpion's hull, and a haggard man in sea-sprayed clothes climbed aboard.

Blood stained his sleeve—not his own from the way he moved, but concerning, nonetheless.

"Captain Magnus," he gasped, clearly having fought treacherous waters to reach us. "Three more constables dead in Senton. The killers left something this time."

He held out a blood-stained piece of parchment, its edges curling inward.

Kuchoff took it carefully, unfolding the missive to reveal flowing script in rich purple ink:

[The blood of the faithful sustains the Renewal.

The time of reckoning approaches.

Justice remembers Dournan.]

I leaned closer, studying the parchment.

"That's not Lemac's handwriting," I observed.

Having seen the wizard's notes in Exland Mountain, I recognized his distinctive, sharp-edged script.

This was more flowing, almost poetic in its curves.

"Dournan," Balt frowned. "Tat's the ruins near Larix, ain't it? Ta one what got abandoned after ta campaigns across ta Strait?"

"Yes," Loher confirmed. "Many who fought in those campaigns returned to find their lands seized for 'failure to fulfill feudal obligations' while they were away fighting."

"So, this could be veterans seeking revenge," Meeka suggested. "Men who lost everything while serving the previous King."

"Perhaps," Kuchoff agreed, though he looked unconvinced. "But this mention of 'Renewal' and blood sustaining something..."

He exchanged a glance with me that confirmed we shared the same suspicion.

"Blood magic," I said quietly, the rats at my feet growing increasingly agitated. "These aren't just killings. They're sacrifices."

"For what purpose?" Meeka asked, examining the parchment more closely.

"That," Kuchoff said grimly, "is what we need to discover." He turned to the messenger. "Return to Senton. Tell them The Scorpion is on its way."

As the exhausted man was led below for food and rest before his return journey, Kuchoff turned to us, his decision made.

"Change of plans. We're not waiting for The Dragonfly at Dewarg. We'll sail directly to Senton, investigate these latest killings while the trail is fresh." His gaze swept over each of us. "Something isn't right about this. If Lemac *is* involved, there's more at stake than murdered constables."

"The celestial portal opens soon," I reminded him quietly. "If these killings are related to his search for the Scepter of Dourn..."

"Then we have little time," Kuchoff agreed. "Wyrmfall Moon or not, we need to understand what we're facing."

Above us, Chron circled lazily, the bronze wyrmling's scales catching the morning light.

He had been unusually quiet since our return from battle, offering few of his cryptic prophecies.

But as The Scorpion's crew prepared to cast off, his voice drifted down from above.

"Blood paints the path where stars will align. Faithful fall in seven measures, feeding what sleeps beneath ancient stone."

"Any idea what that means?" Loher asked, directing her question to Avilyn who had emerged silently from below decks.

His expression remained carefully neutral.

"Nothing specific," he replied, though something in his ancient eyes suggested otherwise. "But prophecies rarely reveal themselves until the moment of fulfillment."

As The Scorpion pulled away from her moorings, guided carefully through the narrow channel that led to open water, I found myself watching the horizon with growing unease.

The rats at my feet had formed a circular pattern, all facing outward as if defending against some unseen threat.

"What is it?" Loher asked, noticing my attention.

"I'm not sure," I admitted. "But whatever's happening with these constable killings, I don't think it's about revenge or justice."

"Blood sustains the Renewal," she quoted softly. "What renewal requires the blood of law-keepers?"

I had no answer, but as The Scorpion entered the open sea, cutting through waves toward Senton, I couldn't shake the feeling that we were already several moves behind in a game whose rules we didn't fully understand.

And somewhere ahead, whether directing these murders or pursuing his own agenda, Lemac waited—a wizard with nothing left to lose and knowledge that could tear the realm apart.

The hunt had begun anew, but this time, the stakes remained hidden in shadows and blood.

Chapter Sixteen

ECHOES OF JUSTICE

The moon hung low over Senton as The Scorpion rocked gently at her moorings.

Unlike our triumphant return from the battle with Nerium, this arrival had been met with wary eyes and hushed whispers.

News of the constable killings had spread quickly through the coastal villages, leaving fear in their wake.

I stood at the ship's rail, watching as darkness claimed the small fishing community.

Most windows were already shuttered tight despite the early hour, residents huddling behind locked doors rather than risking the night air.

Only the tavern, The Rusted Hook, according to its weather-beaten sign—showed signs of life, dim light spilling from its windows onto the worn dirt path.

The rats at my feet grew increasingly restless, their tiny claws clicking against the wooden deck as they formed unusual patterns—defensive circles that suggested danger lurked beyond our immediate perception.

Albi, the largest of my companions, stood on his hind legs, nose twitching frantically toward the village.

"Still troubled?" Loher asked, materializing beside me with silent grace.

Her daggers remained carefully concealed beneath her cloak, but I could sense her readiness—the subtle tension in her shoulders that spoke of anticipated violence.

"Something about this doesn't sit right," I replied, watching Albi organize the other rats into a defensive formation I'd rarely seen them adopt without direct command. "It's too... purposeful for simple revenge killings."

"The purple fletching," she observed. "The Grand Ascendancy's color, Lemac's color."

"But not his style," I countered. "Lemac was many things, but subtle wasn't one of them."

"People change," Loher shrugged, her eyes scanning the darkened shoreline. "Especially after defeat. Nerium's death would have shattered his plans, possibly his sanity as well."

Before I could respond, heavy footsteps announced Balt's approach.

"Captain wants us in his quarters," Balt informed us, his axe gleaming in the moonlight. "Seems our messenger friend brought more'n just bad news."

As we made our way below deck, I sensed a change in the ship's atmosphere.

The usual banter was absent, replaced by focused preparation.

Crew members checked weapons with methodical precision, while others studied maps of the surrounding countryside.

The losses from our battle with Nerium had left us short-handed, but those who remained were hardened veterans, ready for whatever came next.

Captain Magnus waited in his quarters.

Maps and reports covered the table before him, with Meeka studying them intently at his side.

"Three constables dead here in Senton," Kuchoff began without preamble as we entered. "Similar killings reported in Bom Dabo and near Larix. All with the same methodology—arrow to the heart, throat slit afterward, purple fletching."

"Signs of struggle?" I asked, watching as more of my rats slipped into the room, forming a circle near my feet.

"None," Meeka answered, looking up from the reports. "Professional work."

"The King expects us to investigate these murders and bring the perpetrators to justice," Kuchoff finally said.

"We start tomorrow at first light. Thunor, Loher, Balt—you'll come with me to examine the bodies and crime scene. Meeka will coordinate with Tatenda to maintain ship readiness."

"Any word from The Dragonfly?" I asked.

Captain Rina's smaller vessel had been scouting for signs of Lemac since our battle with Nerium.

"Expected to rendezvous with us at Dewarg," Kuchoff replied. "But these killings take priority. We'll send word of our change in plans."

As the meeting concluded, I found myself drawn to the small porthole in Kuchoff's quarters.

Beyond the glass, Senton slumbered uneasily under starlight, its simple buildings seeming suddenly vulnerable.

Whatever forces were at work here, they extended beyond the death of a few law-keepers.

I thought of Dournan—a place I hadn't visited in years.

Even then, it had been a crumbling ruin, swallowed by swamp and decay.

What connection could it possibly have to these methodical killings?

What "justice" needed to be remembered?

My rats shifted anxiously, sensing my unease.

Tomorrow we would begin our hunt for answers, tracking the echo of violence across this quiet fishing village.

And somewhere, perhaps watching us even now, Lemac—or whoever was behind these killings—waited.

Planning.

Calculating.

Preparing for the next sacrifice in whatever dark ritual they had begun.

The hunt had started anew, with higher stakes than any of us realized.

⸻◆⸻

Morning brought no relief from the sense of foreboding that had settled over The Scorpion.

Gray clouds hung low over Senton, promising rain before midday.

The village itself remained eerily quiet—fishing boats sat unrepaired on the shore, nets hung abandoned on their racks, and the usual bustle of commerce was notably absent.

I joined Kuchoff, Loher, and Balt on the pier as we prepared to meet with the village elder who'd agreed to take us to where the bodies were being kept.

The rats at my feet scattered the moment we touched land, disappearing between buildings and under docks—my silent scouts searching for dangers human eyes might miss.

"Not much o' a welcome party," Balt observed as we approached the small group waiting for us.

Just three men—one in formal robes clutching an ornate staff of office, flanked by two nervous-looking villagers carrying poorly maintained spears.

"Can ye blame 'em?" Balt added quietly. "Three dead constables and now The Scorpion arrives. From their perspective, we're as likely to bring more trouble as we are to solve it."

As we drew nearer, I could see the deep shadows beneath the elder's eyes—he likely hadn't slept since the bodies were discovered.

The men beside him gripped their spears with white-knuckled determination, though neither appeared to have any real combat training.

"Captain Magnus," the elder greeted with forced bravado. "I am Elder Torval. We... we are grateful for your swift response to our plight."

"The King takes the murder of his constables seriously," Kuchoff replied, his tone measured and authoritative. "As do we. I understand three men were killed?"

"Yes, dreadful business," Torval nodded vigorously, gesturing for us to follow him into the village. "Found two days ago, just outside the northern boundary. All three were passing through on rotation from Carrington."

"Has Senton had troubles with lawbreakers before?" Loher asked, her eyes constantly scanning our surroundings, missing nothing.

"Nothing serious," Torval insisted, a bit too quickly. "Occasional drunkenness, disputes about fishing rights, petty theft during lean seasons. We're a peaceful community, Captain. These killings... they're an aberration."

Albi returned from his scouting, circling my feet with obvious agitation.

Through our connection, I sensed confusion rather than immediate danger—something unseen but troubling hovered at the edges of his perception.

"Where are the bodies?" Kuchoff asked, his gaze sweeping methodically across the buildings we passed.

"The tavern cellar," Torval replied, gesturing toward The Rusted Hook. "It's the coolest place we have. We've preserved them as best we could, but..."

"We understand," I assured him. "Death waits for no one."

The tavern was empty save for a heavy-set woman polishing glasses behind the bar. Her arms were corded with muscle from years of throwing out unruly patrons, but her eyes widened with undisguised awe at the sight of Captain Magnus.

"This way," Torval directed, leading us toward a narrow door beside the bar. "Mind the steps, they're steep and slick."

The cellar air was cool and damp, heavy with the copper-sweet scent of blood and the beginning stages of decay.

Three forms lay covered with sailcloth on makeshift biers constructed from emptied wine barrels and planks, surrounded by bowls of strong-smelling herbs in a futile attempt to mask the odor.

Kuchoff approached the bodies without hesitation, pulling back the cloth to reveal the first victim.

The man had been young—not much older than twenty—with the weathered face of someone accustomed to outdoor duty.

His skin had taken on the waxy pallor of death, but the wound that killed him remained stark and explicit—a purple-fletched arrow protruded from his chest directly over his heart, while a precise cut across his throat had ensured his death.

"Clean work," Loher observed, examining the wound without touching it. "Single stroke with a very sharp blade. Professional. The throat was cut after death—there's minimal blood spray, suggesting his heart had already stopped pumping."

"Too professional for common bandits," I agreed, moving closer.

Something about the blood didn't feel right to my vampiric senses—it carried a resonance, a subtle magical signature that ordinary human perception would entirely miss.

It felt... hungry somehow, as if it were still actively seeking something even days after it had spilled.

I leaned closer, inspecting the arrow without removing it.

Purple fletching, as reported, but with subtle markings etched into the shaft—symbols I didn't recognize but which carried unmistakable magical intent.

They reminded me vaguely of binding runes I'd seen in ancient texts, but with perverse modifications that suggested darker purpose.

"The other victims show the same wounds?" I asked, moving toward the second body—a middle-aged man with graying temples and hands calloused from years of wielding a constable's staff.

"Identical," Torval nodded, his voice barely above a whisper. "Arrow to the heart, throat slit. Like they were killed by the same hand, following some sort of ritual. We found them arranged in a triangle, faces pointing inward."

The word 'ritual' hung in the air between us, confirming our suspicions without Torval realizing what he'd implied.

Kuchoff and I exchanged a glance, his slight nod acknowledging our shared concern.

"Their weapons and insignia pouches are missing," Loher noticed, gesturing to empty belt loops where short swords and official documentation would normally be secured.

"Taken as trophies," I suggested, "or proof of kill."

"The message," Kuchoff prompted. "Where was it found?"

Torval produced a small wooden box from his pocket, handling it with obvious reluctance.

"We placed it in here, touched it as little as possible. It was pinned to the middle one's chest with this."

He retrieved a dagger from behind a nearby barrel—a wicked-looking blade with a purple gem set in its pommel.

The metal seemed to absorb the lantern light rather than reflect it, giving it an unnaturally dull appearance.

Kuchoff examined the dagger carefully before opening the box.

He held up the blood-stained parchment we'd already received, the purple ink seemed to shimmer slightly in the cellar's dim light, as if still wet despite having been written days ago.

As Kuchoff studied it, I focused on the blood staining its edges.

Unlike the corpses' blood, which had begun to darken with decay, the stains on the parchment remained vibrant crimson, almost alive in their intensity.

My vampiric senses detected subtle magic at work—preservation spells, but with something else beneath them, a pulsing rhythm like a distant heartbeat.

"May I?" I asked, extending my hand.

Kuchoff nodded, passing me the box.

As my fingers neared the parchment, Albi became frantic, circling and squeaking in obvious distress.

He actually nipped at my boot, tiny teeth sinking into the leather with surprising force, trying to warn me away from the blood-stained message.

I hesitated, then deliberately pricked my finger on a splinter from the box, letting a single drop of my blood fall onto the wooden edge—not touching the parchment directly, but close enough to test my suspicions.

The reaction was immediate and violent.

The stains on the parchment pulsed once, a brief flash of light that would have been invisible to normal human sight, and my drop of blood seemed to leap from the wood to the parchment's edge, absorbed instantly into the larger stains.

Albi let out a pained squeak and scurried behind my other boot, his tiny body trembling.

"Blood magic," I confirmed quietly, returning the box to Kuchoff.

The cut on my finger throbbed with unnatural heat, forcing me to resist the urge to plunge my hand into the cool cellar dirt.

"Active, not residual. The parchment itself is part of the ritual. It's... feeding somehow, drawing power from blood it comes in contact with."

"What does that mean?" Torval asked nervously, taking an involuntary step back from the box, his weathered face paling beneath his beard.

"It means," Kuchoff replied grimly, closing the box with careful precision, "that these men weren't just murdered. Their deaths are feeding some larger purpose—a ritual that remains active even days after the killing."

"Where exactly were the bodies found?" Loher asked, her practical nature focusing on concrete details.

"About half a league north," Torval answered. "On the main road toward Carrington. A trader discovered them as he was traveling south."

"We need to see the site," Kuchoff decided. "Elder Torval, we'll need horses and a guide."

The elder hesitated, then nodded.

"I'll arrange it. Though I must advise against remaining there after sundown. The killers may still be watching."

"Let them watch," Kuchoff replied, a dangerous edge entering his voice. "Perhaps they'll learn something about who they're dealing with."

As Torval hurried upstairs to make arrangements, Loher moved closer to us, her voice dropping to ensure we wouldn't be overheard.

"These killings are different from what we know of Lemac," she observed. "Too ritualistic, too public. His work was secretive, calculated."

"Agreed," I said, the throbbing in my finger finally beginning to subside. "The magic in that blood... it's being channeled somewhere. These deaths are powering something, feeding a ritual that extends beyond the killings themselves."

"But what?" Kuchoff wondered, his hand unconsciously touching the hilt of his katana.

"Whatever it is," I replied, "it connects to Dournan somehow. And possibly to this 'Renewal' they keep mentioning."

Dournan.

The name stirred memories from years past—a ruined settlement in the southwestern quadrant near the Charon Swamp, far from Senton and Dewarg.

The town had been largely abandoned after the previous King's failed campaigns across the Strait of Avilyn, its buildings crumbling into the encroaching swamp, fields reclaimed by brackish water and twisted vegetation.

We'd passed through once, seeking information.

I recalled the rotting remains of buildings, bodies left to decompose in the streets, scavengers of unnatural size feasting on the carnage.

It had become a lawless place, inhabited by the desperate and the dangerous.

I'd encountered a lychee there—one of the rare undead scholars who retain their intelligence after death.

The creature had been ancient even then, its withered corpse preserved through necromantic arts long forgotten.

It had given me directions to another location in exchange for a few coins, its dried lips forming words that seemed to whisper directly into my mind.

"We've been to Dournan," I reminded them quietly. "Years ago. The settlement was already in ruins then—buildings crumbling, fields reclaimed by the swamp. But there was magic there, old magic sleeping beneath the decay."

"You think these killings are connected to whatever power lies dormant in Dournan?" Kuchoff asked, his expression thoughtful.

"I don't know," I admitted. "But this 'Justice remembers Dournan' phrase keeps appearing. There's a connection we're missing."

"We need more information," Loher concluded, practical as always. "Local context. These killings may be part of a pattern we're not seeing."

Kuchoff nodded, his decision made.

"I'll signal Balt to prepare a larger ground team. If the murder site yields nothing, we'll need to expand our investigation—perhaps to Dournan itself."

As Kuchoff headed upstairs, I knelt to comfort Albi, who was still trembling from his exposure to the blood magic.

His reaction troubled me deeply.

Whatever power the killers were harnessing resonated in a way that disturbed even the simplest creatures—creatures who normally thrived in the presence of blood and death.

"You felt it too," Loher observed, watching me stroke Albi's scarred back.

"Yes," I admitted, noting how the other rats kept their distance from my pricked finger. "It's old magic, Loher. Blood sacrifice filtered through ritual intent. Whoever's behind this isn't just killing constables—they're harvesting power."

"For what purpose?"

"I don't know," I said, rising to my feet as Albi finally calmed enough to rejoin his companions. "But I'm starting to think these killings are connected to Lemac's search for the Scepter of Dourn. The timing is too convenient."

"Several constables dead," Loher mused. "Seven sacrifices. Seven dragons to bind."

The parallels were becoming difficult to ignore.

What ritual required the blood of men sworn to uphold order and law?

What power grew stronger with each constable slain?

And more troubling still, what would happen when the celestial bodies aligned?

The answers, I suspected, lay in Dournan and its mysterious connection to this "Renewal."

But as we ascended the cellar steps to rejoin Kuchoff and Balt, I couldn't shake the feeling that we were already too late to prevent whatever dark purpose had been set in motion.

The northern road out of Senton was little more than a cart track, rutted from recent rains and flanked by scrubby pine trees that bent against the coastal wind.

Our small party—Captain Magnus, Loher, Balt, I, and two of our surviving crew members, Elias, and Tara—followed our guide, a nervous young fisherman named Deren, as the afternoon light began to fade.

"Not much farther," Deren assured us, glancing repeatedly at the darkening sky. "Just beyond that rise. Though I don't see what good it'll do—they moved the bodies two days past."

"The land remembers," I replied, watching Albi and my other rats fan out ahead of us. "As do those who witness."

Balt snorted.

"Verra poetic, McLaaud. Are ye startin' ta speak in riddles like our scaly prophet now?"

Before I could respond, Albi froze, his tiny body rigid with alarm.

The other rats immediately formed their defensive circle, all facing outward as if warding against an unseen threat.

"Hold," I commanded, raising my hand. "Something's wrong."

Kuchoff signaled the party to stop, his hand moving to his katana with practiced ease.

"What do your rats sense?"

"Magic," I replied, watching Albi's behavior carefully. "Recent, powerful. Not ambient—directed, purposeful."

"Like the parchment?" Loher asked, her bow already in hand though she hadn't nocked an arrow.

"Similar, but stronger." I knelt, communing silently with Albi.

The rat's heightened senses transmitted impressions rather than clear images—patterns in the earth, blood soaking into soil, power flowing along invisible channels.

"There's a ritual site ahead. Recently used, still active."

Deren looked ready to bolt, his weathered face pale beneath his sea-tanned skin.

"The constables were just killed here, nothing more. We should head back before dark—"

"Calm yourself," Kuchoff commanded, his voice carrying subtle psionic reinforcement. "No harm will come to you under our protection."

The fisherman subsided, though his eyes continued to dart nervously toward the lengthening shadows.

"Balt, Elias, take point," Kuchoff ordered. "Thunor, let your rats scout ahead. Loher, watch our backs. Tara, stay with Deren."

We advanced more cautiously now, weapons ready, senses alert for any sign of danger. The trees thinned as we crested the rise, revealing a small clearing beside the road, unremarkable but for the dark stains still visible on trampled grass.

"This is where we found them," Deren confirmed, hanging back as we approached the site. "Arranged in a triangle, faces pointing inward, like you were told."

The clearing seemed ordinary enough at first glance—a small open space where travelers might stop to rest, or merchants might make camp for the night.

But as we drew closer, my vampiric senses detected subtle wrongness—the grass was dying in unnatural patterns, and the air itself felt charged, as if a lightning strike were imminent.

My rats converged on the center of the clearing, where the bloodstains were most concentrated.

They began moving in precise patterns—not their usual chaotic exploration, but deliberate formations that followed invisible lines in the earth.

"There's a design here," I noted, watching their movements. "Carved into the soil beneath the grass, then deliberately covered."

Balt knelt to examine one of the bloodstains, his dwarf's eye for detail noting what others might miss.

"No signs o' struggle," he observed, pointing to subtle markings in the soil. "They was ambushed, taken down all quick like." He pointed to a slight depression in the disturbed earth. "Archer positioned there, elevated shot. Professional work."

"How many attackers?" Kuchoff asked, scanning the surrounding trees.

"At least five," Balt assessed, moving methodically around the clearing. "Maybe more. Coordinated, disciplined." He paused at a distinctive boot print, partially preserved in firmer soil. "Military training, if I had ta guess. These ain't common bandits or angry farmers."

Loher had moved to the edge of the clearing, examining the underbrush with careful precision.

"Tracks here," she called. "Heading northwest, toward the deeper forest."

I joined her, studying the faint impressions.

"Five men," I confirmed. "One heavier than the others, possibly carrying something. They knew these woods—stepped carefully, stuck to harder ground where possible."

As the sun continued to sink, casting the clearing in deepening shadows, my rats returned from their exploration, forming a strange pattern at my feet—a seven-pointed star, with each rat positioned at a point or the center.

"What've they found?" Balt asked, noticing their unusual behavior.

"I'm not sure," I admitted. "They're responding to something in the soil, some pattern we can't see."

Kuchoff approached, kneeling beside the rats.

His psionic senses often perceived things others couldn't.

"There *is* a design here," he said after a moment of concentration. "Carved into the earth beneath the grass, then deliberately covered."

"A ritual circle," I guessed, the pieces falling into place. "The constables were positioned over specific points of the pattern."

Deren had backed away nervously, clearly uncomfortable with talk of magic and rituals.

"Elder Torval said we should head back before dark," he reminded us, eyes darting toward the shadows between the trees.

"Soon," Kuchoff assured him, though his attention remained fixed on the ground. "Thunor, can your rats dig?"

I nodded, directing Albi and the others to excavate small sections of the pattern.

They set to work immediately, their tiny paws scraping away soil to reveal what lay beneath—precise lines carved into the earth, forming intricate symbols that radiated outward from the center of where the triangle of bodies had been placed.

"I've seen these before," Loher said suddenly, her perfect elven memory recalling details from ancient texts. "They're binding runes—used to channel energy from one location to another."

"The constables' blood," I concluded grimly. "Their deaths weren't just killings—they were feeding points for a larger ritual."

"Look here," Balt called, having moved to the center of the clearing.

He'd pushed aside a carefully arranged pile of leaves to reveal a small stone tablet embedded in the soil.

Carved into its surface was a crude but recognizable map of Be-ornan Heafod, with seven locations marked by tiny, precise indenta-tions.

"Sacrifice sites," Kuchoff said quietly, examining the stone. "Including this one."

Three of the marks were filled with what appeared to be dried blood—Senton, Bom Dabo, and one near Larix.

Four remained empty.

"They're creating a pattern," Loher observed, tracing the marks with her finger. "A seven-pointed star across the realm. And look," she pointed to the center, where all lines converged. "Dournan. The Shrine."

The Shrine at Dournan was one of the oldest structures in Beornan Heafod, built atop what many believed to be a nexus of magical energy.

If someone were channeling blood magic through sacrifice sites arranged in a star pattern...

"We need to get to Dournan," I said urgently. "Whatever ritual they're performing, it culminates there."

"Four more sacrifices to complete the pattern," Kuchoff agreed, studying the stone. "But why constables specifically? What makes their blood special for this ritual?"

The answer came from an unexpected source.

Deren, who had been hovering anxiously at the edge of the clearing, cleared his throat.

"Begging your pardon, Captain, but constables take an oath when they're sworn in. A blood oath to uphold the King's law. My cousin joined the service last year in Carrington."

Kuchoff and I exchanged grim looks.

Blood oaths carried powerful magic—a willing sacrifice of blood tied to a specific purpose.

When such blood was spilled in violence, the magical potential multiplied.

"They're not just killing law-keepers," I realized. "They're harvesting oath-bound blood to power something at the Shrine."

"But what?" Balt demanded, hefting his massive axe. "What requires seven blood sacrifices arranged in a star?"

Before anyone could answer, Albi let out a warning squeak.

The other rats froze, then scattered in all directions, disappearing into the grass.

A moment later, I sensed what had alarmed them—movement in the trees beyond the clearing, the subtle shift of shadows that indicated we were being watched.

"We're not alone," I warned quietly, my hand moving to my sword.

Loher had already nocked an arrow; her elven senses pinpointing threats faster than human eyes could track.

"Three in the trees to the north," she murmured. "Two more circling east."

"Deren," Kuchoff said calmly, "go back to your horse. When I give the word, ride for Senton as fast as you can."

The young fisherman nodded, terror plain on his face as he backed slowly toward where we'd left the horses.

"Should we wait for dem to make a move, Captain?" Elias asked, sword already drawn.

"No," Kuchoff decided. "Loher, discourage our visitors. Balt, Thunor, Elias, Tara—defensive formation. Deren, go now!"

As Deren sprinted for his horse, Loher's bow sang out, sending two arrows in rapid succession into the tree line.

A cry of pain confirmed she'd found her mark, followed by the sounds of hasty movement through undergrowth.

"They're retreating," she reported, already nocking a third arrow.

"Let's encourage 'em," Balt grinned, hefting his massive axe. "Nothin' like a wee bit o' aggression ta keep tings interestin'!"

"Hold," Kuchoff commanded. "We need one alive for questioning."

A flash of purple light suddenly erupted from the trees, streaking toward us like malevolent lightning.

Kuchoff raised his hand, his psionic power flaring to life, intercepting the magical attack and dispersing it into harmless sparks.

"Magic user," I warned, my vampiric senses detecting the familiar residue of combat sorcery. "Fairly powerful."

"Looky what we have here," came a mocking voice from the trees. "The famous Scorpion crew, poking their noses where they don't belong."

A figure stepped into view at the edge of the clearing—a young man, barely out of his teens, with close-cropped dark hair and a face marked by elaborate tattoos that seemed to writhe in the fading light.

He wore simple leather armor beneath a purple-trimmed cloak, and half a dozen wickedly sharp throwing knives gleamed at his belt.

"You must be the one they call Swift-Knife," Kuchoff said, recognition dawning as he matched the figure to descriptions in the reports we'd studied.

The young sorcerer offered an exaggerated bow.

"My reputation precedes me! I'm flattered, Captain Magnus. Though I think you'll find I'm faster than stories suggest."

"Reputation?" Captain Magnus laughed, "I've heard no stories about you." He simply held up a crude drawing, "All I have is this likeness of you and I have to say...it's pretty accurate!"

Swift-Knife frowned, disappointed at his apparent lack of fame.

Without warning, his hand blurred with unnatural speed.

Three knives flew toward us simultaneously, each trailing a streak of purple light.

Kuchoff's shield deflected one, while Loher's arrow intercepted another mid-flight.

The third would have found my throat had I not dropped into a crouch, letting it whistle overhead.

"Impressive reflexes," Swift-Knife laughed. "This might actually be entertaining."

"Why constables?" I demanded, buying time as I sensed my rats returning—not fleeing the danger but circling through the underbrush to flank our opponent. "What does your ritual require their blood for?"

Something flickered across the young sorcerer's face—surprise, perhaps, that we'd discerned the purpose behind the killings.

"Clever vampire," he acknowledged. "Or half-vampire, isn't it? The Grand Ascendancy keeps thorough records."

"Answer the question," Kuchoff commanded, his voice carrying the subtle resonance of psionic influence.

Swift-Knife's eyes narrowed, recognizing the attempted manipulation.

"Nice try, Captain. But I've trained against thought manipulation." He tapped a metallic circlet partially hidden beneath his hair. "Protection against *your* particular talents."

"Won't protect ye from me axe," Balt growled, stepping forward menacingly.

"Ah, the famous dwarf berserker," Swift-Knife grinned. "Balt, isn't it? I counted the skull beads in your beard from the trees. Impressive collection. Perhaps I'll add mine after I've finished with you."

"Ye welcome to try, Boy-o," Balt invited, hefting his axe higher. "I've been needin' a fresh skull bead ta even 'em out. Yers will do nicely."

Throughout this exchange, I noticed Loher had vanished—slipping into the shadows with the stealth of her cloak of invisibility.

Swift-Knife seemed unaware of her absence, his attention focused on Kuchoff and Balt.

"You didn't answer my question," I pressed. "Why constables?"

"Why does *anyone* kill law-keepers?" Swift-Knife shrugged dramatically. "Because they interfere. They represent a system that benefits the few while crushing the many. Ask the families of Dournan how well the King's justice served them."

"Flowery speech," Kuchoff observed. "But it doesn't explain the ritual pattern. The blood runes. The targeting of specific locations."

Something shifted in Swift-Knife's expression—a subtle hardening of his features.

"You understand less than you think, Captain. The Renewal isn't just about justice for Dournan. It's about remaking the world." His hand moved to his belt, fingers caressing another knife. "Starting with the destruction of everything you hold dear."

As he spoke, I sensed Albi and the other rats completing their circle, now positioned directly behind Swift-Knife.

I gave them the silent command I'd trained them for in combat situations: attack.

With perfect coordination, a dozen rats swarmed up Swift-Knife's legs, their tiny teeth finding gaps in his leather armor.

The sorcerer cursed; his concentration broken as he tried to dislodge the unexpected assault.

In that moment of distraction, Loher struck.

She emerged from the shadows behind him, her dagger pressing against his throat with just enough pressure to draw a thin line of blood.

"Drop the knives," she commanded softly, "or I'll show you how a master thief finishes her work."

Swift-Knife froze, then slowly raised his hands in surrender.

As Balt moved to secure him, a flicker of something that might have been amusement crossed the young sorcerer's face.

"You think you've won something here," he laughed, addressing Kuchoff directly. "But you're already too late. The stars align in three days' time. The Wyrmfall Moon rises over Dournan."

"Lemac," I concluded. "He's behind this after all."

Swift-Knife laughed—a brittle, manic sound that echoed unnervingly through the darkening clearing.

"Lemac? He's merely a vessel. A worthy one, but still just a vessel."

His eyes gleamed with fanatical intensity.

"The Master's return requires seven sacrifices of sworn blood, placed at the points of power across Beornan Heafod. Four remain to complete the pattern."

"What master?" Kuchoff demanded.

Instead of answering, Swift-Knife suddenly bit down hard on something hidden in his mouth.

Foam immediately appeared at his lips, his body convulsing violently.

Balt grabbed him, trying to force his mouth open, but it was already too late.

"Poison capsule," Loher reported grimly, examining the dying man. "Fast-acting. Northern hemlock, if I'm not mistaken."

Within moments, Swift-Knife lay dead at our feet, his face frozen in a grotesque smile.

The rats abandoned his now-still form, returning to me with agitated squeaks.

Albi pawed at my boot, urging retreat from the corpse.

"Clever bastard," Balt growled, kicking the corpse in frustration. "Had it all planned out."

"He wanted to be caught," I realized. "To deliver a message."

"The Wyrmfall Moon," Kuchoff repeated, his expression troubled. "Three days from now, over Dournan."

"The same timing as the celestial portal," I pointed out. "The one Lemac sought information about in the archives."

"It can't be coincidence," Loher agreed. "The constable killings, the ritual pattern, the portal opening... they're all connected."

Kuchoff knelt beside the stone tablet, studying the pattern of marked locations.

"Three sacrifice sites completed. Four to go." He looked up at us, his decision made. "We split up. Cover the remaining likely targets, try to prevent the next killings."

"Against a coordinated group with magic users?" I questioned. "We're already stretched thin after losing so many in the battle with Nerium."

"We have allies," Kuchoff reminded me. "The Dragonfly was headed to Dewarg. We'll send word, coordinate forces." He rose to his feet, brushing dirt from his knees. "Whatever this 'Renewal' is, whatever 'master' they serve, it requires all seven locations. If we can disrupt even one, we disrupt the whole ritual."

I nodded, seeing the logic.

"And Dournan? The Shrine is clearly their ultimate target."

"I'll contact the King," Kuchoff decided. "Request reinforcements from Salvus Hus to secure the shrine. Meanwhile, we investigate

Dournan—find out what connects these killings to that old settlement."

As we prepared to depart, gathering what evidence we could from the murder site, I cast one last look at Swift-Knife's body.

Something about his fanatical confidence troubled me deeply.

He'd died willingly, believing in some 'master' whose return was worth his sacrifice.

More disturbing still was the realization that Lemac—the wizard we'd been hunting since Nerium's defeat—might not be the ultimate threat.

If he was merely a 'vessel' as Swift-Knife had claimed, then what power was he seeking to channel?

What entity required the blood of oath-sworn constables, spilled at specific points across Beornan Heafod?

The answers, I suspected, lay in Dournan and its mysterious connection to this 'Renewal.'

And we had three days to uncover them before the Wyrmfall Moon rose over Dournan, completing whatever dark ritual had already claimed three lives.

As we rode back toward Senton in the gathering darkness, Albi formed a protective circle with the other rats around my horse's hooves.

Their usually random movements had given way to precise patterns—alert, watchful, aware of dangers I could not yet perceive.

The hunt for Lemac had evolved into something far more complex.

No longer were we pursuing a rogue wizard seeking power, we were racing against a coordinated cult performing blood sacrifices to bring about some cataclysmic "Renewal."

And somewhere at the center of it all was the Scepter of Dourn, a weapon forged to kill dragons, waiting beyond a celestial portal that would open in three days' time.

Chapter Seventeen

BLOOD TIDE

The morning fog clung to the Scorpion's hull as we sailed south through the Strait of Avilyn.

Three days had passed since we discovered the ritual site in Senton, and with each passing hour, the sense of foreboding had grown stronger.

"Sail ho!" the lookout called from the crow's nest. "The Dragonfly approaches from the east!"

I moved to the port rail, watching as the familiar silhouette of Captain Rina's vessel emerged from the mist.

Unlike our last encounter, her ship flew scarlet banners of urgent news rather than the customary greeting colors.

Balt joined me at the rail.

"That cannae be good," he muttered, watching The Dragonfly cut through the waves with unusual haste.

"Rina's never one ta waste wind unless there's trouble."

Captain Magnus ordered the helmsman to heave to, allowing The Dragonfly to come alongside.

As the vessels drew parallel, I could see Captain Rina at her rail—her dark face grimmer than usual, her normally immaculate black wool jacket stained with what appeared to be dried blood.

"Captain Magnus!" she called across the narrowing gap, dispensing with pleasantries. "Powell and Heroston have fallen. Constables slaughtered, just like the others."

Kuchoff's expression remained steady, though I noted the subtle tightening around his eyes.

"How many?"

"Four in total," Rina replied, her voice carrying over the sound of waves lapping between our hulls. "That makes seven altogether."

Seven.

The number hung in the air between our vessels like a death knell.

"When?" Kuchoff demanded.

"Yesterday at dawn," Rina answered. "All at once, in perfect synchronicity according to witnesses. Purple-fletched arrows, throats cut after death. The pattern is complete."

Meeka stepped up beside Kuchoff, her face pale in the morning light.

"The ritual circle," she said softly. "Seven points sealed with blood. Did you recover any messages from the bodies?"

Rina nodded, gesturing to her first officer—Commander Cyrus, a muscular man with a grim countenance.

He passed her a small wooden box, similar to the one Elder Torval had shown us in Senton.

"Same as before," Rina confirmed, opening the box and revealing a blood-stained parchment. The crimson stains still looked wet despite being a day old. "But this one's different. Listen: 'The seven are fallen. The wheel turns. In Dournan's heart, the Master rises at Wyrmfall Moon.'"

"Dournan," I repeated, the name conjuring images of the ruined town we'd passed through years ago. "It's not just about justice for those who lost their lands. Dournan itself is part of the ritual."

"What's so special about Dournan?" Rina asked, clearly unaware of the settlement's significance.

"It's what once stood tall as a proud, bustling town," I explained, recalling our brief but memorable visit. "Now it's a crumbling ruin of sorrow and despair. When we passed through, there were bodies lying in the streets—some fresh, some rotted to bone. The carnage was worse than any battlefield I could imagine."

"Lawless," Balt added with a grim nod. "Scavengers roamin' about, breedin' stronger vermin—rats the size of dogs, crows like eagles, vultures big as dwarves."

"Only a few buildings were still standing," I continued. "The tavern, an armory, and a few well-built homes occupied by unsavory creatures. But beneath it all was a current of old magic—dormant, but powerful."

"The heart of Dournan," Loher mused, joining our conversation. "That's where they'll complete the ritual when the Wyrmfall Moon rises tonight."

Rina's expression hardened.

"We captured one of Lemac's men yesterday—a thin, nervous fellow who called himself Brother Elric. Before he took his own life, he raved about 'the Renewal' and how Dournan would become the center of a new order."

"Did he mention the Scepter of Dourn?" Kuchoff asked sharply.

"No," Rina replied, looking puzzled. "What's that?"

"A weapon forged to kill dragons," Kuchoff explained quickly. "Lemac seeks it through a celestial portal that opens tonight—during the Wyrmfall Moon."

"When dragon magic is at its weakest," Avilyn added, his elven features grave as he joined us at the rail. "The timing is not coincidental."

Captain Magnus turned to address both crews.

"The pattern is clear now. The constable murders were a ritual to channel power to Dournan, strengthening whatever lies dormant there. Tonight, when the Wyrmfall Moon rises, Lemac will use that power to open the celestial portal and claim the Scepter."

"But why constables specifically?" Rina pressed.

"They took a blood oath to uphold the King's law," I explained. "Oath-bound blood carries powerful magic, especially when spilled in violence. By sacrificing twenty-one law-keepers at specific points across Beornan Heafod, Lemac created a ritual circle with Dournan at its center."

"And now he has the power he needs," Meeka concluded grimly.

Kuchoff's decision was swift.

"We sail for Dournan immediately. Captain Rina, can The Dragonfly match our speed?"

"We'll keep pace," she assured him, already barking orders to her crew. "Commander Cyrus! Full sail! We follow The Scorpion!"

As The Dragonfly peeled away to execute a tight turn, Kuchoff gathered his officers.

"The Strait narrows ahead. We'll need to navigate carefully to reach Dournan by nightfall."

"The old trade passage through the Charon Swamp," Loher suggested. "It's treacherous, but it could save us hours. We'll have to swing around to the northern edge."

"Agreed," Kuchoff nodded. "Tatenda, you'll need to navigate with utmost precision."

"Me bring us through, Captain," the Drow assured him, a determined gleam in his eye. "The Scorpion, she dance through dem waters like mist on morning waves."

As the crew dispersed to their stations, I found myself at the bow, watching the coastline scroll past.

The rats at my feet had grown increasingly agitated throughout the morning, their movements jerky and unpredictable.

Even Albi, normally the most composed, scurried in circles, occasionally stopping to rise on his hind legs and sniff the air with alarming intensity.

"They sense it too," Loher observed, silently appearing beside me. "The wrongness."

"It's more than that," I replied, watching Albi's erratic behavior. "They're afraid—not just of what lies ahead, but of what's happening now. Whatever ritual Lemac completed with the twenty-first killing, it's already changing things."

"Look there," she said suddenly, pointing to the shoreline.

Where the morning mist thinned briefly, I could see birds rising from the trees—not in the natural patterns of feeding or migration, but in panicked, chaotic flights.

Entire flocks abandoned their roosts, heading northwest, away from the direction of Dournan.

"The animals are fleeing," I noted grimly. "They sense what's coming."

Chron swooped down from above, landing on the rail beside us.

His bronze scales caught the weakening sunlight as clouds began to gather on the horizon.

"The blood path is complete," the wyrmling intoned, his ancient eyes fixed on the darkening southern sky.

"Twenty-one fallen guardians feed what stirs beneath the ruins. Time splinters as the Wyrmfall Moon approaches."

For once, Balt, who had joined us at the bow, didn't threaten to make boots from the prophetic dragon.

Instead, he reached out a thick finger and gently stroked Chron's metallic scales.

"What stirs beneath Dournan, wee dragon?" he asked, uncharacteristically somber. "What manner o' beastie are we sailin' toward?"

Chron's eyes seemed to look through time itself as he answered.

"Not beast, Stone-Heart. What sleeps beneath Dournan once walked as man. A king of old, betrayed by his own, whose dying curse twisted blood and magic into chains that bind him to the ruined earth. Each drop of oath-sworn blood loosens those chains."

"A king?" Meeka questioned, joining our growing assembly. "You mean from before the current dynasty?"

"Long before," Chron confirmed. "When Beornan Heafod was young, and the first Shrine rose in Dournan. His name is lost to all but the oldest scrolls."

"But Lemac knows it," I concluded. "He found records in the castle archives—the same place he learned about the celestial portal and the Scepter of Dourn."

"The Master's return requires seven sacrifices," Loher quoted from Swift-Knife's dying words. "He wasn't talking about Lemac returning to power. He meant this ancient king."

Kuchoff approached, having overheard our conversation.

"And Lemac plans to use the Scepter of Dourn to control this awakened king? Or to become its vessel?"

"Both, perhaps," Avilyn suggested, his elven features troubled. "The Binding of Draconic Essence could grant Lemac the power to dominate even an ancient magic-user. And with a weapon forged to kill dragons..."

"He could threaten even you," Kuchoff finished, looking at the disguised Dragon King.

The sky continued to darken as The Scorpion sliced through increasingly choppy waters.

The wind had shifted, now blowing directly from the south, heavy with the scent of stagnant water and decay—the unmistakable odor of the Charon Swamp that surrounded Dournan.

"Storm's brewing," Balt observed unnecessarily as lightning flickered on the distant horizon. "Not natural, neither."

"No," Avilyn agreed. "The ritual's power disturbs more than just the physical world."

We fell silent as The Scorpion entered the narrow channel that would lead us through the swamp to Dournan.

On either side, twisted trees rose from brackish water, their gnarled branches reaching like skeletal fingers toward our vessel.

The usual sounds of wildlife—birds calling, insects buzzing—were eerily absent, leaving only the splash of our hull through the water and the creaking of The Scorpion's timbers.

The channel twisted like a serpent through the swamp, forcing Tatenda to make constant adjustments at the Creature Controls.

Behind us, The Dragonfly followed carefully in our wake, her crew visibly tense as they navigated the treacherous passage.

"There," Loher said suddenly, pointing to a half-submerged structure on our port side. "That's the old lighthouse that marked the approach to Dournan when it was still a trading post."

The crumbling tower listed at a precarious angle; its upper portion long collapsed into the murky water.

Yet as we passed, I noticed something disturbing—fresh blood smeared across its weathered stones, forming symbols similar to those we'd found at the constable murder site.

"They've been marking the approach," I realized aloud. "Preparing the way for whatever's about to emerge."

"Or ensuring we can find our way to the main event," Meeka suggested darkly. "Lemac may be expecting us."

As we rounded the final bend in the channel, Dournan came into view—or what remained of it.

The ruined town sprawled across a slight rise in the otherwise flat swampland, its crumbling structures resembling broken teeth against the darkening sky.

At its center, where once a town square might have stood, an unnatural purple light pulsed rhythmically, like the heartbeat of some massive creature.

"The ritual site," Kuchoff identified grimly. "Lemac's already begun."

The Wyrmfall Moon, though not yet risen, cast an eerie glow along the eastern horizon—a sickly green luminescence that seemed to bleed into the gathering storm clouds.

Within hours, it would reach its zenith, directly over Dournan, completing whatever dark purpose Lemac had set in motion.

"No safe approach by water beyond dis point," Tatenda announced, guiding The Scorpion toward a dilapidated dock that somehow still stood among the ruins of Dournan's waterfront. "Too shallow for De Scorpion, Captain."

"Then we proceed on foot," Kuchoff decided, turning to address the assembled crew. "Tatenda, remain aboard with a skeleton crew. Keep The Scorpion ready to depart at a moment's notice. The rest of you, prepare for ground assault."

He turned to where The Dragonfly was maneuvering alongside us. "Captain Rina! We'll need your fighters as well!"

"Already preparing the landing party!" she called back, gesturing to where her crew was checking weapons and donning armor.

As Tatenda skillfully brought The Scorpion alongside the ancient dock, I felt a chill that had nothing to do with the evening air.

The rats at my feet had gone completely still—not scurrying for safety as they normally would before battle, but frozen in place, as if paralyzed by whatever power emanated from the town's center.

Albi alone moved, climbing up my boot to tug insistently at my trouser leg.

When I knelt to check on him, his beady eyes conveyed a message clearer than words—whatever waited in Dournan was something even the rats feared to face.

The hunt for Lemac had led us to something far more ancient and terrible.

As we prepared to disembark, I couldn't shake the feeling that we were walking into the culmination of a plan centuries in the making—and that before the Wyrmfall Moon set, Beornan Heafod would either be saved or changed forever.

CHAPTER EIGHTEEN
THE HEART OF DOURNAN

Dournan's remains stretched before us like a corpse left to rot in the sun.

Buildings that had once housed families and businesses now stood as hollow shells, their roofs collapsed, walls crumbling into the mud.

The streets—if they could still be called that—were little more than trails through the debris, occasionally punctuated by the skeletal remains of those who had died when the town fell.

Our landing party advanced cautiously through this landscape of decay—Kuchoff in the lead, with Balt, Loher, Meeka, and me close behind.

Avilyn had remained aboard The Scorpion, maintaining his elven disguise but preparing draconic magic that might be needed if things went poorly.

Behind us came Captain Rina with a dozen of her best fighters, including Commander Cyrus, whose massive frame dwarfed even the stoutest of his companions.

The rats—all except Albi, who clung tenaciously to my shoulder—had refused to leave the ship, a fact that troubled me deeply.

In all our adventures, they had never shown such reluctance to follow where I led.

"I don't like this," Loher murmured, her elven eyes scanning the ruins for threats. "Too quiet. Even for a dead town."

She was right.

The eerie silence was broken only by our footsteps and the occasional creak of settling timbers.

No birds called, no insects buzzed—even the ever-present sounds of the swamp had faded to nothing, as if the entire area held its breath in anticipation.

"The tavern still stands," I noted, pointing to a two-story structure ahead that seemed remarkably intact compared to its surroundings. "Last time we were here, it was the only building with signs of occupation."

The Salty Mermaid's weathered sign still hung from rusted chains, though the paint had long faded, leaving only the vague outline of the buxom, scaled woman it had once depicted.

The windows were dark, shuttered from within.

"Approach from three sides," Kuchoff decided quickly. "Balt, take four of Rina's crew around back. Loher, circle right with Commander Cyrus. Thunor, with me through the front. Meeka, hold position here with Captain Rina and provide magical support if needed."

As we divided into our assigned groups, I caught a flicker of movement from the corner of my e—a shadow passing briefly behind one of the tavern's shuttered windows.

I tapped Kuchoff's arm and nodded toward it, receiving a grim nod of acknowledgment in return.

"They know we're here," he whispered. "Be ready for anything."

Balt and his group disappeared around the side of the building, while Loher and Commander Cyrus moved with silent efficiency toward the right flank.

Kuchoff and I approached the tavern's front entrance, weapons ready, senses alert for any sign of ambush.

The door hung partially open on worn hinges, revealing a slice of darkness beyond. I extended my vampiric senses but encountered a strange resistance—as if something within actively worked to block my perception.

"Magic," I warned softly. "Strong. Obscuring."

Kuchoff nodded, his hand resting on his katana's hilt. "On three," he mouthed silently, holding up fingers to count down.

At his signal, we burst through the door, weapons drawn—and froze in confusion.

The tavern's interior was immaculate.

Unlike the decaying ruin we'd expected, the common room before us gleamed with fresh polish, the wooden tables and chairs arranged in perfect order, the bar stocked with gleaming bottles.

A fire crackled in the hearth, casting dancing shadows across walls decorated with tapestries that looked newly woven.

Most striking of all was the complete absence of people, despite the clear signs of recent habitation—half-filled mugs of ale sat on several tables, still frothing as if just poured.

A pot bubbled over the fire, the scent of stew wafting through the room.

"Illusion?" I wondered aloud, stepping cautiously across the threshold.

"No," Kuchoff replied, his voice tight. "Something else."

Albi chittered nervously on my shoulder, his tiny claws digging into my cloak as he pressed himself against my neck.

From the back of the tavern came the sound of a scuffle, followed by Balt's distinctive battle cry.

Moments later, the dwarf appeared from the kitchen, dragging a struggling figure—a thin, balding man in simple robes who bore a remarkable resemblance to the tavernkeeper I'd encountered on our previous visit.

"Look what I found hidin' in the pantry," Balt announced, shoving the man roughly into a chair. "Says his name's Tomas, claims he's just the barkeep."

"I am!" the man protested, his watery eyes darting between us. "Just serving drinks, that's all. Don't want no trouble."

Loher and Commander Cyrus entered from the side door; the elven thief's expression troubled.

"The rooms upstairs are all prepared," she reported. "Beds made, fresh water in the basins—as if they're expecting important guests."

"The ritual participants," Meeka suggested, joining us after Kuchoff signaled the all-clear. "This must be their base of operations."

Captain Rina followed, her keen eyes taking in the incongruously pristine surroundings.

"How is this possible? The town is in ruins, yet this place looks freshly built."

"Not built," I corrected, studying the familiar layout of the room. "Restored. This tavern existed when we passed through years ago, but it was dilapidated, filled with the worst sort of clientele." I turned to the nervous barkeep. "Isn't that right, Tomas?"

He licked his lips anxiously. "Don't know what you mean, sir. The Mermaid's always been kept up proper-like."

"Liar," Balt growled, leaning closer with menace. "Last time we were here, this place was filled wit' cutthroats an' murderers. They were tormentin' a young orc, if I recall correctly."

A flash of recognition crossed Tomas' face before he could mask it.

"The purple light in the town center," Kuchoff interjected, leaning over the barkeep. "What is it?"

Tomas's eyes widened with genuine fear.

"Don't know nothing about that, sir. We were told not to look at it, not to go near it."

"Who told you?" Meeka demanded.

"The wizard and his followers," Tomas answered, shrinking into his chair. "They came about a month ago. Started with just a few, then more arrived. Said they were preparing for the Renewal."

"Lemac," I said, receiving a nod of confirmation from Kuchoff.

"Didn't get no names," Tomas insisted. "The wizard paid good coin to use the tavern as their headquarters. Had us fix it up, serve food and drink. Said more important folk would be arriving soon—folk who'd appreciate civilized comforts."

"Where are they now?" Captain Rina asked, her hand resting meaningfully on the hilt of her cutlass.

Tomas pointed a trembling finger toward the window, in the direction of the pulsing purple light.

"The center of town. Been there since sunrise, chanting and carrying on. Said tonight's when it happens—when He returns."

"He?" Commander Cyrus pressed, his deep voice rumbling with threat.

"The Ancient King," Tomas whispered, terror evident in his voice. "The rightful ruler of Beornan Heafod, come to reclaim what was stolen."

Kuchoff and I exchanged grim looks.

"The ritual is further along than we thought," he said quietly.

"We need to see what we're facing," I agreed.

"Captain Rina," Kuchoff decided quickly. "Secure this building with half your force. If this is their headquarters, others may return. Commander Cyrus, you're with us."

He turned to Tomas, who cowered under his intense gaze.

"Is there a way to observe the town center without being seen?"

The barkeep nodded jerkily.

"The old church belltower. Still standing, mostly. Best view in Dournan."

"Lead the way," Kuchoff commanded, gesturing for Balt to bring the man along.

As we exited the tavern, the contrast between its immaculate interior and the devastation outside was even more jarring.

The purple light at the town's center had intensified, pulsing faster now, like a heart beating with growing excitement.

Above, the storm clouds had gathered into an unnatural spiral directly over the light's source, occasionally illuminated from within by silent lightning.

Tomas led us through the rubble-strewn streets, taking a circuitous route that kept us concealed within the shadows of crumbling buildings.

Twice we had to duck out of sight as robed figures hurried past, heading toward the center of town, their faces concealed beneath deep hoods.

"The faithful," Tomas explained in a whisper after they'd passed. "Come from all over to witness the Renewal. Most don't even know what they're participating in—just desperate folk looking for something to believe in."

"And what do you believe in, barkeep?" Commander Cyrus asked, his massive hand gripping the man's shoulder to prevent any thoughts of escape.

Tomas shrugged.

"Coin, mostly. And surviving another day."

The shrine, when we reached it, was a shadow of whatever glory it might once have claimed.

The main structure had partially collapsed, its stone walls cracked and leaning inward as if exhausted by the weight of years.

The belltower, however, remained remarkably intact, rising a good forty feet above the surrounding ruins.

"No bell no more," Tomas informed us as we approached the narrow door at the tower's base. "Took it when the town fell. But the stairs still hold, last I checked."

Balt tested the first few steps cautiously.

"Seem solid enough," he confirmed, though the ancient wood creaked ominously beneath his weight.

"I'll go first," Loher decided, her lighter elven frame less likely to stress the worn stairs. "Follow in single file, keep your weight against the wall where the supports are strongest."

We ascended carefully, the staircase spiraling up the interior of the tower in tight, dusty circles.

Near the top, arrow slits provided glimpses of the town below, but it wasn't until we reached the belfry itself that we had a clear view of what awaited us.

The center of Dournan had been transformed.

Where once a town square might have stood, a perfect circle had been cleared of debris, its circumference marked by seven tall poles.

Atop each pole, clearly visible even from this distance, was the head of a constable, their lifeless eyes staring inward toward the circle's center.

Within that circle, a design had been carved into the earth—an intricate pattern of interlocking symbols that glowed with the same purple light we'd observed from a distance.

At seven points around this pattern, robed figures knelt in attitudes of worship, their hands raised toward the sky where the Wyrmfall Moon would soon rise.

At the very center stood a raised stone dais that hadn't been visible from ground level.

Upon it, two figures commanded attention—one I recognized immediately as Lemac, his purple robes impossible to mistake even at this distance.

Beside him stood a taller figure in elaborate ceremonial armor of an ancient design, a crown of twisted metal upon his head.

"Who is that with Lemac?" Meeka whispered, straining to see through the gathering darkness.

"Sir Victor," Tomas answered, surprising us with his knowledge. "Used to be a knight before the campaigns across the Strait. Lost everything—lands, title, wife. They say he'll be the vessel when the Ancient King returns."

"The vessel," I repeated, the pieces clicking into place. "Not Lemac himself."

"Look there," Loher interrupted, pointing to a structure near the dais. A stone archway stood alone, supporting nothing, leading nowhere—yet the space within its frame shimmered with an otherworldly light. "The celestial portal. It's already forming."

Kuchoff studied the scene with military precision.

"I count at least forty cultists in the circle, plus, however many are still in the surrounding buildings. Lemac and this Sir Victor are our primary targets, but we'll need to disrupt the ritual itself."

"The heads," I suggested grimly. "They're channeling the power of the sacrifices. Remove them, and we might break the connection."

"And the archway," Meeka added. "If we can collapse it before the portal fully forms, Lemac won't be able to retrieve the Scepter of Dourn."

As we strategized, Albi suddenly tensed on my shoulder, his body going rigid with alarm.

A moment later, I heard it too—the soft scrape of a foot on the stairs below us.

Kuchoff raised his hand for silence, drawing his katana with slow precision.

Loher melted into the shadows of the belfry, while Balt and Commander Cyrus positioned themselves on either side of the stairwell opening.

The footsteps grew closer, measured and unhurried, as if whoever approached had no fear of what awaited them.

Then a voice—calm, cultured, and chillingly familiar—called up to us.

"Please, don't waste your energy on an ambush. I'm quite aware of your presence."

A moment later, a figure emerged into the belfry—a tall, thin man with aristocratic features and streaks of premature gray at his temples.

He wore simple traveling clothes rather than cultist robes, but the purple trim on his cloak marked him as one of Lemac's followers.

"My name is Lord Di Garath," he introduced himself with a small bow. "Until recently, Baron of Swapton. I believe you were looking for me?"

Kuchoff kept his katana trained on the newcomer.

"You seem rather calm for someone facing armed enemies."

Di Garath smiled thinly.

"Oh, I'm not here to fight. I'm here to negotiate."

"Negotiate?" Commander Cyrus scoffed. "While your people prepare a ritual to resurrect some ancient king?"

"The term 'resurrection' is imprecise," Di Garath corrected mildly. "The Ancient King never truly died—merely transformed, bound to the land through magic and sacrifice. Tonight, he merely awakens to his rightful place."

"As ruler of Beornan Heafod?" Meeka questioned.

Di Garath nodded.

"Of course. The current dynasty are usurpers—descendants of those who betrayed the last true king. The Renewal simply restores proper order."

"Through blood sacrifice and dark magic," I countered, my fangs extending slightly as my vampiric nature responded to the tension.

For the first time, Di Garath's composure slipped, his eyes widening as he took in my partially revealed nature.

"Fascinating," he murmured. "Lemac mentioned you might be... unusual."

"What exactly do you want to negotiate?" Kuchoff demanded, bringing the conversation back to its purpose.

Di Garath turned his attention from me with visible effort.

"Quite simple, really. Your non-interference. The ritual will proceed with or without your blessing, but Lemac prefers to avoid unnecessary bloodshed." His gaze swept over our small group. "Particularly when it comes to such legendary warriors as The Scorpion's crew."

"And why would we agree to stand aside?" Kuchoff asked, his voice dangerously calm.

"Because the alternative is far worse than you imagine," Di Garath replied, his confidence returning.

"Look below. Count our numbers. Consider the magic already in motion."

He stepped closer to the belfry's edge, gesturing toward the purple light that now pulsed with increasing intensity.

"But more practically, because Lemac offers you something invaluable in return for your neutrality."

"What could he possibly offer that would make us ignore countless murdered constables?" Loher asked from the shadows, her voice cold with disdain.

Di Garath's smile widened.

"A cure," he said simply, looking directly at me. "For vampirism."

The words hit me like a physical blow.

Since being bitten years ago, I had managed to control my condition, to use its benefits without succumbing to its darker urges.

But the promise of a cure—to be fully human again, free from the constant thirst and the slow deterioration of my more civilized instincts...

"Don't listen to him," Loher warned, stepping from the shadows to grip my arm. "It's a trick."

Di Garath shrugged.

"Perhaps. Or perhaps Lemac truly does possess knowledge lost for centuries—knowledge that includes both how to bind an ancient king to a modern vessel and how to reverse vampiric infection."

He watched my face carefully.

"After all, the Ancient King was renowned for his mastery of blood magic."

Kuchoff's eyes narrowed.

"Even if such a cure exists, the price is too high. Too many men are dead, and you plan to unleash a power you barely understand on the realm."

"A small price for justice," Di Garath countered. "Do you know how many died in the campaigns across the Strait? How many returned to find their lands seized, their families starved or displaced? The previous king sent men like Sir Victor to fight and die for his ambitions, then punished them for answering the call." His voice hardened. "The current dynasty inherited that blood-debt. Tonight, it will be repaid."

"And the constables?" I asked. "What was their crime?"

"They upheld an unjust system," Di Garath replied without hesitation. "Enforced laws that protected the powerful while punishing the weak. Their oath-bound blood was necessary—symbolic as much as practical."

"You cannot be seriously considering this," Cyrus growled in my direction.

I met Di Garath's gaze steadily.

"I'm not surprised that you would think such a cure would be... tempting to one such as me. But there's something you've overlooked."

"Oh?" Di Garath raised an eyebrow.

"I stopped wanting to be cured long ago," I said, allowing my fangs to extend fully. "The vampiric gifts have saved my companions' lives more times than I can count. They're part of who I am now."

Di Garath's smile faded.

"A pity. Lemac thought you, at least, might see reason."

"We've seen enough," Kuchoff declared, raising his katana. "This negotiation is over."

"Indeed, it is," Di Garath agreed, stepping backward toward the stairwell. "But don't worry—you'll have excellent seats for the Renewal. Lemac insisted you be allowed to witness history unfolding."

Before any of us could move to stop him, Di Garath raised his hand and uttered a single word in a language I didn't recognize.

Purple light flared around the belfry, forming a shimmering barrier that separated us from the stairs.

"A containment spell," Di Garath explained, already descending the first few steps. "Nothing fatal, merely... restrictive. It will dissipate after the ritual is complete." He offered another small bow. "Do enjoy the view. It should be quite spectacular."

As his footsteps receded down the spiral staircase, Balt lunged at the barrier, only to be thrown backward with considerable force.

"Magic," Meeka confirmed after a quick examination. "Powerful, but specific. We're trapped until the spell breaks."

"Or until we break it," Kuchoff countered, turning to her. "Options?"

As Meeka began assessing the magical barrier, I moved to the belfry's edge, studying the ritual site with growing concern.

The purple light had intensified further, now pulsing in perfect rhythm with the distant thunder that rolled across the swamp.

More concerning still, the shimmering within the stone archway had solidified into what appeared to be an actual opening—a tear in reality through which another place was becoming visible.

The celestial portal was forming, hours ahead of the Wyrmfall Moon's zenith.

"Something's wrong," I called to the others. "The ritual is accelerating."

Kuchoff joined me, his expression grim as he surveyed the scene below.

"Lemac's not waiting for the moon. He's forcing the portal open prematurely."

"That's impossible," Meeka argued, joining us. "The celestial alignment is necessary for the portal to stabilize. If he's forcing it open early..."

"The consequences could be catastrophic," Loher finished, her elven senses detecting what their human perceptions missed. "Look at the edges of the portal—they're unstable, fluctuating wildly."

She was right.

The shimmering border of the opening wavered like heat over desert sand, occasionally sending out lashes of purple-white energy that scarred the ground where they struck.

"He's using the constables' blood to force it," Meeka realized, her face pale in the eerie light. "The oath-bound magic is powerful enough to temporarily override the natural celestial alignment."

Below, the cultists had begun chanting in earnest, their voices rising and falling in a rhythm that matched the pulsing light.

Lemac stood at the center of it all, arms raised toward the stone archway, while Sir Victor knelt before him, head bowed as if in prayer or preparation.

"We need ta get out o' here," Balt growled, testing the barrier again with the haft of his axe. The magic flared where he struck but held firm. "Can ye break it, Meeka?"

"I'm trying," she replied, her fingers tracing complex patterns in the air as she worked counter-spells against the barrier. "It's warded against standard dispelling techniques. I need time."

"Time, we don't have," Kuchoff noted grimly, watching as the portal widened further. Through it, a barren landscape became visible—a desolate plain beneath a blood-red sky where something metallic gleamed in the distance. "The Scepter of Dourn," he identified. "It's already visible."

"Wait," Commander Cyrus spoke up, his deep voice cutting through our growing tension. "What about Albi? Can he get through?"

All eyes turned to Albi, who still clung to my shoulder, trembling slightly but alert.

I considered the suggestion.

"The barrier is meant to contain people, not animals," I mused, gently lifting Albi into my palm. "It might be worth trying."

"What good will one rat do against all those cultists?" Tomas asked, speaking up for the first time since we'd reached the belfry.

"Albi isn't just any rat," I replied, bringing the scarred rodent to eye level. "He's been with me for years, learned commands, tactics. And rats can cause... distractions."

"Send him to The Scorpion," Kuchoff suggested. "If we can't warn them, perhaps he can."

I nodded, lowering Albi to the floor near the barrier.

"Go to The Scorpion," I instructed, using the simple commands we'd developed over years of partnership.

"Bring help. Avilyn."

Albi's whiskers twitched as he processed my words, his beady eyes reflecting understanding.

He approached the magical barrier cautiously, nose working as he tested the edge.

Then, with sudden decisiveness, he darted forward—and passed through with no resistance, the magic rippling slightly but allowing him passage.

"It worked!" Meeka exclaimed, watching as Albi scurried down the stairs. "The barrier only affects humans."

"And non-humans," Commander Cyrus added, gesturing to himself. "I tried pressing through while you were all watching the rat."

"So, we're still trapped," Loher concluded, turning her attention back to the ritual below. "And things are accelerating."

She was right.

The portal had expanded further, now large enough that a person could easily step through.

The landscape beyond was more clearly visible—a wasteland stretching to a distant horizon where what appeared to be the ruins of massive structures loomed against the crimson sky.

"What realm is that?" I wondered aloud, the scene triggering no recognition despite my extensive travels.

"That's no realm I know," Meeka replied, her voice hushed with awe and fear. "It looks... dead. Like a world that died long ago."

As we watched, Lemac lowered his arms and turned to address the assembled cultists.

Though we couldn't hear his words clearly at this distance, the effect was immediate—a surge of anticipation rippled through the crowd, many falling to their knees in attitudes of worship.

Sir Victor rose to his feet, removing his ornate helmet to reveal a face weathered by years of hardship, yet alight with fanatic fervor.

He approached the portal with measured steps, stopping just short of the shimmering boundary.

"He's going through," Kuchoff realized. "To retrieve the Scepter."

"Meeka, any progress on the barrier?" I asked urgently.

"Almost," she replied, sweat beading on her brow as she worked a complex counterspell. "I've identified the anchor points. Just need to... there!"

The barrier flickered once, twice, then collapsed with a sound like shattering glass.

We didn't wait for explanation, already racing down the spiral staircase, weapons drawn.

Behind us, Tomas remained in the belfry, either too frightened or too wise to join in the coming confrontation.

We emerged from the church at a full sprint, Kuchoff in the lead with his katana drawn, the rest of us fanning out behind him.

The cultists had their attention fixed on the ritual, giving us precious seconds to close the distance before being noticed.

"The heads first," Kuchoff commanded as we ran. "Disrupt the power flow. Balt, Thunor—right flank. Loher, with me to the left. Meeka, target Lemac directly. Commander, watch our backs."

We separated according to his orders, using the ruins for cover as we approached the circle.

The purple light was now so intense it hurt to look at directly, casting everything in an unnatural glow that distorted shapes and shadows.

We were perhaps fifty yards from the nearest cult member when the alarm was raised—a shout of warning that quickly spread through the assembly.

Instantly, robed figures rose to their feet, many drawing weapons from beneath their ceremonial garments.

"Go!" Kuchoff shouted, abandoning stealth for speed.

I surged forward with vampiric swiftness, outdistancing even Balt as I targeted the nearest pole bearing a constable's severed head.

The cultists moved to intercept, but they were too slow—my sword flashed in a silver arc, severing the pole at its base.

As it toppled, I caught the grisly trophy before it could hit the ground, respectfully lowering it to the earth.

The effect was immediate.

The purple light near this point faltered, its steady pulse becoming erratic.

"It's working!" I called to the others, already moving toward the next pole. "Destroy the circle!"

Balt had reached his first target, his massive axe making short work of the wooden pole.

Rather than catch the falling head, he used his momentum to continue toward his next objective, leaving a path of destruction in his wake.

Across the circle, Kuchoff and Loher worked with brutal efficiency, she providing covering fire with her bow while he struck down cult members who attempted to interfere with our plan.

But Lemac had not remained idle.

Seeing the disruption of his carefully constructed ritual, he raised his hands and unleashed a bolt of purple energy directly at Meeka, who had been casting a spell of her own.

She barely managed to deflect it, the resulting collision of magic sending up a shower of arcane sparks.

"Sir Victor has entered the portal!" Loher shouted, her elven eyesight picking out details we missed.

I turned to confirm and saw the former knight's armored form silhouetted against the crimson sky of the dead world beyond, already striding toward the distant gleam that marked the Scepter's location.

"We need to collapse the portal!" Kuchoff commanded, cutting down another cultist who attempted to bar his path.

"Not yet!" Meeka countered, deflecting another of Lemac's attacks. "If we close it while he's inside, he'll be trapped forever!"

"Better him than the Scepter in Lemac's hands!" Commander Cyrus argued, his massive frame providing a bulwark against cultists attempting to flank us.

As we argued, a new sound cut through the chaos—the deep, resonant toll of a dragon's roar.

Heads turned skyward as Avilyn appeared in his true form, his iridescent scales shifting through impossible colors as he descended toward the ritual site.

Behind him came Jade and Emeral, their green forms sleek and deadly in the purple-tinged twilight.

Cultists scattered in terror at the sight, many abandoning the ritual entirely to flee into the surrounding ruins.

Only the most devoted—or perhaps the most terrified of Lemac's retribution—held their positions.

"Albi made it," I realized with a surge of pride for my small companion.

Lemac's reaction was immediate and violent.

Abandoning his attack on Meeka, he redirected his magic toward the approaching dragons, sending a concentrated beam of purple energy skyward.

Avilyn banked sharply to avoid it, but Emeral was less fortunate—the beam caught his wing, sending him into a spiral that ended with a crash among the ruins several hundred yards away.

"ENOUGH!" Lemac's voice boomed across the ritual site, amplified by magic to a volume that shook dust from the remaining structures. "You are too late, Captain Magnus! The wheels are in motion!"

As if to punctuate his words, the portal flared with renewed intensity.

Through it, we could see Sir Victor had reached the Scepter—a gleaming object that appeared to be embedded in a raised stone dais.

As we watched, he grasped its haft and pulled, freeing it with surprising ease.

Even at this distance, the weapon's power was palpable.

Unlike any scepter I'd seen before, its head was composed of what appeared to be crystallized light, constantly shifting in color and intensity. The haft was bone-white, wrapped in what could only be dragon hide, inscribed with runes that glowed with inner fire.

Sir Victor raised it triumphantly over his head, then turned back toward the portal, the Scepter clutched firmly in his gauntleted hands.

Lemac's attention had shifted entirely to the portal, his expression a mixture of reverence and greed as he awaited Sir Victor's return.

This distraction gave us the opening we needed.

"Now's our chance," Kuchoff called to Meeka. "Can you disrupt the remaining power points?"

She nodded grimly, gathering her magic for a concentrated effort.

"Three remain intact. If I can break the connection between them and the portal..."

"Do it," he commanded, then turned to the rest of us. "Protect her at all costs."

Balt, Loher, Commander Cyrus and I formed a defensive circle around Meeka as she began a complex incantation.

Above, Avilyn and Jade continued to harass Lemac, forcing him to divide his attention between defending himself and maintaining the ritual.

Cultists pressed in from all sides, their initial fear replaced by desperate determination.

They seemed to understand that the ritual's success hung in the balance, driving them to reckless courage.

"Here they come," Balt growled, hefting his gore-streaked axe. "A proper fight at last!"

The first wave broke against us like water on stone.

Balt's axe carved a bloody path through robed figures, while Loher's bow sang a deadly song, each arrow finding a vital target.

Commander Cyrus's massive sword swept in wide arcs that kept the cultists at bay on his side, while my vampiric speed and strength allowed me to strike with near impunity, my blade a silver blur in the purple light.

Behind us, Meeka's voice rose in a crescendo as her spell neared completion.

The air around her shimmered with building power, focusing toward the remaining ritual poles.

Through the chaos, I caught glimpses of the portal.

Sir Victor had nearly reached its threshold, the Scepter of Dourn glowing more intensely as it approached our realm.

Lemac had positioned himself directly before the opening, hands outstretched in welcome or command—or perhaps both.

"Almost," Meeka called, her voice strained with effort. "Just need... a few more... seconds!"

The air crackled with competing magics—Meeka's counterspell building toward release, Lemac's ritual fighting to maintain cohesion, and the portal itself, a wound in reality that pulsed with increasing instability.

Suddenly, Sir Victor emerged through the shimmering boundary, the Scepter held before him like an offering.

The moment it passed completely into our realm, a shock wave of power emanated from its crystalline blade, knocking cultist and Scorpion crew alike to the ground.

I recovered first, vampiric reflexes allowing me to regain my footing before the others.

What I saw froze me in place.

The Scepter's face had changed—no longer shifting in color, it now glowed with a steady, mesmerizing purple light that matched exactly the hue of the ritual circle.

In Sir Victor's hands, it seemed to pulse with eager anticipation, like a predator scenting prey.

Lemac approached the kneeling knight, his hands outstretched.

"The Scepter," he commanded. "Give it to me."

Sir Victor raised his head, and even from this distance, I could see something was wrong.

His eyes glowed with the same purple light as the Scepter, and when he spoke, his voice carried harmonics that no human throat should produce.

"The Scepter is not for you, wizard," he said, rising slowly to his feet. "It is for the King."

Lemac's expression shifted from triumph to confusion.

"Yes, of course. You will wield it in the King's name, once the binding is complete."

Sir Victor smiled, but there was nothing human in the expression.

"There will be no binding. The King returns on his own terms."

Behind me, Meeka gasped.

"The Scepter," she whispered. "It's not just a weapon. It's a conduit."

"For what?" Kuchoff demanded, regaining his feet beside me.

"For the Ancient King himself," Meeka replied, horror dawning in her eyes. "The Scepter wasn't kept beyond the portal to protect our realm from it. It was keeping something contained within it."

As if in confirmation, Sir Victor raised the Scepter high.

The purple light intensified, flowing from the blade down the haft and into his armored form.

His body convulsed, back arching at an impossible angle as the light enveloped him completely.

Lemac stumbled backward, final understanding coming too late.

"No," he gasped. "This isn't what was written! The King requires a vessel prepared through ritual and sacrifice!"

"Fool," Sir Victor's voice replied, though his lips didn't move.

The voice seemed to emanate from the Scepter itself, deep and resonant with ancient power.

"I AM the ritual. I AM the sacrifice. The blood of law-keepers has freed me from my prison, and now I return to claim what was stolen."

The purple light surrounding Sir Victor pulsed once, twice, then exploded outward in a silent detonation that knocked us all backward.

When my vision cleared, the knight's form had changed.

Where Sir Victor had stood now towered a figure at least eight feet tall, clad in armor that seemed to be crafted from shadow and bone.

A crown of twisted metal sat upon a head that was somehow both skull and flesh, eyes burning with purple flame within cavernous sockets.

The Scepter in his hand had transformed as well, growing to match his new proportions, its face now a writhing mass of purple energy that seemed to drink the very light from around it.

"The Ancient King," Meeka breathed beside me.

"At last," the figure rumbled, its voice shaking dust from the ruins, "I have returned."

Lemac had recovered enough to attempt retreat, backing away with hands raised defensively.

"My lord," he stammered, "I am your faithful servant. It was I who orchestrated your return, who discovered the ritual—"

"Silence!" The Ancient King commanded, and Lemac's voice cut off abruptly, his mouth working silently as he clutched at his throat. "You sought to bind me to your will, little wizard. For that alone, you deserve oblivion."

The Scepter moved in a casual arc, almost too fast to see.

Where it passed, reality itself seemed to part.

Lemac had no time to scream as his body separated into perfect halves, the cut so clean that for a moment both sides remained standing before collapsing in opposite directions.

The remaining cultists fell to their knees, terror and worship mingled on their faces as they beheld their master's true form.

The Ancient King surveyed them impassively, then turned his burning gaze toward us.

"The Scorpion's crew," he intoned, recognition evident in his sepulchral voice. "How fitting that you should witness my return. Your reputation precedes you, even across centuries of imprisonment."

Kuchoff stepped forward, katana held ready though he surely knew it would provide little defense against the being before us.

"Whatever you were," he challenged, "whatever you believe was stolen from you—this is not your realm anymore. These are not your people to rule."

The Ancient King's laughter rolled across the ritual circle like distant thunder.

"Bold words from one so temporary. But then, that has always been humanity's failing—the belief that your brief lives grant you ownership over time itself."

He gestured with the Scepter toward Avilyn, who hovered above in dragon form.

"Ask your draconic ally about the true nature of rule and succession. He was old when I first claimed my throne."

Avilyn descended slowly, transforming as he did so into his elven form.

Though he appeared as a merely aged elf to human eyes, there was an ancient power in his stance as he faced the returned King.

"I remember you," Avilyn said simply. "You were not what the legends now paint you to be."

"No?" the Ancient King questioned; amusement evident in his burning gaze. "And what do they say of me, Dragon King? That I was cruel? Tyrannical? Perhaps they speak of the blood magic that extended my reign beyond natural limits?"

"They say nothing of you at all," Avilyn replied calmly. "Your name was struck from every record, your deeds attributed to others or forgotten entirely. The greatest punishment for one such as you—complete erasure from history."

The amusement vanished from the Ancient King's manner, replaced by a cold rage that sent cracks spreading through the stone beneath his feet.

"A mistake that will be rectified, beginning tonight."

He raised the Scepter, its face flaring with intensified light.

"The Wyrmfall Moon rises, and with it, my power returns in full. All of Beornan Heafod will know their true King has returned, and those who betrayed me will find their descendants pay the price."

"Not if we stop you first," Kuchoff declared, signaling to Meeka.

She nodded, unleashing the counterspell she had been holding in reserve.

Pink energy erupted from her hands, targeting the remaining ritual poles.

The magic struck with devastating force, shattering the wooden structures and sending the grisly trophies atop them rolling across the ground.

The effect was immediate and violent.

The ritual circle's light flickered erratically, and the portal behind the Ancient King began to contract, its edges becoming unstable.

"No!" the King roared, turning his attention to the failing magic.

He thrust the Scepter toward the circle's center, purple energy streaming from its face to reinforce the failing spell.

"You cannot undo what has been wrought!"

"Maybe not," Balt called, charging forward while the King was distracted, "but we can sure as hell try!"

His axe struck the Ancient King's armored leg with enough force to shatter ordinary metal but merely produced a discordant ringing against the shadowy surface.

The King barely seemed to notice, focused entirely on maintaining the ritual's integrity.

"The portal," Meeka called to Avilyn. "If we can collapse it completely, it might draw him back in!"

Avilyn nodded grimly, reverting to his true form.

With a roar that shook the very foundations of the ruins, he unleashed his dragon-breath upon the portal—not fire, but a beam of pure iridescent energy that struck the shimmering boundary with devastating precision.

The Ancient King howled in rage as the portal began to collapse inward, the dead world beyond rapidly receding.

He redoubled his efforts, channeling more power through the Scepter to maintain the opening.

"It's working!" Loher shouted, nocking another arrow. "Keep pressing!"

Commander Cyrus had joined Balt in direct assault, his massive sword striking the King's armor with little effect but serving as distraction, nonetheless.

I circled wider, looking for any vulnerability in the ancient being's defenses.

The King was powerful but divided—part of his attention maintaining the failing portal, part defending against physical attacks.

This division gave us an opening.

"Kuchoff!" I called, indicating the ritual circle beneath the King's feet. "The symbols—they're anchoring him to this realm!"

Understanding flashed across the Captain's face.

Using his katana, he began systematically defacing the nearest arcane marking.

Where his blade passed, the purple light dimmed, the symbol's power disrupted.

I joined him, targeting another section of the circle.

Loher, seeing our strategy, directed her arrows at a third section, the impacts scoring deep gouges in the carefully prepared ground.

The Ancient King noticed our efforts too late.

As the final symbol was disrupted, a change came over him—his form wavering slightly, becoming less substantial.

The Scepter in his hand pulsed erratically, as if struggling to maintain connection with its wielder.

"ENOUGH!" he thundered, abandoning the portal to face us directly.

The Scepter swept in a wide arc, sending a wave of purple energy racing across the ground toward us.

"Shields!" Kuchoff commanded.

Our errfords responded instantly, creating a protective barrier that deflected most of the deadly wave.

Even so, the force that broke through was enough to send us staggering backward.

The portal, no longer maintained by the King's power, collapsed rapidly.

The crimson landscape beyond winked out of existence, leaving only the empty stone archway standing alone in the ritual circle.

"You think this defeats me?" the Ancient King raged, his form solidifying once more as he drew power from the Scepter. "That was merely my prison, not my source! I am here, in my realm once more, and I will not be banished again!"

Above, Avilyn circled lower, preparing another attack.

Jade had recovered enough to join him, though he flew awkwardly with his injured wing.

Together, they unleashed twin blasts of draconic energy directly at the Ancient King.

The King raised the Scepter, intercepting the attacks with its face.

The purple energy writhed and twisted, somehow absorbing the dragons' power rather than being overwhelmed by it.

"Fools," the King laughed, his voice echoing through the ruins. "The Scepter of Dourn was forged specifically to kill dragons. Your own powers feed it!"

Avilyn roared a warning, but too late—the Scepter unleashed the absorbed energy back at him, amplified tenfold.

The beam struck the Dragon King squarely, sending him tumbling through the air to crash among the ruins beyond the ritual site.

"Avilyn!" Meeka cried out, her face pale with shock.

"He lives," the Ancient King assured her mockingly. "For now. I have plans for the Dragon King—old debts to settle."

Jade retreated higher, unwilling to risk a similar fate.

With Avilyn temporarily disabled, our strongest ally was removed from the fight.

The King turned his burning gaze upon us once more.

"Now, for the vermin who would oppose their rightful ruler."

He raised the Scepter to strike, but before he could bring it down, a new sound cut through the night—a sharp, rhythmic drumming that seemed to come from everywhere at once.

The King hesitated, head tilting as if listening.

"No," he whispered, an emotion close to fear entering his voice for the first time. "It cannot be."

The drumming grew louder, faster.

From the ruins around us, hundreds of small shapes emerged—rats, pouring from every crevice and shadow, moving with unnatural coordination.

At their head ran a familiar scarred figure—Albi, leading his kin in a coordinated attack.

"Blood calls to blood," Meeka realized aloud. "The constables' blood—it's attracting every rat in Dournan."

The swarm converged on the ritual circle, focusing particularly on the spots where the constables' heads had fallen.

As they reached the blood-soaked earth, something extraordinary happened—the rats began to change, growing larger, their eyes glowing with the same purple light that emanated from the Scepter.

"Blood magic cuts both ways," Meeka explained, wonder and horror mingled in her voice. "The ritual's power is being redirected through the rats!"

The Ancient King seemed genuinely disturbed by this development.

He swept the Scepter in wide arcs, sending waves of energy to incinerate the approaching swarm.

But for every rat that fell, ten more took its place, and those that reached the ritual circle continued to transform, becoming the size of small dogs, their teeth elongating into fangs that could tear through armor.

"This is impossible," the King snarled, retreating a step as the first of the transformed rats reached his armored feet. "Mere vermin cannot challenge me!"

But challenge him they did.

The rats swarmed up his legs, their enhanced fangs finding purchase in the joints of his otherworldly armor.

Where they bit, purple light leaked out like blood from a wound.

"Now!" Kuchoff commanded, seeing our opportunity. "Attack while he's distracted!"

We charged forward as one, weapons ready.

Balt's axe struck the King's knee with renewed purpose, finding weakness where moments before there had been none.

Commander Cyrus's massive sword focused on the opposite leg, while Loher's arrows targeted the joints in his armored torso.

I leapt higher than humanly possible, vampiric strength carrying me to eye level with the ancient being.

My sword thrust directly at the burning orbs within his skeletal face, causing him to jerk backward to avoid being blinded.

The King roared in fury and pain, sweeping the Scepter in desperate arcs to dislodge both rats and attackers.

But the coordinated assault was taking its toll—purple energy leaked from a dozen wounds, his once-imposing form now hunched and defensive.

"The Scepter," Meeka called from where she was crafting a complex binding spell. "It's the source of his power! Separate him from it!"

Easier said than done, I thought grimly, watching how the King clutched the weapon with both hands now, using it as much for support as attack.

Even wounded, his strength was inhuman, his connection to the Scepter absolute.

Then I noticed something—where Albi and his transformed kin bit into the King's gauntleted hands, the purple light dimmed momentarily.

The connection between wielder and weapon wavered.

"The rats!" I shouted to the others. "They're disrupting his bond with the Scepter!"

Understanding flashed across Kuchoff's face.

He focused his psionic power, creating a battering ram of pure mental energy directed at the King's grip.

At the same moment, Balt swung his axe at the exposed wrist of the King's right hand, while Commander Cyrus targeted the left.

The combined assault, along with the rats' continuous harassment, finally broke the King's grip.

The Scepter tumbled from his hands, landing head-first in the blood-soaked earth of the ritual circle.

The effect was immediate and catastrophic.

The moment the face of the Scepter touched the ground, the accumulated power of the ritual and the constables' blood reacted violently.

Purple light erupted from the contact point, shooting skyward in a pillar that pierced the storm clouds above.

The Ancient King screamed—not in rage but in genuine agony.

His form began to unravel, threads of shadow and bone being pulled inexorably toward the Scepter as if it were drinking him in.

"No!" he howled, reaching desperately for the weapon. "I will not be contained again!"

But it was too late. The Scepter had become a vortex, drawing in the very essence of the being it had momentarily freed.

Around us, the transformed rats began to revert to their normal size, the purple light fading from their eyes as the power that had changed them was likewise sucked into the growing maelstrom.

"Fall back!" Kuchoff ordered, recognizing the danger. "Everyone, retreat to safe distance!"

We didn't need to be told twice.

Grabbing any wounded companions, we raced away from the ritual circle as the vortex intensified, consuming not just the Ancient King but the very fabric of the ritual site itself.

Stone, earth, and remnants of the cultists who hadn't managed to flee were all pulled inward, disappearing into what had become a tear in reality.

From the ruins beyond, Avilyn emerged in his dragon form, battered but alive.

He took to the air, circling the vortex at a safe distance, observing the catastrophic collapse of the ritual.

The Ancient King made one final, desperate attempt to escape his fate.

His partially dissolved form reached out, trying to grasp anything that might anchor him to our realm.

Finding nothing, he turned his burning gaze toward us, his voice barely audible above the roar of the collapsing ritual.

"This is not the end," he promised, the words seeming to burn themselves into my mind. "I will return when the stars align once more. And when I do, I will remember those who opposed me."

With that final threat, the last of his form was sucked into the vortex.

The Scepter itself followed, the purple light condensing to a single point before imploding with a thunderclap that shook the very foundations of Dournan.

Then, silence.

Where the ritual circle had been, only a smoking crater remained, perfectly round and impossibly deep.

We approached cautiously; weapons still ready in case of further danger.

"Is it over?" Loher asked, peering into the darkness of the pit.

"For now," Meeka replied, her voice weary but certain. "The ritual collapsed in on itself. the Scepter and the Ancient King have been banished once more."

"Banished, not destroyed," Kuchoff noted grimly.

"Some things cannot be destroyed," Avilyn said, landing nearby and reverting to his elven form. "Only contained, bound, forgotten."

Balt snorted, wiping gore from his axe.

"Easy fer you ta say, Dragon King. Ye'll still be around next time tat ancient nightmare finds a way back."

"Perhaps," Avilyn acknowledged with a slight smile. "Though I suspect The Scorpion's legacy will endure as well, in one form or another."

As the immediate danger passed, I searched for Albi and the other rats.

They had returned to normal size, scurrying among the ruins in typical rat fashion, though many seemed disoriented by their brief transformation.

Albi, however, made his way directly to me, climbing up my leg to reclaim his position on my shoulder.

"Brave little warrior," I murmured, stroking his scarred back with one finger. "You saved us all."

Captain Rina and the rest of her crew from The Dragonfly arrived, having secured the tavern and surrounding buildings.

Their expressions showed a mixture of awe and disbelief as they surveyed the devastation.

"By all the gods," Rina breathed, staring at the smoking crater. "What happened here?"

"Justice, of a sort," Kuchoff replied enigmatically. "The Ancient King has been returned to his prison, and the Scepter of Dourn with him."

"And Lemac?"

"Dead," I confirmed, gesturing to where his bisected corpse lay at the edge of the ritual site. "Along with most of his followers."

Rina nodded grimly.

"Good. The constables are avenged, then."

"Not just avenged," Meeka added thoughtfully. "In a way, they saved us all. Their oath-bound blood was meant to free the Ancient King, but in the end, it helped bind him again."

"The ritual went wrong," Kuchoff explained, piecing together what had happened. "Lemac forced the portal open prematurely, thinking he could control both the Scepter and the King. But the King had plans of his own, and the Scepter..." He shook his head. "The Scepter was more than just a weapon."

"It was a prison," I finished. "Designed to contain the King's essence after his physical form was destroyed centuries ago."

"And now it contains him once more," Loher concluded. "Back beyond the celestial portal, waiting for the next fool to seek its power."

Commander Cyrus gestured toward the crater.

"Should we... I don't know, fill this in? Mark it somehow as a warning?"

"No," Avilyn said firmly. "Let nature reclaim it, as it has the rest of Dournan. The less attention drawn to this place, the better."

Kuchoff nodded in agreement.

"We'll report to the King that the threat has been eliminated. The details can remain known only to those who witnessed them."

As we prepared to depart, Balt approached the crater's edge one final time, peering into its depths.

"Ye know," he said thoughtfully, "fer all ta trouble, I never did get ta make a proper new skull bead. Seems a waste o' perfectly good killin'."

Despite the grim circumstances, I found myself laughing. Some things never changed—and perhaps that consistency was what we needed most after facing a power from beyond time itself.

"There's always next time, Stone-Heart," Chron said, gliding down to land beside the dwarf.

The bronze wyrmling had remained aboard The Scorpion during the battle but had apparently decided to join us for the aftermath.

"Aye," Balt agreed, surprising us all by gently stroking the dragon's metallic scales. "I suppose tere's always next time."

We made our way back through the ruins of Dournan, leaving behind the broken ritual site and the secret it would keep for centuries to come.

Above us, the storm clouds had begun to disperse, revealing glimpses of the night sky—including the Wyrmfall Moon, now past its zenith, its green light fading as it continued its celestial journey.

The threat had been contained, the constables avenged, but as The Scorpion and The Dragonfly prepared to depart, I couldn't shake the Ancient King's final promise.

I recalled his burning gaze, the absolute certainty in his voice as he vowed to return.

Some enemies, it seemed, transcended death itself.

And some hunts never truly ended.

But that was a concern for another day.

For now, we had done what The Scorpion's crew always did—faced the impossible, suffered losses, but ultimately prevailed.

And whatever the future held, we would face it together, as we always have.

Chapter Nineteen
FULL CIRCLE

The Scorpion's Den welcomed us home with its familiar embrace of stone and sea.

Six weeks had passed since our confrontation with the Ancient King in Dournan, and the realm had settled into an uneasy peace.

The King had received our report with grave concern, particularly the revelation that an entity of such power had nearly returned to Beornan Heafod.

He'd ordered all records of the Ancient King sealed once more, accessible only to the Royal Wizard and The Scorpion's highest-ranking officers.

"Home, sweet home," Balt declared as The Scorpion sailed through the narrow channel into our hidden sanctuary.

His dwarven features relaxed visibly as the ship's hull kissed the familiar dock.

"Nothin' like returnin' ta yer own den after months o' chasin' dragons an' ancient kings."

I found myself nodding in agreement, watching as the crew expertly secured mooring lines.

The rats at my feet scurried eagerly toward the gangplank, as anxious as I was to feel solid ground beneath them once more.

Only Albi remained at my side, his scarred body perched regally on my shoulder as if surveying his domain.

Loher materialized beside me, her elven grace undiminished despite the rigors of our recent adventures. Something had changed in her demeanor these past weeks—a softness to her normally sharp edges, a thoughtfulness behind her practical observations.

"The provisions we ordered from Dewarg should arrive within the week," she commented, though her eyes were focused on the deeper caverns that led to our personal quarters within the Den. "We'll need to inventory what we have until then."

"Worried about running short?" I teased gently, knowing her methodical nature often manifested as heightened concern for logistics.

A smile touched her lips, secretive and warm in a way that stirred something primal within me.

"Perhaps I'm simply thinking ahead more than usual," she replied cryptically.

Before I could question her further, Captain Magnus approached, his katana secured at his hip.

"Thunor, Loher," he greeted us with the easy familiarity of long friendship. "Once you're settled, join me in the strategy room. There's something we need to discuss."

His tone carried neither urgency nor alarm, but after years of serving under Kuchoff's command, I recognized the subtle tension in his shoulders.

Something required our attention, though perhaps not our immediate concern.

"Trouble?" Loher asked, her hand instinctively moving to the dagger at her hip.

"Not exactly," Kuchoff replied, his eyes briefly tracking to where Meeka supervised the unloading of essential supplies. "Let's call it... unfinished business."

With that enigmatic statement, he strode off to confer with Tatenda, who was already making notes on repairs The Scorpion required after our long journey home.

The ship had weathered our adventures remarkably well, though her wooden scales bore new scars that told tales of battles survived.

"Unfinished business," Loher echoed thoughtfully. "That could mean many things coming from our captain."

"Indeed," I agreed, watching as Balt organized a team to transport our wounded to the healing chambers deep within the Den.

Despite our victories, we'd suffered injuries that would take time to mend—both physically and otherwise.

The losses from our confrontation with Nerium still haunted us, empty spaces at mealtimes where friends should have sat.

We disembarked together, finding the familiar comfort of the Den's main cavern largely unchanged since our departure.

The massive space had been carved generations ago by untold years of erosion, its walls smoothed by the sea and time.

Cleverly positioned mirrors captured sunlight from hidden apertures in the mountain above, casting the entire area in a warm, natural glow.

As we made our way toward our quarters, Loher's hand found mine, her fingers intertwining with unusual tenderness.

The simple gesture held meaning I couldn't quite decipher, though it stirred a warmth in my chest that had nothing to do with my vampiric nature.

"I need to speak with you," she said quietly once we were alone in our chambers. "Before we meet with Kuchoff."

Something in her voice, a vulnerability rarely displayed, caused me to give her my full attention.

She moved to sit on the edge of our bed, her graceful composure momentarily betrayed by a nervousness I'd rarely witnessed in all our years together.

"What is it?" I asked, sitting beside her.

She took a deep breath, her eyes meeting mine with uncharacteristic uncertainty.

"I've been waiting for the right moment, and perhaps there is none better than now, returning to the place we've made our home."

A pause, weighted with significance.

"I'm with child, Thunor. twins, according to the midwife in Senton."

The world seemed to still around me as her words penetrated my consciousness.

"Twins?" I repeated my voice barely above a whisper.

She nodded, a smile breaking through her composure like sunlight through storm clouds.

"Three-quarters elven and one-quarter... whatever your vampiric nature contributes. She couldn't say for certain how that might manifest."

"When?" I managed, my mind racing through calculations and memories.

"Before Dournan," she replied. "Perhaps even before our confrontation with Nerium. Elven pregnancies progress differently than human ones. We have time—nearly a year still—but I'm certain."

A thousand emotions crashed through me at once—joy, fear, wonder, panic—leaving me momentarily speechless.

I'd never imagined myself as a father, had never dared to hope for such a future given my condition.

Yet here it was, offered like a gift I'd never thought to receive.

"Twins," I repeated, finding my voice at last. "A family. Our family."

Loher's hand found mine once more.

"I want them to know this place," she said quietly. "To grow up here, surrounded by the Den, by The Scorpion, by the strange collection of beings we call family. They'll have plenty of playmates their own age—the eline kits, human children, young elves, and all those errford cubs running about."

"Balt as an honorary uncle," I mused, envisioning the dwarf teaching small children how to wield miniature axes. "Kuchoff as their godparent. Chron telling them cryptic prophecies they're too young to understand."

"Exactly," Loher laughed, the sound lighter than I'd heard from her in months. "A proper upbringing for the children of The Scorpion's crew."

I pulled her into an embrace, overwhelmed by the future suddenly unfolding before us.

"I love you," I whispered against her hair. "And I will love them, with everything I am."

"I know," she replied simply, her certainty a balm to fears I hadn't yet voiced.

After a moment of shared silence, she straightened, her practical nature reasserting itself.

"Now, let's see what 'unfinished business' requires our attention. I suspect it involves the remaining Grand Ascendancy followers."

I nodded, though my thoughts remained tangled in visions of small hands and laughter echoing through the Den's stone hallways.

Together, we made our way to the strategy room, where Kuchoff, Meeka, Balt, and surprisingly, Captain Rina from The Dragonfly awaited us.

The strategy room was a natural chamber enhanced with carved shelves and a massive stone table at its center.

Maps covered the polished surface, weighted with various objects to keep them flat.

A single spot was illuminated by a shaft of sunlight from a hidden aperture, highlighting a location I immediately recognized.

"Exland Mountain," I observed, noting the mark on the nautical chart. "I thought we were done with that place."

"So did we all," Captain Rina replied, her weathered face grim in the cave's dim light. "Until my scouts reported activity there three days ago."

"What kind of activity?" Loher asked, joining the others around the table.

Kuchoff gestured to a small pile of purple-trimmed fabric scraps.

"Grand Ascendancy robes. And this."

He pushed forward a sealed parchment bearing a wax seal I'd never seen before, a crown sitting on what appeared to be a scepter.

"Unopened?" I questioned, studying the seal without touching it.

"After what happened with the blood-magic messages, we thought it prudent to wait," Meeka explained. "I've examined it for spells and found nothing dangerous, but..."

"Better safe than sorry," Balt finished for her. "Especially when it comes ta purple-robed fanatics."

"It was left deliberately for us to find," Captain Rina added. "Placed at the entrance to the mountain, along with this."

She produced a small object wrapped in black velvet. Unwrapping it carefully revealed a miniature carving of The Scorpion in exquisite detail, down to the tiny wooden scales along its hull.

The craftsmanship was remarkable, but what made my blood run cold was the material—it appeared to be carved from human bone.

"A message and a threat," Loher observed quietly.

"Lord Di Garath," I guessed, recalling the aristocratic cultist who had offered me a "cure" in Dournan. "He escaped during the chaos at the ritual site."

Kuchoff nodded grimly.

"And apparently, he's appointed himself Lemac's successor. The scouts reported approximately twenty individuals entering Exland Mountain in the past week. All wearing purple."

"Ye'd think they'd learn ta wear a different color after all ta trouble we've caused tem," Balt grumbled, stroking his beard thoughtfully.

"They want to be recognized," Meeka pointed out. "The color is part of their identity now—a symbol of their cause."

"Which brings us to the decision at hand," Kuchoff said, his gaze sweeping across our faces. "Do we open the message and potentially walk into whatever trap Di Garath has set? Or do we ignore it and risk allowing the Grand Ascendancy to rebuild under his leadership?"

The question hung in the air between us, weighted with the memory of all we'd sacrificed to defeat Lemac and the Ancient King. Part of me—the part now acutely aware of Loher's pregnancy—wanted nothing more than to seal Exland Mountain permanently and forget it existed.

But another part—the hunter who had tracked Lemac across realms—knew that unfinished business had a way of returning at the worst possible moment.

"Open it," I decided, my voice steady despite my conflicted thoughts. "If it's a trap, better to know its nature now than be surprised later."

Kuchoff nodded, producing a thin blade to carefully break the seal.

The parchment unfolded to reveal flowing script in purple ink:

'To the esteemed crew of The Scorpion,

What was begun cannot be undone.

Though Lemac has fallen, and the Ancient King returned to his prison,

the Renewal continues in forms you cannot yet perceive.

I offer a simple exchange—your presence for the lives of those who would otherwise perish.

Come to Exland Mountain at the new moon.

Captain Magnus,

the half-vampire,

the elven thief,

and the dwarf.

No others.

Refuse, and the deaths that follow will serve a purpose beyond your understanding.

The faithful remember.

Lord Di Garath,

Voice of the Ascendancy'

"Well, that's not ominous at all," Balt remarked sarcastically, though his hand had moved to rest on his axe.

"It's obviously a trap," Loher stated flatly.

"Of course it is," Captain Rina agreed. "The question is why? What does Di Garath hope to accomplish by facing you directly? He must know he's outmatched."

"Unless he isn't," Meeka suggested thoughtfully. "We know very little about him beyond his title and his role in the Grand Ascendancy. He could possess abilities we haven't witnessed."

Kuchoff studied the message again, his expression calculating.

"He's being deliberately vague about the threat. 'Those who would otherwise perish' could refer to hostages, or it could be another ritual sacrifice in planning."

"Either way, we can't ignore it," I said, thinking of the constables whose deaths had nearly brought about catastrophe. "If he's planning something similar to the ritual in Dournan..."

"Agreed," Kuchoff decided. "But we'll approach this with caution. Captain Rina, can The Dragonfly remain nearby as reinforcement?"

"Of course," she replied without hesitation. "My crew is at your disposal."

"Then we have five days until the new moon," Kuchoff noted, his tactical mind already forming plans.

"Balt, I want you to work with Tatenda on specifically equipping The Scorpion for close quarters combat within the mountain."

"Wit pleasure," the dwarf grinned, already mentally designing new implements of destruction.

"Meeka, consult with Avilyn about magical countermeasures. If Di Garath has access to any of Lemac's spell books or artifacts..."

"I'll ensure we're prepared," she promised grimly.

"Thunor, Loher," he continued, turning to us, "scout the mountain's exterior. Find any changes since our last visit, any new entrances or guard positions."

I exchanged a quick glance with Loher, seeing the same thought reflected in her eyes.

With her pregnancy, caution would be even more essential, though I knew better than to suggest she remain behind.

Her skills would be crucial to our success.

"Consider it done," I replied for both of us.

"Very well," Kuchoff concluded. "We have our tasks. Dismissed until tomorrow's planning session."

As the others filed out, I lingered, waiting until only Kuchoff remained.

"Something on your mind, Thunor?" he asked, gathering the maps from the table.

"Loher is with child," I said simply, seeing no reason to delay the news. "Twins, according to the midwife in Senton."

Kuchoff's hands stilled, surprise momentarily overtaking his usual composure. Then a goofy toothy grin—rare these days—transformed his features.

"That's... wonderful news," he said warmly. "Truly. Have you told the others?"

"Not yet," I admitted. "We only just confirmed it ourselves."

He nodded understanding.

"I won't speak of it until you're ready. But know this—The Scorpion and the Den will always be home to your family. We'll ensure these children grow up surrounded by protection and love, whatever the future holds."

"Thank you," I replied, throat unexpectedly tight with emotion. "That means more than you know."

He clapped a hand on my shoulder.

"We've faced ancient kings and dragon-human hybrids. I suspect raising children might be our greatest adventure yet."

With that surprisingly lighthearted comment, he departed, leaving me alone with thoughts of the future, both the immediate confrontation with Lord Di Garath and the longer path that stretched beyond, now populated with small figures I couldn't yet visualize but already loved fiercely.

◆

The new moon brought perfect darkness to Exland Mountain, its jagged silhouette barely visible against the star-strewn sky.

The Scorpion lay anchored in deep water half a league offshore, while The Dragonfly maintained position behind the nearest islands, hidden from casual observation.

Our approach to the mountain came not by ship but by smaller craft, a rowing boat crewed by silent oars wrapped in cloth to muffle their sound. Kuchoff sat in the bow, his katana secured across his back, while Balt and Loher took positions amidships.

I handled the oars, my vampiric strength making quick work of the distance.

The mountain's silhouette loomed before us, dark and forbidding against the starlit sky.

Each stroke of the oars brought us closer to what could easily be an elaborate trap.

The weight of our weapons—familiar and reassuring—did little to ease the tension that had settled over our small party.

"No guards visible on the exterior," Loher reported, her elven vision penetrating shadows that would blind human eyes. "The entrance appears unchanged since our last visit."

I scanned the rocky shore and the carved entrance, my vampiric senses reaching out for any sign of an ambush.

There was something unsettling about the stillness—no birds, no night insects, just the gentle lapping of waves against our boat and the distant mountain.

"I don't like it," I whispered. "It's too quiet."

Albi chittered nervously on my shoulder, his tiny claws digging into my cloak as if warning me away from the approaching shore.

"Too easy," Balt grumbled, absently fingering one of the skull beads in his beard. "Di Garath's waitin' inside, I'd wager me best axe on it."

"No doubt," Kuchoff agreed, his voice pitched low to avoid carrying across the water. "The question is where and with what surprises."

Our scouting over the past few days had revealed little beyond confirming that members of the Grand Ascendancy had indeed taken up residence within Exland Mountain.

They maintained no exterior guard posts, no visible defenses, almost as if they wanted us to enter unimpeded.

The boat's keel scraped gently against the narrow strip of pebbly beach below the mountain's main entrance.

We disembarked silently, securing the craft with a length of rope that would allow for quick departure if necessary.

I sent Albi and a small contingent of rats ahead to scout, their tiny forms melting into the shadows of the carved entrance.

The rodents had proven invaluable as an early warning system, and I'd spent additional time training them since Dournan to respond to more complex commands.

"Remember," Kuchoff said as we prepared to enter, "we're here to assess the threat and neutralize Di Garath if possible. This isn't about vengeance."

The last comment seemed directed particularly at Balt, whose expression suggested he had a different perspective on our mission's purpose.

"Course not, Captain," the dwarf replied with exaggerated innocence. "Just a friendly visit ta our purple-robed acquaintances."

The fact that he'd brought not only his primary battle axe but also three smaller throwing axes and what appeared to be several explosive devices suggested his definition of "friendly" differed substantially from most.

As we entered the mountain's carved passageway, I noted with surprise that torches illuminated the corridor at regular intervals, a marked change from the darkness that had greeted us on previous visits.

The Grand Ascendancy had clearly been busy making Exland Mountain their own.

Albi returned after we'd progressed about fifty yards into the mountain, his excited chittering conveying that he'd found something of interest further ahead.

The other rats remained deployed throughout the passageways, an invisible network of sentinels.

"Lead on," I instructed him quietly.

The scarred rat scurried ahead, pausing occasionally to ensure we followed.

The main corridor branched several times, but Albi unhesitatingly chose a path that led deeper into the mountain, gradually descending.

"This isn't the way to Ficolus' chambers," Loher observed, her perfect recall of the mountain's layout evident in her concerned tone.

"No," Kuchoff agreed. "We're heading toward the lower levels—areas we haven't explored before."

The air grew noticeably damper as we descended, the carved walls giving way to natural stone formations.

Stalactites hung from the ceiling like stone daggers, while corresponding stalagmites rose from the floor in places, creating a landscape that required careful navigation.

Finally, Albi paused at the entrance to what appeared to be a large natural cavern.

Unlike the torchlit corridors behind us, this space was illuminated by an eerie purple glow emanating from crystalline formations embedded in the walls.

The effect was both beautiful and unsettling, reminding me uncomfortably of the ritual site in Dournan.

"Welcome to the Heart of the Mountain," a cultured voice echoed from within the chamber. "I'm pleased you decided to accept my invitation."

Lord Di Garath stepped into view from behind a particularly large crystal formation.

He looked much as he had in Dournan—tall, aristocratic, his silver-streaked hair tied back neatly.

He wore purple robes similar to Lemac's, though of simpler design, and carried no visible weapons.

"How long would've ye waited if we dinna show up?" Balt asked rhetorically, his axe half-raised in readiness.

Di Garath's lips twitched slightly at the dwarf's bluntness before he regained his composed demeanor.

"Longer than you might think, Master Dwarf. Patience is a virtue I've cultivated."

"Where are your followers, Di Garath?" Kuchoff asked, his hand resting casually near his katana's hilt.

"Elsewhere in the mountain," Di Garath replied with a small smile. "I thought a private conversation would be more productive than a confrontation."

"Funny thing about that," Balt growled, his axe already in hand. "I find confrontations plenty productive."

Di Garath's smile didn't waver.

"I'm sure you do, Master Dwarf. But I invited you here for a purpose beyond violence—though I came prepared for that eventuality as well."

He gestured to the surrounding crystals.

"Do you know what these are? They're remnants of the portal stones' magic, crystallized over centuries within the mountain. They respond to certain... influences."

"Like blood magic," I guessed, noting the similarities to the purple light we'd witnessed in Dournan.

"Precisely, Master McLaaud," Di Garath nodded approvingly. "Though not necessarily in the crude fashion Lemac employed. There are subtler applications."

"Get to the point," Loher said coldly, her patience visibly thinning. "You mentioned an exchange in your message. What exactly are you proposing?"

Di Garath's expression grew more serious.

"The Grand Ascendancy has lost its way. Lemac's obsession with the Ancient King and the Scepter of Dourn led us down a path that nearly destroyed everything. I seek to rebuild with a different purpose."

"Which is?" Kuchoff pressed.

"Balance," Di Garath replied simply. "The realm needs checks against absolute power—be it kings or dragons. The Grand Ascendancy was originally founded as such a check, before Lemac's grandfather twisted it toward personal ambition."

"You expect us to believe you've had a change of heart?" I asked skeptically. "After participating in the murder of so many constables?"

A shadow passed across Di Garath's features.

"I won't pretend my hands are clean. I believed in the cause as Lemac presented it—justice for those abandoned by the crown, power to protect the vulnerable. I didn't understand the true nature of what we were unleashing until Dournan."

"So, what do you want from us?" Kuchoff asked, his voice neutral but his posture still ready for combat.

Di Garath spread his hands in a surprisingly open gesture.

"An armistice. Allow those of us who remain to continue our work within these chambers, away from the realm's notice. In exchange, we will serve as an early warning against threats similar to what we faced in Dournan."

"Threats like what?" Loher questioned, her suspicion evident.

"The Ancient King isn't the only power that sleeps beneath Beornan Heafod," Di Garath replied grimly.

"There are others—entities sealed away by magic now largely forgotten. The crystals in this chamber can detect disturbances in those seals long before they become dangerous."

"And we're supposed ta trust you wit tis responsibility?" Balt scoffed. "After everything yer group has done?"

"Trust is earned," Di Garath acknowledged. "I propose regular reports to Captain Magnus, transparency about our activities, and if necessary, a permanent representative of The Scorpion stationed within Exland Mountain to observe our work."

The offer was surprisingly reasonable—suspiciously so.

I exchanged glances with Kuchoff, seeing the same calculation in his eyes. If Di Garath was sincere, such an arrangement could indeed benefit the realm.

If he wasn't...

"And the alternative?" Kuchoff asked carefully.

Di Garath's expression hardened slightly.

"We've prepared contingencies should you refuse. Nothing as dramatic as Lemac's plans, but effective, nonetheless. The Grand Ascendancy has supporters throughout Beornan Heafod—many in positions of influence. A shadow war would benefit neither of us."

"You're threatening us," Loher stated flatly.

"I'm being pragmatic," Di Garath countered. "We both have power. We both want stability. I'm proposing we find it together rather than at each other's throats."

A tense silence fell over the cavern, broken only by the faint humming emanation from the purple crystals.

I found myself studying Di Garath carefully, looking for signs of deception or hidden threat.

To my surprise, I detected neither—only a weariness beneath his composed exterior, and what appeared to be genuine concern.

"How many of you remain?" Kuchoff finally asked.

"Seventeen," Di Garath answered without hesitation. "Mostly scholars and mages who joined seeking knowledge rather than power. Those who followed Lemac for more violent purposes either died in Dournan or have been... encouraged to pursue other paths."

Kuchoff nodded slowly, then looked to each of us in turn, seeking our input without words.

Balt looked distinctly unhappy but gave a grudging nod.

Despite his love of combat, the dwarf was no fool—he recognized the practical value of Di Garath's proposal.

Loher's expression remained skeptical, but she too inclined her head slightly.

Her thief's instincts told her there was more to discover here, and an armistice would provide that opportunity.

As for myself, I found the idea strangely appealing.

After all we had endured, the prospect of converting an enemy into a resource had undeniable merit.

And with the future now stretching before me in ways I'd never anticipated—a family to protect, children to raise, I found myself less eager for unnecessary conflict.

"A trial period," Kuchoff decided, turning back to Di Garath. "Three months during which a representative of The Scorpion will reside here. Full access to your activities, regular reports to me personally, and immediate notification of any... disturbance you detect."

Di Garath bowed his head in acceptance.

"Agreed."

"If we discover any hint of deception, any continuation of Lemac's work..." Kuchoff let the threat hang unspoken.

"Understood, Captain," Di Garath replied solemnly. "We seek only to serve the realm in our own way, as you serve it in yours."

"Then we have an accord," Kuchoff extended his hand, which Di Garath shook firmly. "My first officer, Commander Ashpin, will select our representative. Expect them within the week."

With formal arrangements made, Di Garath offered to show us the crystals' function in more detail.

As Kuchoff and Balt followed him deeper into the cavern, Loher drew me slightly aside.

"What do you think?" she asked quietly, her eyes searching mine. "Is this a mistake?"

I considered carefully before answering.

"A calculated risk," I decided. "But one with potential benefits that outweigh the dangers, especially with our oversight."

Her hand brushed unconsciously across her abdomen, still flat beneath her leather armor.

"I find myself thinking differently now," she admitted softly. "Seeing threats and opportunities through the lens of what they mean for... for them."

"I know," I replied, covering her hand with mine. "But that's not weakness, Loher. It's wisdom—the kind that comes from having more to protect than just ourselves."

She smiled then, a rare full smile that transformed her features.

"When did you become so philosophical, McLaaud?"

"I've always had hidden depths," I replied with mock seriousness. "You were simply too distracted by my obvious charms to notice."

Her laughter, quiet but genuine, echoed slightly in the crystal cave, drawing curious glances from the others.

In that moment, surreal as our surroundings were, I felt a peace I hadn't experienced since before Nerium's appearance on the horizon—a sense that perhaps, just perhaps, we had weathered the worst of the storm.

Autumn came to The Scorpion's Den with surprising beauty.

Though hidden within a mountain, the changing season made itself known through subtle shifts in the light that filtered through the carefully engineered apertures in the rock ceiling.

The water in the hidden lagoon cooled, while the air carried hints of woodsmoke from the settlements along the coast.

Three months had passed since our unexpected armistice with Lord Di Garath and the remnants of the Grand Ascendancy.

True to his word, he had accepted Meeka's choice of representative—she had chosen herself.

Her weekly reports described a group genuinely focused on research and monitoring, with no signs of the darker pursuits that had characterized Lemac's leadership.

The Scorpion herself rested in her berth, undergoing extensive renovations under Tatenda's exacting supervision.

The ship had earned a period of recovery as much as her crew, and the Drow took particular pride in incorporating improvements based on lessons learned during our recent adventures.

Within our private chambers deep in the Den, Loher's pregnancy had begun to show visibly, her normally slender frame now gently curved around the twins she carried.

The changes to her body were matched by subtle shifts in the Den itself—baby furniture crafted by Balt in his spare time appeared piece by piece, while Meeka had begun assembling a collection of books suitable for young minds.

On this particular evening, we gathered in the Den's great hall for a feast marking the successful completion of the first phase of ship repairs.

Lanterns hung from iron brackets set into the stone walls, casting warm light across long tables laden with food and drink.

The reduced crew of The Scorpion mingled with workers from nearby villages and the occasional visitor from further afield, creating an atmosphere of comfortable camaraderie.

"To The Scorpion," Kuchoff proposed, raising his tankard high. "May her next adventures be slightly less apocalyptic than her last."

"Hear, hear!" came the enthusiastic response, followed by the clinking of mugs and cups.

I sat beside Loher, watching as Balt regaled a group of wide-eyed villagers with increasingly embellished tales of our encounter with the Ancient King.

The dwarf had added several dramatic confrontations that existed solely in his imagination, including a one-on-one axe duel that apparently lasted "three hours by the shadow-clock."

"He'll be telling them he defeated the Ancient King single-handedly by year's end," Loher observed dryly, though affection colored her tone.

"Let him have his stories," I replied, smiling as Balt mimed an especially improbable axe maneuver that would have dislocated both shoulders if attempted in reality. "The truth is remarkable enough—who could blame him for adding a few flourishes?"

Chron glided down from his usual perch near the ceiling, landing gracefully on our table.

The bronze wyrmling had developed a particular fascination with Loher's pregnancy, often remaining near her for hours, his ancient eyes studying her with solemn attention.

"The future divides and multiplies," he observed cryptically. "Two becoming four, circles closing only to reopen."

"Any chance you could be more specific about our children's futures?" Loher asked, having grown accustomed to the dragon's mysterious pronouncements.

Chron tilted his head, scales catching the lamplight.

"One bears your gift for shadows, the other carries their father's affinity for blood. Both will find their own paths, separate yet entwined. They will sail on The Scorpion when stars align and danger threatens, continuing the cycle begun before their birth."

For Chron, this was surprisingly straightforward information.

I exchanged a meaningful glance with Loher, who seemed equally startled by the dragon's unusual clarity.

"Thank you," I told him sincerely. "That's... actually helpful."

The wyrmling made a sound suspiciously like a chuckle before taking wing once more, returning to his lofty observation point.

As the evening progressed, I found myself increasingly content to simply observe—Meeka deep in conversation with Avilyn about some arcane matter, their hands sketching complex patterns in the air; Tatenda demonstrating the functioning of a new rigging design to fascinated shipwrights; Captain Rina and her first officer enjoying The Dragonfly's shore leave in our company.

Eventually, Kuchoff made his way to our table, sliding onto the bench across from us with uncharacteristic relaxation.

The months of relative peace had eased some of the tension he habitually carried, though his eyes retained their watchful quality.

"Enjoying the celebration?" he asked, nodding toward Loher's untouched ale.

"Just taking it all in," she replied, her hand resting comfortably on her growing abdomen. "It's not often we have moments like this."

"True enough," he agreed, his expression growing more serious. "Though I sometimes wonder what we're meant to do during peacetime. The Scorpion was built for adventure, for facing threats others can't or won't confront."

"There will always be another adventure," I assured him, thinking of Chron's prophecy regarding our as-yet-unborn children. "The realm never stays quiet for long."

"I suppose you're right," Kuchoff acknowledged, a faint smile tugging at his lips. "And in the meantime, we have renovations to complete, a new crew to train, and apparently, twins to prepare for."

"Speaking of which," Loher interjected, reaching beneath the table to retrieve a small wooden box she'd kept hidden until now. "We have something for you."

She slid the box across the table to Kuchoff, who accepted it with a curious expression.

Opening it revealed two identical silver pendants, each shaped like a miniature version of The Scorpion, expertly crafted down to the smallest detail.

"For the twins," she explained. "A reminder of their heritage and their extended family. We'd like you to be their godfather, Kuchoff."

A goofy toothy grin spread across his usually composed features.

"I... would be honored," he replied, carefully closing the box. "Truly."

"Good," I said firmly. "Because Balt is already planning to teach them axe-throwing as soon as they can walk, and someone needs to be the voice of reason."

Kuchoff laughed, the sound drawing surprised glances from nearby crew members who rarely heard their captain express such unguarded mirth.

"Between the three of us, we might just manage to raise them with some semblance of normalcy."

"Normal is overrated," Loher declared with unexpected conviction. "Let them be extraordinary, like the family they're born into."

As if in response to her words, a commotion arose near the entrance to the great hall.

Heads turned to see a messenger in the King's colors being ushered in, his travel-stained appearance suggesting urgency.

Kuchoff rose immediately, all traces of relaxation vanishing as he moved to intercept the newcomer.

The hall quieted as they spoke in hushed tones, the messenger gesturing emphatically while Kuchoff listened with growing concern.

"What now?" Loher sighed, although without real annoyance.

The rhythm of crisis and resolution had become so familiar that it carried a certain comfort of its own.

Kuchoff returned to our table, his expression once again the captain rather than the friend.

"Reports of strange creatures emerging from the Western Forest," he explained briefly. "Nothing apocalyptic—just unusual enough to warrant investigation."

"The Scorpion sails at dawn?" I guessed, already calculating what preparations would be.

EPILOGUE

LEGACY OF BLOOD AND SHADOW

The Scorpion cut through the midnight waters of the Strait of Avilyn, her wooden scales gleaming in the moonlight.

Fifteen years had wrought changes to the legendary vessel—enhanced weaponry, reinforced hull sections, more efficient sail configurations—but her essence remained unchanged.

She was still the most feared ship in Beornan Heafod, and her reputation had only grown with time.

High in the crow's nest, a slender figure stood motionless against the star-filled sky.

Nilah McLaaud's long dark hair, streaked with her mother's elven silver, whipped about her face in the salt breeze.

At fifteen, she already displayed the unnaturally keen senses inherited from her father's vampiric nature.

Her eyes, a striking amber that seemed to glow in darkness, scanned the horizon with predatory focus.

A small group of bats circled above her, occasionally diving close to receive whispered instructions before disappearing into the night.

Unlike her father's rats, Nilah's winged companions provided aerial reconnaissance, their echolocation abilities allowing them to map terrain and detect movement in absolute darkness.

"See anything interesting?" a voice murmured from seemingly nowhere.

Nilah didn't startle—she'd sensed her twin's approach long before he spoke.

Thorne McLaaud materialized from the shadows surrounding the mast, the darkness reluctantly releasing him like a jealous lover.

Though they shared the same birthday, the twins could hardly have appeared more different.

Where Nilah had inherited their father's predatory grace and affinity for blood, Thorne was purely his mother's son—lean and quicksilver, with eyes the deep blue of twilight forests and shadows that clung to him like faithful pets.

"Movement along the northern cliffs," Nilah reported, pointing to a barely visible outcropping of rock.

"Something large shifting between the caves."

Thorne frowned, his shadows swirling more intensely around his ankles.

"Those caves were supposed to be abandoned decades ago. The mining guild sealed them after the collapse."

"Exactly," Nilah agreed, her gaze never leaving the distant shoreline. "Which makes any activity there worth investigating."

The sound of boots on the ladder interrupted their exchange.

Thunor McLaaud emerged from below, his face hadn't aged despite the fifteen years that had passed.

The vampiric blood that flowed through his veins had slowed his aging to a slow crawl, though hints of silver now threaded his hair at the temples.

As always, rats scurried around his feet, their tiny bodies forming complex patterns across the deck.

"Report," he said without preamble, though the pride in his eyes as he looked at his children was unmistakable.

Nilah provided details with military precision, her posture unconsciously mirroring her father's.

"Movement in the northern cliff caves. No fishing vessels should be operating in that area, and the mining operations ceased years ago. Echo has detected unusual thermal patterns consistent with large creatures."

Thunor nodded thoughtfully.

"Your mother's already informed the Captain. We're changing course to investigate."

"Our first real mission," Thorne murmured, excitement and apprehension mingling in his voice.

Their father's expression softened slightly.

"Reconnaissance only," he reminded them. "You're to observe and report. No engagement without explicit orders."

The twins exchanged a glance that parents throughout history would have recognized as trouble.

"Of course, Father," Nilah said innocently.

"Wouldn't dream of it," Thorne added, his shadows momentarily stilling in a picture of perfect compliance.

Thunor sighed, recognizing the look all too well.

"Your mother was right. You two are more dangerous together than apart."

"Compliment accepted," Thorne grinned.

"It wasn't meant as one," their father replied dryly. "Come below. The Captain wants to brief the whole team."

As they descended to the main deck, The Scorpion's crew moved with practiced efficiency, preparing the ship for potential combat.

Several eline crew members darted across the rigging with feline grace—Liona, daughter of the legendary Roash, led her hunting team through equipment checks, her spotted fur gleaming in the moonlight.

Below, her brother Karesh, The Scorpion's new tactical officer, conferred with other eline warriors, their tails swishing in synchronized anticipation.

The twins had grown up surrounded by the eline children, treating them as cousins rather than simply crew members.

Thorne caught Liona's eye and gave her a quick hand signal—a silent promise to share whatever they discovered.

She acknowledged with a subtle ear twitch that her mother would have recognized instantly.

Loher emerged from the Captain's quarters; her elven beauty undimmed by time.

She wore the same practical leathers she always had, multiple daggers strapped to her thighs and hidden in her boots.

Her eyes immediately found her children, assessing them with the instinctive concern of a mother and the tactical evaluation of a master thief.

"There you are," she said, falling into step beside them. "I hope you're both clear on the parameters of this mission."

"Crystal clear, Mother," Nilah assured her.

"Absolutely transparent," Thorne agreed.

Loher's expression suggested she believed neither of them.

"Thorne, I've counted my daggers. All seventeen are accounted for. They'd better remain that way."

Thorne managed to look wounded.

"Mother, I would never—"

"You would and you have," she interrupted, though there was a hint of amusement beneath her stern facade.

"Just remember what happened last time."

Thorne winced at the memory.

His "acquisition" of his mother's favorite throwing knife had resulted in two weeks of kitchen duty and a particularly grueling training regimen designed by Balt himself.

"That was an accident," he protested weakly.

"Mmhmm," Loher hummed disbelievingly. Her attention shifted to her daughter. "And Nilah, please remember that reconnaissance bats are not the same as attack bats."

Nilah had the grace to look slightly embarrassed.

Her last "reconnaissance" mission had ended with three of her bats diving at a merchant who had tried to cheat the crew on supplies.

The merchant had been so terrified he'd fallen into the harbor.

"They were acting on instinct," she defended.

"Your instinct, perhaps," her mother countered. "Just keep them under control this time."

Captain Magnus waited for them in the strategy room, a circular chamber carved from the heart of The Scorpion herself.

Maps and charts covered the central table, illuminated by enchanted lanterns that never dimmed or flickered.

"Ah, the next generation of trouble," he greeted the twins with unexpected warmth.

Despite his intimidating reputation throughout the realm, Kuchoff had always shown a softer side to his godchildren.

"We prefer to think of ourselves as strategic assets, Captain," Nilah replied with perfect seriousness.

Balt's booming laugh filled the chamber.

"Just like your father! Always with the fancy words when 'trouble' works just fine!"

The dwarf's beard now reached nearly to his knees, intricately braided and decorated with dozens of skull-shaped beads, each representing a significant kill.

The years had softened his once-thick accent to something much more comprehensible, though it still emerged in moments of extreme emotion or battle rage.

He had become, if possible, even more feared in battle over the years, his berserker charges legendary throughout Beornan Heafod.

"Let's focus," Captain Magnus suggested, though he couldn't quite suppress his smile. "We have a situation developing."

Meeka stepped forward, her hands tracing glowing patterns over the map.

"For the past three months, ships have been disappearing along the northern trade route. No distress signals, no wreckage found, simply... gone."

"Seventeen vessels lost," Balt added, his diction clear and precise, so different from the thick brogue of years past. "Including three military galleys sent to investigate the disappearances."

"The King is concerned, understandably," Captain Magnus continued. "But more troubling are the reports from the few survivors who've managed to reach shore after these incidents."

"What reports?" Thorne asked, his shadows swirling with interest.

"They describe massive tentacles emerging from the water," Meeka replied grimly. "Tentacles that glow with an unnatural blue light, capable of snapping a ship's mast with a single strike."

"A kraken?" Nilah suggested, her expression dubious. "They're known to hunt in the deeper waters beyond the strait, but they rarely venture this close to shore."

"Not a kraken," Thunor corrected. "Krakens don't glow blue. And they typically leave wreckage."

A heavy sound of claws on stone drew everyone's attention to the chamber's entrance.

Chron entered, his massive bronze form barely fitting through the doorway.

The bronze dragon had grown to his full size over the past decade, his metallic scales gleaming like freshly minted coins in the lantern light.

Though he could maintain a smaller form, when necessary, aboard The Scorpion he typically remained just small enough to navigate the larger passageways.

His ancient eyes swept over the assembled crew, finally settling on the map with intense focus.

Everyone waited, expecting one of his cryptic pronouncements, but the dragon remained uncharacteristically silent, merely observing.

"The survivors also mentioned caves," Captain Magnus continued after a respectful nod to Chron. "Caves along the northern cliffs where they saw strange lights and movement before the attacks occurred."

"The same caves Nilah's bats detected activity in tonight," Thunor noted.

"Precisely," Meeka confirmed. "We believe whatever is attacking these ships is using the caves as a base of operations."

"Operations implies intelligence," Loher observed. "You don't think this is simply a sea monster."

"No," Captain Magnus shook his head. "Not anymore. The pattern is too deliberate, the targets too specific. Many of the ships were carrying valuable cargo—weapons, alchemical supplies, magical artifacts."

"Someone's building something," Karesh spoke up, the eline tactical officer's ears flicking forward with interest.

"Or preparing something."

"That's our suspicion," Meeka agreed. "The question is: what?"

"And that's where we come in," Thunor said, looking at his children.

Captain Magnus nodded.

"The caves are too narrow for The Scorpion to navigate, and sending a larger party would risk detection. We need a small team to investigate—individuals with unique talents for moving unseen and gathering intelligence."

"Us," Nilah stated simply, a faint smile playing at the corners of her mouth.

"You, along with your father and Liona's hunting team," Captain Magnus confirmed. "Your abilities complement each other perfectly for this mission."

Thorne's shadows danced with excitement.

"When do we leave?"

"Tonight," Captain Magnus replied. "Under cover of darkness. You'll approach by skiff, investigate the cave system, and return before dawn with whatever intelligence you can gather."

"Reconnaissance only," Thunor emphasized again, fixing each twin with a stern look. "We don't engage unless absolutely necessary."

"Of course," the twins chorused, their expressions angelically innocent.

Not a single adult in the room was fooled.

"I'll accompany them part way," Chron announced suddenly, his deep voice resonating through the chamber.

It was rare for the bronze dragon to offer his direct assistance, making his statement all the more significant.

"The narrow passages" Meeka began.

"Need not concern you," Chron interrupted smoothly. "I have my ways."

The cryptic response was so characteristic that it actually relieved some of the tension in the room.

Some things, at least, never changed.

"It's settled then," Captain Magnus declared. "Thunor, the twins, Liona's team, and Chron will investigate the caves. The rest of us will maintain position nearby, ready to provide support if needed."

As the meeting concluded and the crew dispersed to prepare, the twins lingered in the strategy room, their excitement too palpable to contain.

"Our first real mission," Thorne whispered, his shadows coiling and uncoiling around his ankles.

"First of many," Nilah replied confidently, checking her various concealed weapons with practiced precision.

Chron observed them from his position near the door, his ancient eyes holding knowledge he would not share.

The future had many branches, many possibilities, but some things remained constant across all potential timelines.

The McLaaud twins would face danger tonight—that much was certain.

What was less clear was how that danger would shape them, and how the consequences of their actions would ripple outward into the future of Beornan Heafod.

But such concerns were for seers and prophets.

For now, the bronze dragon would simply watch over these children of The Scorpion, these heirs to a legacy of blood and shadow, as they took their first steps into the wider world of adventure and peril that had defined their parents' lives.

The preparations continued throughout the evening, weapons checked and rechecked, plans reviewed, and contingencies established.

As midnight approached, the small team gathered on The Scorpion's deck, ready to embark on their mission.

Thunor embraced Loher briefly before joining the twins at the rail.

"Keep them safe," she whispered against his cheek.

"Always," he promised. "Though they're becoming quite capable of keeping themselves safe these days."

"That's what worries me," she replied with a wry smile. "They're too much like us at that age."

"Precisely why they'll succeed," Thunor countered, pressing a final kiss to her lips before turning to the mission at hand.

The skiff was lowered silently into the dark waters, Liona and two other eline warriors already positioned at the oars.

Their night vision made them ideal for navigating the treacherous waters near the cliffs without lights to give away their position.

As the twins prepared to descend the rope ladder, Captain Magnus approached for a final word.

"Remember your training," he told them quietly. "Trust your instincts, but not at the expense of your judgment. And above all, remember that you're part of a team—you're not alone out there."

"We won't let you down, Captain," Nilah assured him, her amber eyes gleaming with determination.

"Never doubted it for a moment," he replied with a proud smile. "Now go make The Scorpion proud."

Chron waited until they had all boarded the skiff before launching himself from The Scorpion's deck, his massive wings catching the night air with barely a sound.

He circled once overhead before flying ahead toward the distant cliffs, a bronze sentinel against the star-filled sky.

As the skiff pulled away from The Scorpion, Thorne gazed back at the legendary vessel that had been their home for as long as he could remember.

Her wooden scales gleamed in the moonlight, her proud silhouette, a promise of safety and return.

"Nervous?" Nilah asked quietly, noticing her brother's contemplative look.

"Not nervous," he corrected, shadows swirling thoughtfully around him. "Just... aware. This is where it all begins for us. Our story."

"Our chapter in a much longer tale," she amended, nodding toward their father who sat at the bow, his rats already fanning out across the small vessel in defensive formation.

"Think we'll ever have stories as incredible as theirs?" Thorne wondered.

Nilah smiled, a rare full expression that transformed her serious face and revealed the tips of her fangs.

"I think we're about to find out."

Above them, the stars of Beornan Heafod glittered against the velvet darkness.

The same stars that had witnessed their parents' battles, journeys, and countless adventures of The Scorpion's crew throughout the generations.

The wheel turned.

The legacy continued.

And somewhere in the darkness ahead, unknown dangers waited, unaware that the next generation of McLaauds was coming for them—blood and shadow, bat and stealth, carrying forward the mantle of those who had sailed these waters before.

The hunt, as always, continued.

If you enjoyed **Hunt** please post a review
and watch for Book Six of The Scorpion Chronicles.

Coming soon...